Early Prais‹

"*Relatively Normal* by Whitney Dineen is among the best chick lit novels that I have read so far. Not only did it give me a long hearty laugh on many occasions, but the story also comes together splendidly. The unpredictable turns of the plot are adeptly created to grip the attention of any reader. Paired with the humor, the book makes for a must-read for anyone with an appreciation of romantic comedies." —5/5 **Stars, Readers Favorite**

"*Relatively Normal* is a piss-yourself, hold-on-to-your-belly, catch-your-breath, and spill-your-pint-tale. This story is hilarious, off the wall, daft, and you can picture each and every event as it's being unfolded in your mind's eye. This was my first read by Whitney Dineen, but will not be my last. Thinking we should be bancharaids." —A.J. **Book Remarks**

"Whitney Dineen knows how to take the best of the 90s Rom-Com and update it for the 21st Century—*Relatively Normal* had me entranced from the first page. I laughed, I cried, and I laughed some more—this is one you don't want to miss! Reese Witherspoon will be all over this! —**Loretta Nyhan, Amazon #1 bestselling author of Digging In**

"You'll laugh, cry, and scream (in a good way), at the utter hilarious pandemonium this lovable family can cause. Meeting the Mastertons this Holiday season will make you swoon with happiness at the wild, outrageous parties this lovable, kooky Scottish clan can deliver. Bring on the haggis! Whitney Dineen does it again! 5 Humongous Stars!!!" —**Ms. Birdlady Book Blog**

"Dineen has a talent for spinning a tale that is both hilarious and heartwarming. I loved this book!"— **Becky Monson, author of** *Just a Name*

"Whitney Dineen continues to delight and surprise with her latest collection of quirky characters in *Relatively Normal*. You'll laugh, groan, and get all the feels along with heroine Cat when she spends the holidays with her wacky family and finds herself in the center of a very complicated and compelling love triangle. This book is a must-read for fans of Marian Keyes and Kristan Higgins." —**Tracie Banister, author of** *Izzy As Is*

"*Relatively Normal* is Whitney Dineen's best book to date. It will have you laughing out loud one moment and swooning the next. Above all it will make you grateful for all the weirdos in your own life that make life worth living." —**Jennifer Peel, bestselling author of** *The Sidelined Wife*

"Whitney Dineen knocks it out of the park with a laugh-out-loud romantic comedy full of family weirdness and personal revelations. I loved it!" —**USA Today Bestselling Author, S.E. Babin**

"I loved *Relatively Normal* so much! It's rare a book that makes me laugh out loud but this one did … repeatedly! I will be adding it to the top of my list of favorites for 2018!" —Annabella Costa, author of *My Perfect Ex-Boyfriend*

"I've reviewed a number of Dineen's books, so I expected to have a grand time reading this offering. If anything, it exceeded my expectations. *Relatively Normal* is definitely not your normal story about in-laws and holidays!" —Jack Magnus, Readers' Favorite, 5/5-Stars

"So many LOL moments! I loved reading about a family that may just may be zanier than my own! Don't miss out on this feel-good funny by Whitney Dineen." —Kathryn R. Biel, award-winning author of *Made for Me*

"Hilarious and full-of-heart, Dineen has outdone herself. Relatively Normal is fabulous read." —Karin Gillespie, author of *Love Literary Style*

"High-class writing with witty, laugh-out-loud humor. I laughed so hard my face hurt!" —Joslyn Westbrook, author of **Cinderella-ish**

Also by Whitney Dineen

Romantic Comedies
Relatively Normal
Relatively Sane
She Sins at Midnight
The Reinvention of Mimi Finnegan
Mimi Plus Two
Kindred Spirits
Going Up?

Non-Fiction Humor
Motherhood, Martyrdom & Costco Runs

Middle Reader
Wilhelmina and the Willamette Wig Factory
Who the Heck is Harvey Stingle?

Children's Books
The Friendship Bench

Relatively Normal

Whitney Dineen

Made in the United States of America
September 2018

Ebook Edition
ISBN-13: 978-0-9988620-4-0

https://whitneydineen.com/newsletter/
33 Partners Publishing

Some of us are lucky enough to find the loves of their lives in high school. For all of those people, this book is for you.

Brea + Clinton

Kris + Dave

Erin + Steve

Caryn + Ryan

Mary Rose + Philip

Sue + Rick

Rachael + Justin

Brittani + Ben

Vickie + Kurt

Betsy + Matt

Tarah + Brodie

Nicole + George

Heidi + Dave

Candace + Andy

Konnie + Rick

Chanté + Steve

Cameron + Amy

Lisa + Don

Karen + John

Maria + Bruce

Lisa + Case

Kelly + Dan

Joanne + Steve

Suzie + Roger

Annette + John

Aimee + Corey

Tiesha + Russell

Heather + Mike

Lindsey + Greg

Betsy + Matt

Acknowledgments

The thing I enjoy most about being an author is getting to meet all the crazy characters that pop into my brain. The cast of *Relatively Normal* not only knew who they were when they introduced themselves to me, they'd already written their story. It only took them three weeks to share it with me.

There are SO many people to thank for this book, it boggles my mind. First, thank you to my own knight in shining armor, Jimmy. We didn't meet in high school, but we started dating when I was only twenty. I count myself pretty darn fortunate to have met you so young. You're my love, father of my children, and inspirer of my dreams. You have my heart forever.

Thank you to my mom, Libby Bohlen, and dear friend, Beth Boyer, who were the first to lay eyes on this book. Your enthusiasm and support kept me writing deep into the night and on those 4:00 a.m. wake-up calls.

Diana Orgain, Celia Kennedy, and Kathryn Biel, where do I start? Your suggestions, notes, encouragement, and tough love made this book the best it could possibly be. You make me a better storyteller and I would be nothing without you.

To the rest of my writing tribe Tracie Bannister, Becky

Monson, and Jennifer Peel, thank you for being my foundation. You make time for me whenever I need you, and you offer guidance, and words of wisdom. I owe you more than I can ever repay.

To my friends at Chick Lit Chat, you rock! No question is too stupid for you to answer, no idea is too ridiculous for you to consider. I'm grateful you're always there when I need you. Annabella Costa, Sheryl Babin, and Rich Amooi, I'm looking at you!

Authors would be nothing without bloggers and I'm fortunate to have the support of Melissa Amster and Sara Steven at Chick Lit Central, M.S. Birdlady, A.J. Book Remarks, Bethany Clark, Kate Rock, and Barbara Kahn, to name a few. Your love for authors and books is inspiring!

To Paula Bothwell, my grammar police, thank you for making me look literate. Thank God you were paying attention in English class while I was apparently day dreaming out the window.

Finally, thank you to my readers, or as I like to think of you, my partners in crime. You're the peanut butter to my jelly, the ranch dressing to my salad, and the French fries to my cheeseburger. I adore you!

I love Cat and her crazy family so much, they're coming back in another episode in 2019.

Four Years Ago

My best friend is a vision straight out of one of those glossy bridal magazines that costs more than a macchiato and breakfast sandwich at Starbucks. She's well over six feet tall in her heels, slim as a fashion model—except she's sporting a C-cup no emaciated supermodel would be caught dead with—and her silky brown hair is currently twisted in an impossibly complicated up-do that probably required four professional hair stylists and a drag queen to execute. She's elegant beyond words.

I gasp as she spins around, so I can behold her in all her splendor. The sleeveless, beaded-bodice trumpet gown fits her like a glove. "Jasmine Marie, you're glorious!"

She giggles, which is a sound you wouldn't expect to come out of such a stunningly ethereal creature. She spins again, "I've never felt so girly! And that's saying something being that I'm this tall."

"Whoever said a month's paycheck was too much to spend on a wedding dress clearly never saw you in this one. I feel like a proud mother right now."

Jazz heaves a sigh. "Speaking of mothers, you have to do me a favor." My eyebrows raise in interest. She continues, "Watch out for mine and make sure she doesn't murder my dad's new wife during dinner."

I snort. "Puh-leeze, your mom is every ounce a lady. She'd no more commit murder than I would."

"Alas, Brandee—with two e's— the latest of my dad's spouses, has just announced she's pregnant. My mom isn't taking the news gracefully."

"You're kidding me? You're going to have a new brother or sister at twenty-nine?" Then I ask, "How old is Brandee again?"

My friend rolls her big brown eyes. "My dearest stepmother has just turned twenty-four."

"I don't know, Jazz. I think your dad is the one who needs offing in this scenario. I might be persuaded to help."

"I would appreciate if no murders were committed at my nuptials." Then she hugs me, and says, "But I love you for offering."

"Oh, Jazzy," I exclaim, "this day is going to be so wonderful. You deserve every minute of happiness. Dylan is one lucky guy."

Brushing a non-existent wrinkle out of her skirt, she declares, "Now all we need to do is find you the perfect man. Three of the groomsmen are single. You've met two of them, and the third is the one with sandy blond hair. He's Dylan's cousin, Jared, from Detroit."

"Detroit? Hard pass." The sarcasm rolls off my tongue. "I'm not looking for a long-distance love. But have no fear, I'll definitely scope out the other two. I'm not opposed to meeting the future Mr. Catriona Masterton tonight."

She beams. "People often meet their future spouses at weddings. It's a thing."

"So, it's got to be my turn, right?"

Jazz playfully punches my arm. "That's the attitude I love! I just wish you were walking down the aisle with me."

I call out to Jennifer, our assistant, "Make sure you pack up all of Jazz's stuff and take it over to her suite at the hotel. Oh, and before you go, tell Elaine to get the limos turned around out front to transport the wedding party to the reception once the ceremony ends."

In addition to being best friends, Jazz and I own a much sought-after event-planning business in Manhattan. We're the go-to duo known for stylishly executing even the trickiest parties—like weddings where the groom was once married to the bride's sister—without a hitch.

I turn to the current bride. "I wish I were walking down the aisle with you too, but someone has to make sure this shin-dig of yours goes off perfectly. There's a ton of potential business out there, so we have to make sure this is our best party yet. Now, hustle, the bridesmaids are already upstairs, and their procession starts in ..."—I check my watch— "two minutes, which only gives you seven before it's your turn."

I pick up my friend's chapel-length train to keep it from getting dirty on the stairs. "Let's go, lady; your happily-ever-after awaits."

We arrive upstairs in the entrance of St. John the Divine Cathedral just as Emily, the last bridesmaid, starts her goosestep down the aisle. Jazz and I stand side-by-side watching her go. As Emily takes her place in the front of the altar, the first strains of Trumpet Voluntary fill the atmosphere like a heavenly serenade. Chills race through my body as I kiss my friend's cheek and hand her off to her father who will deliver her to her destiny, one Dylan Finch.

Once the ceremony is over and the reception is in full swing at the St. Regis Hotel, I take off my party-planner hat and put on my dancing shoes. It's go time. I have my eye on a particular groomsman, whom I've met on a couple other occasions. He's sweet and shy, but super easy on the eyes. I'm not sure we're destined for matrimony, but a couple of dances would be fun.

I straighten the skinny navy skirt of my evening dress and prepare for the chase. I take a step forward and wind up doing an unexpected split to the ground. *Ouch!* The waiter rushes over to clean up the spilled drink I inadvertently stepped in, and before I can begin the process of restoring my dignity, a pair of shiny, black shoes shows up next to me.

A manly hand stretches out and a deep voice inquires, "May I be of assistance?" He introduces himself. "Ethan Crenshaw, lifelong friend of the groom." I recognize him from the rehearsal dinner, but I didn't get a chance to talk to him. Not only is Dylan's friend chivalrous, but he has gorgeous green eyes that remind me of Maeve's, my childhood cat.

I take his hand. "Thank you. That's very kind."

"Let me help you to a chair and then I'll get some ice for your injury. It'll keep the swelling down," he announces.

Once I'm positioned at table fourteen in the main ballroom, I watch Ethan walk to the bar. He looks good in a way that suggests he's comfortable in formal wear, like James Bond. And bam, just like that, I realize I had totally forgotten about the cute groomsman.

When my knight in shining armor—a.k.a. a black tuxedo—returns, he helps prop my foot up on a chair and states, "There's a nine percent chance of getting injured at a wedding reception."

As far as opening lines to, it's not the best. Yet, his previous gallantry more than makes up for it. "That seems to be an awfully high number," I reply. "I've been to almost two hundred weddings so far and this is my first injury. If my calculations are correct, that puts my risk at point five percent, nowhere near your estimate."

"Two hundred weddings? You must be quite a popular friend."

I inform him, "I'm a party planner. I'm Jazz's partner."

"Ah, well then, surely you've had a blister, a burnt finger, or a stiff neck?"

I laugh. "If you're going to include all the mundane discomforts, I'd think you'd be more accurate to say there's a hundred percent chance of getting injured at a wedding."

He shakes his head. "No, only nine percent, unless my research is wrong." With a pointed look he adds, "Which it never is."

What kind of person researches injuries at weddings? So, I ask, "What exactly do you do for a living?"

"I'm an actuary. Certainly, not as glamorous a profession as party planning, but it pays the bills."

I've heard the job title, but I have no idea what it entails. Kind of like an ornithologist. I know it's something. I just don't know what. At my confused look, he explains, "Insurance companies and brokerage firms hire actuaries to assess the financial risk of investments and people. I currently work at an insurance company and help set rates, based on the statistical probability of natural disasters hitting certain demographics. For instance, earthquake insurance in the Midwest costs you next to nothing compared to what it does in California, for a reason."

"Huh." I can't seem to think of any other response.

"It sounds like a job that could bore the paint off the walls, doesn't it?" he laughs.

I flirt, "Lucky for me, I like numbers."

Ethan sits with me for the next three hours while I ice my ankle, ten minutes on and twenty minutes off, as per his suggestion for the best healing effects. As we get to know each other, I watch Jazz flirt and dance with the man who just promised to love her forever.

Dylan is hands down the sweetest, funniest, and most devoted man I've ever met. He adores my friend with his whole being and treats her like delicate china, even though she's not the kind of woman you'd want to sneak up on in a dark alley. Jazzy is one hundred percent Amazon with a touch of Xena Warrior Princess. She and Dylan are perfect for each other.

I was once in love with a man very much like Dylan and it didn't turn out well, which is why I'm currently in the market for someone more practical. I'm less concerned with grand gestures and flowery compliments, than in a reliable partner who will be there when the chips are down.

Throughout the reception, not only do I discover that Ethan adheres to a strictly regimented life, but I also learn he's a lovely man. He even offers, "Would you like me to see you safely home? No ulterior motives, I promise."

"It's kind of early to leave, don't you think?" And while he claims no other motivation, I wouldn't be opposed to a little romance.

He looks at his watch and explains, "I promised my neighbor,

Mrs. Fein, I'd look in on her cat while she's away. Apparently, Fifi suffers from separation anxiety and needs someone to bat her toy mouse around with her before she can go to sleep."

As the party is winding down, and I can see the staff has everything well in hand, there's nothing more for me to do. I allow Ethan to escort me home. True to his word, he doesn't try any funny business. He just gives me a sweet kiss, leaving me wanting more, and asks, "When can I see you again?"

The Courtship

When my doorbell rings, I quickly apply a fresh layer of lipstick and grab my purse. Tonight, we're celebrating our first anniversary, which happens to coincide with Jazz and Dylan's first anniversary. I'm wearing a cerulean-blue wrap-dress that compliments my blond hair and blue eyes. I bought it especially for this occasion.

Ethan greets me with a bouquet of long-stemmed white roses. "For my beautiful lady."

I pull him in and give him a proper kiss of appreciation. "These are perfect, thank you." Even though red roses are meant for lovers, Ethan's favorite are white ones. He claims they're pure and untarnished, like me. Swoon, right?

Our dating experience has been perfect. There's no rush to jump into bed and burn ourselves out having wild monkey sex six times a day. That's not to say there's isn't any chemistry. There definitely is. It's just not some uncontrollable chemical explosion guaranteed to fizzle once the initial throes of passion are spent. It would be more accurate to conclude we're committed to an adult relationship that involves a lot of other aspects of our union, in addition to the physical. It's exactly what

I'm looking for. I've reached an age where I'm no longer interested in unpredictable and spontaneous men.

Ethan and I have a nice routine together. We eat out twice a week, taking turns picking the location. Sometimes it's breakfast, sometimes dinner, but it's always twice a week. I change up my location depending on what the buzz on the street is. I'm always on the lookout for a new adventure. Ethan seems content to stay with the same handful of locations, which is fine. There are plenty of new things for me to try, though he seems to favor a few select menu items.

We watch television two nights a week and go to the movies on Sunday. I stay over at his apartment twice a week and he stays the same number at mine. All in all, we spend a lot of time together. We also seem to have a thing for the number two.

I put the roses into a vase and inhale their fragrance deeply before saying, "We'd better run. Our reservation is at seven."

"I changed it to seven thirty. I didn't want to run the risk of being late and losing it," he replies.

That's Ethan in a nutshell. He thinks things through and always has a plan. In a world where people constantly fly by the seat of their pants, I think this is a refreshing way to live. "Perfect. Would you like a glass of wine before we leave?"

He holds out his hand. "No. We can always get one at the bar if we're early. I asked the Lyft driver to wait for us."

As we walk out the door of my Chelsea apartment, the world is my oyster. I'm celebrating a year with the same wonderful man, I have a flourishing career, and the air is finally cooling and starting to smell like a New York City fall. Contentment permeates my world.

Ethan and I hold hands in the car on the way to the restaurant. I say, "This is quite a special night, isn't it?" We don't normally eat at restaurants as expensive as Astor Court, but this is a celebration.

"It is. Since we met at the St. Regis Hotel, it's only fitting we return to the scene of the crime a year later."

Ethan guides me from the car into the hotel with his left hand placed gently on my lower back. The lobby is old-world elegant, and I feel like a princess entering a castle.

Once we're seated, our waiter, a middle-aged man wearing black pants with a matching vest and bow tie, greets us, "Mr. Crenshaw, Ms. Masterton, we're so honored to have you dining with us. My name is Frank, and I'll be taking care of you this evening." Wow, that was worth a couple hundred bucks right there. It's the little things like this that make people keep coming back.

Frank pops open a bottle of champagne and pours for us. Ethan has left no detail unattended. He's even requested the same champagne Jazz and Dylan served at their wedding, Veuve Clicquot Rosé.

After our appetizers are ordered—lobster risotto for me, and the caprese salad for him— Ethan surprises me by dropping to one knee beside me. "Catriona ..." My heart starts to beat so loudly I can hear it pounding inside my ears. Before he can say anything else, I start the little camera in my brain clicking away to save this moment for posterity. I never suspected he was going to propose marriage tonight.

I inhale deeply and look up at the mural of a blue sky with white, fluffy clouds painted on the eighteen-foot ceiling. I observe the gold-leaf crown molding and count all six crystal chandeliers. Everything seems to be moving in slow motion.

I always thought that women who claimed they didn't know a proposal was coming were just playing up the drama for the retelling of their story. Turns out, some might really be surprised. I finally look at Ethan and say, "Yes?"

He smiles widely. "Will you do me the great honor of becoming my wife?"

First of all, there's no way I'm not going to say yes. I mean, this is storybook stuff. Secondly, I love Ethan, and thirdly, did I mention the perfection of this night? I semi-shout, "Yes! Yes, I'll marry you!" A crowd of fellow diners give us an encouraging round of applause as the waiter approaches with a ring box on a silver tray.

Ethan opens the lid and removes an emerald-cut diamond from its black velvet pillow. He places it on my ring finger while uttering a heartfelt, "Thank you."

I wish someone was recording this so I could watch it on replay. Even though I'm living it, it feels like it's happening to someone else and I'm sure to forget some detail. Once Ethan gets back into his chair, he announces, "You should move in with me. We'll be able to save more money for the wedding that way."

What he says is true. My thirty-eight hundred dollar a month apartment will add up to a hefty sum for a wedding. I ask, "When would you like me to do that?"

"I've been thinking about it since I bought the ring, and decided if you said yes, you should move in right away. I know your lease is month-to-month, and as this is the last week in the month, how about over the weekend?"

And just like that, my life as a single woman in New York City comes to an end. I've never lived with a man, and suddenly I feel quite grown up. I mean, sure I'm thirty, and have a successful business, but now I'm an engaged woman to boot. If you had told me last year that this would be happening, I would have never believed you.

One Year Later

"Catriona, would you please pass the No-Salt?" Ethan never calls me Cat.

Despite the fact that he's been asking for that god-awful substitute for the year we've lived together, I can't help but crinkle my nose. Still, I hand over his salt replacement and ask, "Why do you insist on using that?"

Over the top of his glasses, he explains, "Based on my heredity, there's a thirty-eight-percent chance I will develop high blood pressure by the time I'm forty. By not using salt to season my food and by doing a minimum of thirty minutes of cardio a day, I reduce my chances to a mere twelve percent. Those are odds I can't afford to ignore."

This is the kind of information Ethan is known for. It's a bi-product of his job, and while I suppose he's right, I'd personally rather die five years early and really enjoy my food than put up with the weird aftertaste of the fake stuff.

If we can ever get confirmation on our preferred wedding venue, I'm fully prepared for an all-out battle about serving real salt at our reception. For me, this is a non-negotiable point.

"Our flight to Chicago leaves at five thirty tomorrow night."

I say this as I grind some pink sea salt onto my scrambled eggs.

"We should have a car pick us up at eleven fifteen, then."

I perform an internal eye roll. I don't care how early Ethan leaves for the airport when he's traveling alone, but I absolutely refuse to spend my life anticipating the worst and winding up sitting at JFK for three hours before getting on a plane. "I have a lunch meeting tomorrow, so I'll have to meet you there—if you insist on going early, that is."

He gives me the look, one that suggests, "Aren't we being a little frivolous?"

I cut him off at the pass before he has a chance to say it. "I'm meeting with the Vanderhauffers, of Vanderhauffer Jewels on Fifth Avenue, about doing their daughter's wedding. The kind of money and exposure we're talking about will more than make up for the extra car fare."

I'm actually not meeting the Vanderhauffers tomorrow; I'm meeting with them today. I have a massage scheduled for tomorrow to preemptively defeat the incoming stress of Thanksgiving. I don't usually lie to Ethan, but sometimes it's just easier than having to explain myself. Also, it avoids a heated disagreement, which I'm against, as a rule.

Plus, let's be honest, there is no way Ethan will appreciate the eccentricities of my family. I firmly believe there is a widely accepted range of behavior—from straight and stodgy to certifiable—that all humans exhibit from one degree to another. Fortunately, or unfortunately, depending on how you look at it, my family is firmly lodged in the quirky range.

Take my mother, for instance. She's plagued by a disorder where kitchen gadgets actually talk to her and beg her to take them home. During my childhood, she would drag me from one garage sale to the next just to see what treasures people were getting rid of. God forbid it was a shortbread pan in a shape she didn't have or some kitchen wonder that promised to peel, slice, dice, or waffle cut any vegetable you could imagine.

She's currently the proud owner of twenty-nine shortbread pans that form every shape from flower bouquets, to hearts, to the Loch Ness Monster. In addition, she has a basket of assorted culinary oddities, which she stores in the laundry room. She doesn't know exactly what they do or how to assemble them. She just knows they might come in handy one day, and God forbid she not have them when they're needed.

Also, my mother is the only human being alive who knows how to properly load a dishwasher—knives down, forks up, and no spoon caught spooning with another, ever. Even if you follow every one of her dictates to the letter, you will still inevitably do it wrong. "Forks up only on the first twenty-two days of the month and never on a full moon!" You think I'm kidding? Don't get me started on what happens when Mercury is in retrograde.

My mother's idiosyncrasies used to bug the absolute crap out of me until I decided to find them charming. Now when she tells me about a new shortbread pan she's found or complains that after thirty-five years of marriage, my dad still doesn't know how to load the dishwasher, I just smile. I'm never going to change her, and darn if I'm not going to miss these conversations someday.

Then there's my nan, who is happily still alive at eighty, and living with my parents. She developed something like Tourette syndrome when I was eight. Up until then, she was a perfectly normal grandma. Then one day, out of the blue, she snapped.

We had all been sharing a pew at the First Presbyterian Church on Easter morning. I couldn't wait to get home and bite the head off my solid chocolate Godiva Easter Bunny, but in the meantime was covertly popping jelly beans into my mouth, slowly sucking off the semi-hard candy coating before letting the delicious gummy center melt on my tongue.

I'd just eaten two pink ones, two white ones and had started on my two yellow, when Pastor Abernathy's wife walked by us. Nan shouted out as loud as you please, "Twat!" You've never heard such silence. The entire congregation was not only rendered mute, but totally immobile by the epithet hanging in the air above them.

Mrs. Abernathy had stopped dead in her tracks, slowly turned around, and scowled at my grandmother—a woman she'd known since they were in elementary school together. She had stared her down in such a way a lesser mortal would have succumbed to the arctic exposure of her glare.

My grandmother, on the other hand, had merely smiled and greeted, "Dorcas, how are you this fine Sunday?" It effectively left everyone wondering if they'd really heard what they thought they heard or if they'd all been victims of some strange audio hallucination.

The doctor hadn't been able to pinpoint the exact cause of her change, but guessed it was the result of a series of small strokes that effectively killed the governor living in her brain. After the incident at church, Nan became proficient at saying whatever she was thinking, wherever she was thinking it. Most people decided to act like they didn't hear her. It was a weird truce between the citizens of our little town and an old lady seemingly bent on offending everyone she came into contact with.

If a proliferation of shortbread pans and curse words weren't enough, my father's quirk is a love of dead rodents. No, I'm not kidding. I only wish I were. He has other peculiarities, but this one stands out as the most glaring.

My brother, Travis, is plagued by overt-selfishness and an inability to grow up. At twenty-nine, he's unemployed, living in my parents' basement, medicating his angst over life not turning out the way he expected with anything he can get his hands on—scotch, pot, Benadryl, sleeping pills. You name it, if it can alter his consciousness in any way, he's all over it like flies on a cow pie.

Why am I telling you all of this? Because up until this point, I've managed to keep Ethan from ever meeting my family. Even with us in New York City, and them in Illinois, it hasn't been easy to keep them apart. Now that we've been official for over a year, and Thanksgiving is just around the corner, Ethan has decreed he *will* meet my family, regardless of any excuse I come up with to keep that from happening. He's also invited his mom and dad along so that we can share our wedding plans with both sets of parents at the same time.

I can only hope my particular quirk, which is an almost mystical belief that all things work out as they should, is less a Pollyanna-ish pipe dream and more a fact-based reality. Otherwise, there's no way I can see this weekend going well for any of us. Is it any wonder I'll be spending two hours with a hulking masseur? I'll probably need another two when we get home.

Unexpected Gifts

When I get to the office, Jazz throws me a tiny package wrapped in Tiffany-blue paper, tied with a white satin bow.

"What's this?" I ask.

She smiles brilliantly. "A thank you gift from the bride of our last wedding. She was so thrilled with everything, she bought us each diamond earrings in appreciation of our hard work."

I tear the paper off with lightning speed and there nestled in the elegant satin-lined flip-top box, are delicate hoop earrings in white gold, accented with three diamonds, each. "Holy crap, these are gorgeous! What do you think they cost?"

My friend smiles radiantly, showcasing her infectious smile, "I just looked online." She lets anticipation hang in the air for a moment before revealing, "Twenty-four hundred big ones!"

I whistle under my breath. "Any chance we can return them for actual cash? We could combine our stash and finally buy those chandeliers we've been wanting to add to our event decoration stores."

Jazz barks out a laugh in response. "Quit being so practical and enjoy an extravagant gift. It's not like you get that many."

She has a point there. Ethan and I have a policy that we set aside any extra money for a rainy day or retirement, whichever comes first. I remember the year my dad was laid off. That was when we discovered my mom had been pilfering funds from the emergency account to support a hummingbird sanctuary in Costa Rica. You can't make this kind of stuff up. We wound up eating a LOT of Top Ramen and mac and cheese during those six months, but at least my mother was happy with the knowledge that the hummingbirds were safe.

I don't ever want to relive that experience.

While scrolling through my texts before leaving for my meeting, I spy a message from EatMeOrganic. It's from my high school friend, Sarah. Unlike me, Sarah moved back home after graduating from college and started an organic produce company, which she's turned into this weird kind of destination location for slow-food-minded millennials like herself. She spent the first five years establishing and expanding the farm, which is situated on ten of her parents' fifty acres. They now supply produce to some of Chicago's swankiest restaurants.

I see her every time I come home. I'm particularly excited to introduce her to Ethan.

Hey, Chick! I've added five yurts to the farm since you've been here to use as a B&B. I can't wait for you to see them. Now, if you're family drives you too nuts, you can always come stay with me! -Sarah

I respond:

I'm half-tempted to come right to your place. I'm terrified what Ethan is going to make of them.

She immediately answers:

You didn't do yourself any favors by keeping them apart for so long.

I type:

Thanks a lot! Are you trying to make this harder?

She responds with a series of emojis that range from terrified faces to those sweating bullets to others outright laughing before answering:

I'm doing the North Shore run myself tomorrow, so I can pick you and your yummy man up at the airport. You mentioned in your email you were planning on renting a car, but please let me do this so we can have a couple hours to hang before I drop you off at the asylum.

Touched, I tell her:

Sounds Great! I just know you and Ethan will hit it off like gangbusters! Don't forget his parents will be with us.

She sends another twenty or so kissy face emojis before signing off.

Life in the fast lane calls. I need to go out to the greenhouse and rotate my compost and feed my worms.

I have to know.

Feed your worms?

Vermiculture, baby! You keep a zillion worms in a plastic worm farm and feed them regularly, then use their waste as fertilizer. It's liquid gold!

I feel my scrambled eggs coming up on me.

Worm poop? You use worm poop? I have no words.

Catriona Fiona Masterton, you've turned into a city slicker. What happened to the country girl I grew up with?

I respond:

I was never into worm poop, even when I lived on the farm with my family. We used good old-fashioned steer manure and it never did us wrong.

She sends another laughing emoji.

The world of poop is ever-changing my friend. Can't wait to see you!!!!!!!!!!!!!!

I smile despite my overall trepidation of going home. Sarah is the perfect person to introduce Ethan to before he meets my family. She'll prepare him a tiny bit for what's to come. It's not everyone who can have a legit conversation about the benefits of fecal matter. Granted, she's the least crazy person from my early life, but she's way more out there than anyone my intended knows. I head out the door to my appointment feeling lighter than I've felt since this trip was planned. Now, all I have to do is nail down the Vanderhauffer wedding and pick up all the things on my mom's list that she wants me to bring home for her. What could possibly go wrong?

The Friendly Skies

"Catriona, can you please pass me the Dramamine I put into your purse?"

Ethan is green. I dig through my bag and hand him the purple and gold box. "Are you feeling motion sick again?"

He nods his head. "It should pass once we stop bumping around up here." Ethan isn't afraid to fly and can quote all kinds of statistics to let you know why you're much safer eighteen thousand feet in the air versus doing something truly dangerous like roller skating in the park. But he is sensitive to motion.

"I'm getting quite excited, actually."

"Why?" I ask.

He opens his eyes and turns to me. "Because I'm finally going to meet your parents. They're my future in-laws, after all."

I offer a noncommittal, "Mmm." I've spent the last fourteen minutes, since our wheels left the ground, wondering if it was still possible to keep this meeting from occurring. Short of a plane crash, which my intended assures me isn't likely, I'm coming up dry.

I smile at Ethan's mom, Natalie, who's sitting across the aisle from me. "How are you doing, Natalie? Would you like a Dramamine?"

She shakes her head. "No, dear, that's okay. I already took one. It should be kicking in any time now." Natalie *is* afraid to fly, but nothing is going to keep her from meeting my parents, either.

"Well, let me know if I can get you anything," I reply. A parachute perhaps?

She reaches across the aisle and takes my hand. "You're a thoughtful girl, Catriona. We're simply delighted to have you joining our family."

Ethan is very like his parents. They're planners, they're staid, always calm. I'm not sure they've ever raised their voices. I've certainly never heard them, anyway. While this may sound boring to some, to me it's downright nirvana. I grew up in a loud, crazy, and unpredictable environment. I don't want to raise my future offspring in an atmosphere like that. I want to know we're having meatloaf on Monday and ordering pizza on Friday, and that we will actually have dinner, the hummingbirds be damned.

Some might perceive Ethan as inflexible and rigid. Yet while he *is* very focused and organized in his own life, he doesn't normally try to control mine. This makes it possible to enjoy the benefits of the order he creates without feeling constricted by it— even though I occasionally tell a little white lie like I did with my massage appointment. This kind of structure is what I've been craving since my life plans blew up in my face, right after high school graduation.

Ethan's dad, Jason, offers Natalie a blow-up pillow for her neck. I overhear him say, "That's it, dear. Just close your eyes. I'm right here. I'll hold your hand while you sleep." How cute is that? They've been married for nearly forty years, and they're still so considerate of one another.

"I bought your grandmother a gift. I know how proud she is to be Scottish, and I wanted to let her know I support that," Ethan announces.

Nan needs Ethan's support about as much as she needs a dictionary of foul words. It's nice he did that, but he should understand my grandmother isn't some insipid frail woman in need of anything he can offer.

I don't know how to articulate that, so I say, "How sweet. You're so thoughtful."

He smiles reassuringly. "We're going to have a wonderful time. Quit worrying." *Yeah, I'll get right on that.*

Ethan dozes off like his mother, whose snoring has begun to resemble a rusty chainsaw. Poor Natalie would be mortified if she knew. Jason is reading a copy of The Atlantic, and I'm contemplating hijacking the plane with my nail scissors and forcing them to turn around.

When Things Start to Go Wrong

Note: When you ask the universe a question like, "What can possibly go wrong?" even casually, you have to be prepared for the answer—which in my case is everything. Everything can go wrong. Sarah picks us up from the airport in her farm truck. I told her we'd have Ethan's parents with us, but she apparently filed that information away and didn't bother checking the file before leaving for Chicago. Short of putting the Crenshaw's on the flatbed on a bale of hay, like a couple of stowaway golden retrievers, there's no way we're all driving the hundred miles to Gelson in the same vehicle.

Natalie and Jason are lovely about the mix-up. Natalie announces, "We'll just get a rental car and follow you."

"We should have an extra vehicle anyway in case we want to run an errand or something," Jason agrees.

This sounds like the perfect solution to our problem, except that Ethan is nowhere near as gracious. He's clearly irritated and doesn't try to hide it. He huffs, "I'll go with you. Catriona can ride with her *friend.*" He says "friend" in such a way one would think he was talking about a particularly virulent strain of STD.

Sarah looks pretty respectable for her, especially considering she's been delivering produce all morning. It's not like she still has dreadlocks or anything. Her shiny blonde hair is cut a bit shorter than mine, which is shoulder length. Granted, her nose ring is a little large and could pass for a sketchy-looking mole, but she's only wearing three eyebrow rings, instead of the eight she had when we were in high school.

My friend opens and closes her mouth three times, as if she's trying to process Ethan's bad manners but doesn't know how. If it were anyone other than my fiancé being so rude to her, she'd probably tell him to pull his head out of his ass and get a life, but for my sake, she demurs. The silence is deafening.

I turn to Ethan, aghast at his behavior. I want to call him on it, but I don't want to fight in front of his parents. Instead, I grab his cell phone and type my parents' address into his GPS app. I smile at his folks. "Again, I'm so sorry about the confusion. We'll see you in a couple of hours."

Natalie waves her hand. "Nothing to worry about, dear. I can't tell you how much we're looking forward to this trip."

Ethan won't even make eye contact with me, so I grab my suitcase and take off in the direction of the parking garage. Sarah catches up to me but remains quiet. Finally, I look at her and abruptly change my route to an escalator that leads to one of the many bars of O'Hare Airport.

When we arrive at the first, my childhood friend walks straight to the counter and demands, "Two microbrews, make it fast." She takes a big swig of hers before saying, "It feels more like a margarita kind of night, but we still have to drive home."

I shake my head. "I have no idea what's gotten into him. Ethan's always so polite. Like seriously, he'll apologize to strangers if they step on his feet, claiming it was his fault for being in their way."

My friend shrugs her shoulders. "Maybe he's nervous about meeting your family. This is kind of a big deal for him."

"*He's* nervous?" I gasp. "I'm petrified! I'd planned on preparing him a little more during the drive home for what he's going to encounter. But now, there's no chance."

Sarah's eyes bug out in alarm. "What do you mean by prepare him? You have told him what awaits, haven't you?"

I tilt my head in an ambivalent fashion. "Well, yeah, sure, I've told him some stuff. Like he knows my brother is currently unemployed, and that my mom loves her shortbread pans." I take a big sip of my beer. "I've mentioned Nan's colorful vocabulary, but he has no idea the extent of what's coming."

"Holy crap, Cat. I think we're going to need a few more of these. We'll have to hit up the liquor store on the way into town for fortification."

"Most definitely. I just haven't been able to figure out how to describe my family without scaring Ethan to death."

"So, you decided to just spring them on him? I'm not sure how sound that reasoning is."

I blow out a breath I didn't realize I'd been holding. "I just figured that once they were all together it would just sort of evolve. You know, just mix."

"You mean like hydrogen sulfide and nitric acid?" She takes in my look of confusion and explains, "High school chemistry. Remember the time we set the science lab on fire?"

I do. "Oh, yeah. You don't really think my family and Ethan are going to explode like that, do you?"

She takes another healthy gulp of her beer. "Only one way to find out." She stands up, grabs my arm and says, "Come on."

The Introduction

Sarah and I hide out in the driveway until Ethan and his parents pull in, which is only a few minutes after we do. Sarah blew right past them on the freeway about thirty miles after we left O'Hare. Ethan is a bit of a Sunday driver. My friend is not.

As soon as the Crenshaws get out of their rental, my dad calls out, "Halloooo! Welcome! Come right on up!" I imagine he's had his faced pressed to the window for the last hour waiting for us to arrive. "Hurry up. It's colder than a witch's tit out here."

My mom smacks him playfully. "Now, Dougal, what kind of thing is that to say?" In truth, it's the kind of expression every member in my family has used my whole life.

My parents are ecstatic about finally getting to meet Ethan. This is the only reason I can think that the walkway in front of the house has actually been cleared of snow. Historically, my father has adopted a policy of refusing to do so, simply on the grounds that it will only fill up again. The house itself appears like it always does: warm, welcoming, and slightly weird.

My mom grabs her guests in a sort of hug meets huddle and declares, "I'm Maggie, this is my husband, Dougal."

Ethan's parents seem pleased, if not a little overwhelmed, by the exuberant welcome.

"What a unique vase display," Natalie announces. She's, of course, referring to the fourteen copper and brass jugs by either side of the front door. I'm not going to be the one to tell her they're spittoons. Like actual things we spit into. I just hope she doesn't look closely and see their engravings. "Spit Your Wad Here" and "Lick and Spit" are just a couple that are sure to give it away.

Sarah doesn't follow us up to the porch. She calls out a greeting to my parents and then says, "I'll call you tomorrow, Cat." Then with an exaggerated wink, adds, "Have fun!"

When we walk into the entryway, Nan appears in a 1960s style house dress of bright yellow and orange. Yes, she's desperately out of fashion, *and* wearing a turban; but other than that, she looks like she's trying to make a good impression. I hug her tightly and whisper in her ear, "You look gorgeous!"

She beams in response and motions to her mouth. "I'm chewing gum. It should help me keep some of my thoughts to myself." Since it is not something she normally cares about, she is obviously trying to not scare Ethan away and I love her for it.

My mom leads the way into the living room and we all follow obediently behind. It's well past eleven pm, but she's still set out her version of appetizers: pistachio nuts— still in the shell, and an uncut salami log. She gushes, "We're just so tickled to have you here! Imagine, after all this time, we're finally getting a chance to meet."

Natalie beams, "We're just as delighted as you are, Maggie. It's past time."

My mom rubs her hands together like she's just had a fiendish idea. "Now, how about something celebratory to drink?"

"I'd love a cold water, please," Natalie says.

"Make that two." Jason adds.

Ethan laughs. "Three it is!"

While she fills requests, my dad runs back outside to gather a few spittoons for the inevitable shells. When he gets back, he picks up the nut bowl to show everyone how it's done at Masterton Hall—his moniker for our old farmhouse, not mine. I'm not even particularly concerned about his demonstration, because in reality it's such a benign thing compared to what's ahead.

Dad grabs a small handful of nuts, throws them all in his mouth, and begins what he refers to as the shuck and chuck. After about forty seconds, he begins to spit the pistachio shells across the room aiming at various spittoons. He hits all the marks, then smiles and explains, "The rules are you have to put a minimum of ten nuts in your mouth at a time or you forfeit victory. The winner is the person who gets the most shells in and you have to get at least one into every spittoon."

Ethan and his parents have no idea what to make of this. They look at me helplessly, wanting me to intervene. "Dad," I say, "maybe this isn't something we have to do on our first day here. Maybe we can build up to it."

"Nonsense!" he booms. "Your future family is my future family. I just know they'll be naturals."

He's so excited I don't have the heart to put an end to this. So, I grab a few nuts and face my soon-to-be in-laws. I instruct, "It's not as hard as it looks. Basically, you shuck all the nuts first, then squirrel them away in your cheek while you line up the shells to fire out." Clearly taking leave of my senses, I add, "Make sure your tongue is dead center in the middle of the shell and then spit for all you're worth."

Natalie looks like she's about to faint. Ethan stares at me like I've grown a second head.

Jason finally manages, "I've never spit a nutshell in my life. I can't imagine I'd be any good at it."

No amount of cajoling on my part encourages the Crenshaws to join in my dad's favorite game. Even Nan gets in on the action, but it's a no-go for Ethan and his parents.

Somewhat defeated by their failure to participate, my mother offers, "Maybe you're all just tired. Would you like me to show you to your rooms?"

They jump at the reprieve.

"Please!" Natalie effuses. "I'm really quite worn-out. I'm sure a good night sleep will be just the ticket."

My mom explains, "Nan is going to bunk down in the basement with Travis while you're here, so you can have her room. She'll just need to come in every now and again to get her whatnots out of the closet."

Natalie and Jason nod politely and share a look, obviously not quite sure what a whatnot is. I'm guessing they're hoping it's not a machete she plans on using on them in their sleep.

Ethan follows me into my girlhood bedroom full of ceramic unicorns and New Kids on the Block posters. He hasn't spoken to me since the airport. When my mom finally wishes us a good night, he turns around and chokes out, "*They* are your parents?" He asks like I've just introduced him to Ted Bundy and his wife, or at the very least Honey Boo Boo and Mama June.

I know he's been thrown for a loop. I get that. But still, I'd hoped he'd have the decency not to be so openly appalled. For a split second I feel very protective of the crazy people that are my family. In that moment, I answer, "Yes, *they* are my parents. What's wrong with them?" I dare him to state the obvious, which he wisely chooses not to do. Instead, he turns his back on me and changes into his pajamas before crawling into the twin bed across the room from mine. Our conversation is apparently over.

In the Light of a New Day

Traveling is stressful. Meeting new people who will soon be related to you by marriage is stressful. My certifiable family is stressful. Given last night's traumas, when I wake-up I decide to cut Ethan some slack and start the day fresh. After all, it's on me that I didn't do more to prepare him for what to expect. I peek over my covers at him and see him lying perfectly still on his twin bed like a soldier lined up for inspection.

I creep across the room, pull the covers back and crawl in next to him. He unconsciously makes room for me, as he's been doing since I moved in with him a year ago. When I playfully run my foot up and down his leg, he groans in his sleep and turns toward me. But before anything can come of it, his eyes pop open and he declares, "Catriona!"

I smile coyly. "Yes, Ethan?"

Shimmying as far as he can toward the wall, he replies, "We can't do this in your parents' house!"

"Why not?"

"W-w-w-well …" he stammers, "it wouldn't be appropriate."

I make a "psh" sound and respond, "We've shared a one-bedroom apartment for a full year *and* we're engaged to be married. I'm guessing my parents know the score."

He shakes his head and pushes me away. "I wouldn't be comfortable."

So much for reconnecting. But at least we're talking to each other. "Ethan, I told you my family was different. Now that we're here, you're going to see that for yourself. Please try to remember you're marrying me, not them."

The memory of the night before seems to rush in all at once and smack him in the head like a low flying bird of prey. He recoils. "Please tell me you don't actually enjoy that nut game."

"Obviously not," I laugh. "As you've never seen me perform the shuck and chuck before, you can be comforted in knowing it's not a tradition I plan on keeping alive."

"Thank God." He sighs audibly, crinkling his nose at the memory.

"But you should also know my parents do things differently"—which is an understatement of epic proportion—"and I'm not going to tell them how to act in their own home." I hope he understands this means he can't control them either and shouldn't bother trying. God knows it's a losing battle.

Ethan doesn't bother acknowledging my warning, he just throws the covers off, and we get up and make the bed. The fact that he's whistling under his breath while he does so, tips me off that he's no longer holding a grudge about yesterday and is back to his old self.

"Come on, let me show you the bathroom. There are a few things you should know about our old plumbing." The look on his face is priceless while I impart, "Let the water run for thirty seconds, so any rust in the pipes can clear out, and never flush the toilet without yelling out 'FLUSH!' first."

"Why in the world would I have to yell flush?" He looks like he's about to be sick.

"To alert the household you're about to flush the toilet," I answer. Lest he think this is another wacky kind of game my family plays for kicks, I explain, "When a toilet is flushed anywhere in the house, scalding hot water pours out of any faucet that happens to be turned on at the time."

Shaking his head, he responds, "That can't be safe. Your parents need to have their pipes fixed."

"What they need is brand new plumbing, but that's costly. In the meantime, this method works just fine."

"Catriona," my fiancé begins, "I cannot announce to the whole house when I've just, you know, used the facilities."

Now seems the appropriate time to warn him that my dad jumped on the whole low-flow toilet craze a few years back, and that sometimes, depending on what's left in the toilet, it needs to be flushed multiple times. But I can't bring myself to share that news quite yet. Instead, I shoo him out the door, relieve my bladder and show him how it's done.

"FLUSH!"

Yes, It's Edible

I walk into the kitchen and hear my mom tell our guests, "Nan is from Scotland. Her family immigrated to the US when she was only three." While, she doesn't have any trace of a brogue or anything, my grandmother's pride in her roots is fierce. She connects to her ancestry as often as possible, normally through cooking and dance. My mother was raised accordingly.

Mom scurries around the kitchen preparing her standard show-off breakfast, which she only does when she's trying to impress. By the looks of it, she's intent on making a good impression on my future in-laws.

Jason appears to have put last night's awkward introduction behind him and announces, "Everything smells so delicious, I can't wait to dig in."

Natalie follows suit, "I'm positively famished." I bet she's wishing she had a few of those pistachio nuts last night after all.

The first thing my mom puts on the table is a plate of shortbread. I look closely and realize she's purchased a new mold. Ethan reaches out to take one and asks, "Is that ET stamped on your cookies?"

Mom, or Maggie, or Mags as her friends call her, beams with

pride. "It is! I've never seen a shortbread pan quite like it. I came upon it on eBay one day and I just had to add it to my collection." Then she confides, "I paid fifty dollars for it, if you can believe it." Which obviously, Ethan can't.

Natalie finishes up a bite in her mouth and declares, "That's the best shortbread I've ever eaten. What's your secret?"

I challenge my mother with my eyes that she is not to share her secret. She's positively chomping at the bit to do it, though. I shake my head in her direction. There are somethings better left a mystery; one of those things is pig lard.

Her mouth forms a half grimace, half smile as she answers, "Alas, I've vowed to never divulge it." Then with a twinkle in her eye, she adds, "But if you figure it out on your own, I promise to confirm your suspicions if they prove correct."

I exhale in relief. My family is not capable of duplicity as a rule, but this one is truly best kept under lock and key. She pulls her Scotch eggs out of the oven and puts them on the table, before retrieving another pan.

"Is that a loaf of rye bread?" Ethan's mom claps her hands and asks in delight.

I answer for my mom, "No, Natalie, that's a traditional Scottish meat dish." I know I should tell them more, but I'm hoping they'll just eat it without ever needing to know its name.

Jason's eyes brighten as he inhales mightily. "It smells wonderful! I can't wait to try it."

"Serve yourselves while the food is hot." My mom instructs. "The rest of the family ate earlier." I'm guessing that's probably true. She most likely fed them cold cereal before hiding them away. My parents are aware they're different. They know I've kept

Ethan from meeting them because I don't know how to explain them. I'm not proud of that and I never wanted to hurt their feelings, but honestly, it's like they're from another planet. A planet where normal, well-thought-out behavior is not tolerated.

My mom cuts into the meat and scoops it on to everyone's plate for them. She announces, "We only serve this on special occasions."

Jason digs in, excitedly. He eats with gusto and praises, "My word, this is something special!" My mom basks in his approval.

Ethan also seems to be enjoying himself, so I make my excuses and head downstairs to check on Nan. I haven't seen her in months, and I want a few private moments alone with her to find out how she's doing.

As I descend the stairs, my nostrils are assailed by the skunky stench any high school student would recognize—marijuana. When I reach the bottom of the staircase, I look across the finished basement and discover Travis and Nan sitting on a sofa sparking up a doobie.

I cross over to them concerned. "Nan, tell me you're not letting my idiot brother corrupt you."

Travis rolls his eyes. "Dude, chill out. They've done some great research that shows pot reduces the symptoms of Tourette syndrome."

I smack the back of his head. "Travis, Nan doesn't have Tourette's. She has damage from strokes which apparently crossed a couple wires in her brain."

My brother blows a plume of smoke in my direction. "Neurological is neurological. If it helps with one, it'll probably help with the other."

I look around at the complete disarray of his living space—piles of clothes scattered about higgledy-piggledy, a garbage can overflowing with beer bottles, and dirty plates strewn about like the fraternity in Animal House. I sarcastically snap, "I'm sorry, all this time I thought you were sucking off our parents like a parasitic tick, but you've been going to medical school the whole time."

Nan exhales a cloud of MaryJane and yells, "Whore!" At my shocked expression, she clarifies, "Not you, dear. I was just thinking about that Dorcas Abernathy."

Nan regularly comments on thoughts running through her head that seem entirely random to anyone she's with. Also, Gramps dated Dorcas in high school and asked her to marry him at graduation. Dorcas declined his offer and Nan has never gotten over being his second choice. Hence, Mrs. Abernathy is at the heart of a lot of my grandmother's complaints.

"Is the pot helping any, Nan?" I ask. I mean, heck, if it is, it's probably better to have a stoned grandmother than one who talks like sailor on shore leave.

Nan smiles as she inhales and holds the smoke in her lungs to work its magic before blowing it out and answering, "I would say it takes away about half of my outbursts. So, that's pretty good, right?"

"That *is* good," I reply. And if my brother weren't such a cretin, I'd probably apologize to him for doubting his mad skills in prescribing help for our grandmother. Just as I'm about to suggest Nan come upstairs and properly meet my future husband, I hear the afore mentioned yell out, "OH, MY GOD! Why didn't you tell me it was haggis?!"

And while ground sheep's innards are not for everyone, they truly are edible.

The Chieftain

After making sure Ethan doesn't throw up his breakfast, I once again reassure him, "Haggis is real food and you're not going to die because you consumed it. In fact"—I recite a favorite tidbit of my dad's— "it's full of vitamin A, D, C, B12, and loaded with minerals—magnesium, selenium, zinc, and copper—just to name a few."

He doesn't look sold and goes upstairs to rest, like his parents have already done. I head outside in search of my father. I know I'll find him in the barn out back. It's where he always goes for his alone time.

I once asked him, "Why the barn?"

"Because I like the smell," he informed me. "It's so earthy and real. It makes me feel like I'm connected to my ancestral clan." There's no better thing on earth than the ancestral clan as far as Dougal Masterton is concerned. Disneyland wouldn't even be a close second.

I put on a pair of snow shoes sitting by the back door and make my way the hundred yards to his hideaway, which is a huge white structure that would probably fit our house twice over. My parents don't currently have much livestock to speak of. We had cows, goats, horses, sheep, chickens, and pigs while I was growing up, which provided a constant source of meat and entertainment. But in the last several years, they've been getting rid of most of the animals since they no longer want the responsibility. They're down to six chickens and a donkey named Heather.

Dad has always bemoaned the fact that he wasn't raised in Scotland during the great Jacobite uprising of 1745. He's always felt he was born in the wrong time and has struggled to live in the modern world his whole life. He doesn't watch television, he rarely talks on the phone, and only drives a car because horses aren't practical everyday transportation. And he golfs, a lot.

When I finally spot him, I ask, "Aren't you cold out here, dressed like that?"

"Lass," he says as he stands up modeling his Masterton plaid kilt and bare knees, "Scots don't chill in their native attire."

He wears the plaid more often than he wears pants, although happily he didn't last night. Yes, that's correct. My dad wears his family kilt around town like it's the most normal thing in the world, and to him, it is. Asking him to stop would be akin to asking him to cut his legs off at the knees.

I indicate the old bagpipes next to him. "I see you've been polishing great-grandad's pipes. Any chance you've been practicing?" I ask hopefully.

"No time, I'm getting the boys ready for battle."

I look and see he's fastidiously dressing his assorted taxidermied field mice in the Masterton plaid. From the looks of it, they're fighting the French today. "Want to help?" he asks. *As if.* "No, I just came out to see how you're doing."

He puts down the mouse chieftain in his hand and comes

over and wraps his arms around me. "I'm good, honey. How are you?"

I smile. There's nothing like the safe feeling I get wrapped in my father's embrace. My dad is a big hugger and he always makes sure we know how much he loves us by the copious number of them he gives us.

I shrug my shoulders in response. "Doing okay, I guess. Kind of nervous about everyone getting to know Ethan."

"Oh, come on, he's not so bad," he jokes. "A little boring maybe, but I'm sure we'll all like him just fine."

My dad knows I'm more worried about what Ethan will make of them, but he's so confident in his weirdness he easily teases me about it. He asks, "Has he had any conversations with Nan yet?"

I shake my head. "Not yet. She's downstairs getting high with Travis."

My dad tips his head back and forth. "Yeah, that's something new, but it seems to be helping, so we're supportive of her efforts." And why wouldn't they be? A stoned grandmother fits right into their definition of normal.

"What about my idiot brother? Why do you keep supporting him like you do? Don't you think it's time he gets a life and starts taking care of himself?"

"Actually, I do. Your brother has never had your innate confidence, and he seems determined to make his life as difficult as possible." He puts the chieftain down and picks up another mouse. "Your mom and I have talked recently, and we think it's time we kick him out of the nest and force him to take some responsibility for his life. We're giving him until the New Year and then we're going to tell him he needs to find work."

Wow. I did not see that coming. My parents have always seemed quite content to let Travis do his own thing and try to find his own path. They invested in his pipe dream to make his own microbrew corn beer, thinking it was a good use of the five acres they still use after renting out the rest to a neighboring farmer. Of course, nothing came from it as Travis drank all the beer he ever made.

"Are you going to finally make him use his degree from clown college?" I ask. My parents paid for Travis to go to clown college when he decided it would be lucrative to be the only clown for rent in a hundred-mile radius.

My dad rolls his eyes heavenward. "God, no! That boy drastically overestimated people's desire to pay money to a creepy man wearing big shoes and makeup to entertain their children at birthday parties."

"Shirley Shyster was not a moniker that instilled confidence," I agree. "He was such a normal little kid, too."

Even though we were three years apart, I still remember a lot of fun times with my brother. While I currently find him as pleasant to be around as a nasty case of bronchitis, I still hold out hope he'll grow up one day and become a productive member of society.

Time and again my mom and dad have stood by him, but thus far, nothing has gotten Travis off his butt, to ever stick with anything. He always quits before he can gain any momentum. I'm glad they're finally going to give him the push he so obviously needs.

"So, what are your plans for today?" my dad inquires.

My eye is drawn to a mouse half the size of the others. I can't for the life of me imagine how someone ever stuffed something so small. I answer, "I'm going to take Ethan and his parents over to Sarah's farm and show off her growing empire. I know the farm stand is closed this time of year, but she says she keeps the gift shop open and sells herbs from the greenhouse. She's going to make us lunch."

He puts a pair of mouse spectacles on the rodent he's working on. "That sounds like fun. Just be back in time for dinner. We have a fantastic surprise for you tonight."

Life on Another Planet

Before we climb into my mom's car, I pull Ethan aside. "You owe Sarah an apology."

He practically growls in response. "I know. I'll take care of it." It's not the right time to ask why he was so rude to my friend at the airport, as we're about to see her. I don't want to pull a fresh scab off his irritation, but I am going to find out later. Ethan's not acting at all like himself, and I can only assume it's the stress of being with my family.

I open the car doors for Natalie and Jason and discover my mom's backseat is full of gin. And by full of gin, I mean like four cases full.

Natalie's eyes bug out and she exclaims, "My goodness, that's a lot of gin!"

I just smile and ask Ethan, "Will you to help me carry the boxes to the garage?"

"Why does she have so much?" he asks while trudging through the snow.

I half shrug my shoulders. I can't do a full shrug because I'm currently hauling fifty pounds of hooch. "I have no idea."

He's obviously expecting more of an answer, but I don't have one for him. My mom has gone through several phases that simply defy explanation. The year I was in seventh grade she collected every kind of cozy like they were a valuable commodity nearing extinction. Tea cozies, toilet paper cozies, mug cozies, beer can cozies, toaster cozies. You've never seen so many cozies. It seemed like there were thousands of them.

When I asked her what was going on, she answered, "I like the word cozy. It makes me happy there's something out there that wants to hug all the treasures in my kitchen." The weird thing is—correction, the extra weird thing is—she never used any of them. She just hoarded them for fifteen months before donating them all to the hospital. I have no idea what they did with them.

So why does she have a carload of gin? God knows. Maybe she's fallen in love with juniper berries and has decided that having their essence close by makes her feel loved. Maybe she's making her own astringent. Maybe she's inviting the whole town over for martinis. One guess is as good as the next.

When my mom's sedan is booze-free, we climb in, and I give the Crenshaws a short tour of town. We turn onto the brick Main Street, and I tell them, "We have seven churches, two pharmacies, two diners, three clothing stores, one library, two banks, one grocery store, one movie theater, and one stop light. The whole town is only thirty-two hundred people." It doesn't take that long to get through.

Ethan's mom comments from time-to-time, "How delightful!" or "How charming!" or "What a sweet village!" I think she means it, too.

Gelson truly is the perfect small-town backdrop. People wave to each other on the street, you never go anywhere without knowing ninety percent of the folks you run into, and your neighbors will always help you out in a pinch.

They also always know your business—often before you do, they gossip about you like you're Kim Kardashian, and they make up stories when they get bored. It's like living in an idyllic world full of chocolate cake and vipers. But you never know what you're going to encounter when you walk out your front door.

Jason wants to know things like, "What kind of crops do you grow?" or makes comments such as, "You'd definitely need a riding mower if you lived here." Which isn't true at all. People in Gelson either mow their own lawns on foot, or they hire a neighbor kid to do it for next to nothing. Kids in rural towns are used to working hard for their spending money.

"My first jobs were detasseling corn and walking beans," I inform them. "Which were the only jobs underage kids could get and still make a decent amount of money."

"I would have never taken you for a farm laborer. I bet you miss it," Ethan teases.

I shoot him a look and brag, "I got up at four in the morning to eat, pack my lunch, and ride my bike to the IGA, where the bus picked us up at five to start our workday. We were out in the fields by five thirty." With a prideful tone, I add, "Riding lawnmowers weren't for us. They were for suburbanite softies who didn't like to break a sweat." Growing up in this town certainly toughened me up. Having said that, I'm glad those days are behind me.

There are signs announcing we're nearing Sarah's farm miles before we get there. "Eat Me Organic in 5 Miles!," "You Can Eat

Me Organic in Only 3 Miles!" And my personal favorite, "Eat Me Now! Next Right!"

Pulling into her driveway is like landing on another planet.

"My goodness, isn't this interesting!" Natalie exclaims.

Jason seems genuinely excited, as well. "These bird windmills are delightful."

Ethan makes no comment, but the look on his face suggests he just got a whiff of bad meat. Although that might still be the lingering effects of his breakfast.

The yurts are awesome looking, big and imposing, but also seemingly out of place—like a pop-up village on the moon. There are multi-colored windmills shaped like various birds everywhere. They're startlingly bright against the snowy white landscape. Roadrunners, pelicans, birds of paradise—you name it, they're flapping their wooden wings in the breeze like they're trying to pick up enough speed to take off. The look of distaste on my intended's face is palpable. I look at Ethan and warn, "Be nice. I mean it." He rolls his eyes in response.

Sarah flies out of the yurt closest to our car, jumping up and down like she's seven and I'm Santa Claus. I love her excitement. I get out and throw my arms around her and whisper in her ear, "My mom served haggis this morning."

She pulls away and makes a retching sound. "Oh, my GOD! Are you sure they're up to eating again today?" As a dedicated vegetarian, there is no food more repugnant to my friend than haggis.

I don't have a chance to answer before the Crenshaws are upon us. Natalie reaches out to take Sarah's hand and gushes, "What a beautiful property! You must be so proud of it."

"Do you have any windmills for sale?" Jason asks. "I'm particularly taken with the parrot."

"I sure do," she assures him. "I'll show you the gift yurt after lunch." Then she leads us inside.

"Surprise!" Sarah shouts. The space has been set up as the most charming little café you've ever seen. There are eight small tables, each with a different brightly colored Indian print batik table cloth and mismatched napkins. It's eclectic to the max, but one hundred percent my friend's style. "I'm officially opening it this summer, but I couldn't wait to show you. Guess what I'm naming it?"

I start laughing, because there's only one thing Sarah would name her restaurant given the name of her produce business. "Eat Me!" She nods her head up and down so fast she looks like a bobble head on the dashboard of a speeding car.

When we sit down, she announces, "I went totally vegan today and made garbanzo bean cutlets with cashew sour cream, assorted steamed vegetables, and naan bread."

I tear off a piece of bread and it's so good I want to fill my purse with it, so I can eat it all day. She ends the meal with dark cherry and coconut ice cream. I gorge myself until all I want to do is lie on the ground and unbutton my jeans.

The elder Crenshaws clean their plates, and even Ethan claims to have enjoyed it. "I never knew vegetarian food could be so good." While it's not a winning endorsement, it's still a compliment.

Sarah smiles graciously. "Thank you, Ethan. That means a lot." I can tell she's not harboring any hard feelings over his previous mistreatment of her. He seems to take her comment to mean he doesn't need to apologize for his bad manners yesterday. I can't wait to get back to New York and get the old Ethan back. I do not like this Midwestern version of him very much.

The gift shop is just as charming as the café. One-of-a-kind pottery abounds, along with wind chimes, incense, and books on out-there topics like past-life-regression and casting runes. I pick up some tea lights made out of lightning glass and say, "These are gorgeous! Do you make them yourself?"

"I wish!" she laughs. "No, I get them from this cool guy I went to college with. He lives in a shack on Lake Michigan and specializes in all kinds of glass art. He's going to make me a line of hookas to sell this summer."

"Are you going to sell opium, too?" I joke.

"Nah, they're just decorative and cool looking. If people don't buy them to use for pot, they'll use them as objects d'art."

I pick up a few things to take back to Jazz. I even order two cases of tea lights made with lightning glass to use for our beachy weddings in the Hamptons.

When it's time to leave, I hug my friend. "I wish we lived closer. I miss having you in my everyday life."

She hugs me back even harder. "I'll never live in a concrete jungle like New York, so if you ever want that to happen, it's up to you to come home."

I snort, "I guess I'll just have to keep missing you." Then I promise, "I'll see you again before I leave."

We all climb into the car nearly in a food-induced coma. As tomorrow is Thanksgiving, I'm not sure it was wise to eat so much today, but boy, was it yummy. I suddenly remember my parents' surprise and try not to worry.

Surprise!

Surprises from my parents are one of the things I couldn't wait to leave behind when I left home.

"Surprise, we're taking a family sheep shearing class and learning how to spin our own wool!"

"Surprise! We're renting a cottage without electricity or indoor plumbing for the summer on a lake where you can't swim because of the eels!"

"Surprise, we're hosting a foreign exchange student from Venezuela, who doesn't use deodorant and gets to share your room with you for a year!"

You see where I'm going here? Their surprises never consisted of family cruises, nice dinners out, or lottery winnings. They were always weird and guaranteed not to delight.

So, when we get home and I see a car in the driveway that I don't recognize, I immediately know my parents' newest surprise involves a person. Historically, that's never gone well. I cite the Venezuelan foreign exchange student, and the homeless person my dad picked up at the grocery store who came to dinner and refused to leave until we gave him bus fair to go to South Dakota.

"It appears we have company," I tell the Crenshaws. "Don't

feel like you have to hang around. You can all go take a rest if you'd like."

Natalie looks relieved. "Thank you, dear. I really could use a little lie down." Jason nods his head in agreement.

Ethan yawns loudly and declares, "As you know, I'm not a napper, but I could definitely benefit from some quiet time." He never sleeps during the day, but I imagine he's worn out from all the new people, not to mention the constant conversation. Ethan likes his alone time, and there's been precious little of that here.

So, with that settled, I sneak us through the side door and send them up the back stairs before they can be bombarded by whomever is lying in wait. Then I walk into the kitchen and surprise! It's Sam Hawking, in the flesh—the only person in this world I'd hoped to never see again. The only person I've ever allowed to take my heart, stomp on it, give it back to me, and then shoot an arrow through it. Sam. Flipping. Hawking. In my parents' kitchen.

Sam is the one who got away. And I'm not the one who let him go, either. We were young and so completely entwined in each other's lives that it felt like we were the same person. I knew him like I knew myself, or I thought I did anyway, until the dumping.

We were in the same class from second grade (when his family moved to Gelson) until we graduated from high school. We both tried on different identities throughout our formative years, like kids do. Early on, he was an egghead, totally engrossed in studying, then he became a band geek and remained so until the summer after our freshman year. When he came back to school in the fall, he was one hundred percent jock. I don't know what they fed him, or what his fairy godmother sprinkled on him, but man-oh-man when I laid eyes on him after his transformation, I was blinded by my need to always be at his side.

My metamorphosis was almost diametrically opposed to Sam's. When he was in his geek phase, I was the only girl and best player on the little league team. When he was a band nerd, I was a junior high school cheerleader. When he transformed into Mr. Hunky Pants, I was the president of the National Honor Society. We were total opposites, but you know what they say about opposites. And in our case, they were one hundred percent correct.

We were like TNT and a match until Sam broke my heart by not going to the University of Illinois like we'd decided. Instead, he took a scholarship to Northwestern, two-and-a-half hours away. Not only did he not honor our plan, but on the night of our high school graduation, he broke up with me. Three years as a couple and poof. Over. Like we never meant anything to each other. Like we hadn't already decided what to name our kids, Isla and Oliver.

We'd spent our entire senior year planning how we would both go to school in Urbana. We'd get engaged our junior year, and then the summer after graduation we'd get married and move to Chicago to start our lives.

Apparently, Sam had been cooking up some other plans for himself, like applying to Northwestern, without telling me. The night of graduation, when I thought we were going to spend a romantic night dancing and dreaming under the stars, he broke my heart. And now he's here, in my parents' kitchen, fourteen years later, looking better than I could have ever imagined. The bastard.

All I can say is that my parents have outdone themselves this time. This is by far their worst surprise ever, and that includes the time they took us to see Barry Manilow in concert instead of the Backstreet Boys, like they'd promised.

Sucker Punched

I feel like I was casually walking down the street, minding my own business, when out of nowhere a fist the size of a Mack truck walloped me right in the solar plexus. BAM, sucker punched!

My mom sees me and jumps up like a fully wound jack-in-the-box. "Cat, look who's here!"

I want to smile casually and ask, "I'm sorry, have we met?" I want to not have just eaten my body weight in Indian bread, and more than anything I want to be unaffected by the man who gets up and turns toward me.

I can't help myself; when Sam Hawking looks into my eyes, I start to move toward him like we're magnets and he's pulling me in. I have to force myself to stop before I rub up against him like a cat in heat. I have a choice to make. I can either hock a loogie right in his face and top it off with a knee to the groin, or I can shake his hand like a maiden aunt visiting from Cleveland. I choose the latter. "Sam, what a surprise." No exclamation point.

He grins from ear to ear like he's the happiest man on earth and exclaims, "Kitty Cat! Let me look at you." Then he does. He gives me the slow peruse from head to toe, followed by a grunt of appreciation and low growl of something else altogether. *Jesus, Mary, Joseph, all the saints, and maybe an apostle or two*—that's how Nan used to swear before she discovered real cussing.

I grab a chair at the table and sit down before my knees buckle. I demand, "What are you doing here?" I hope my tone imparts disbelief as well as a healthy dose of incredulity at his sheer audacity to be darkening my doorstep.

"I saw Sam's mom at the IGA last week," my dad answers. "She said he was asking about you. So, I made her promise to send him by." Then he looks at Sam and gushes, "We've missed you, boy!"

Boy smiles sheepishly. "I've missed you all, too." His eyes linger on me a moment too long for someone who once threw me out of his life like yesterday's news.

I quirk my head and eyebrow as if to say, "Stick it where the sun don't shine, smooth-talker. The only reason I'm not welcoming you is because you walked out on me. When you crap where you eat, you're no longer invited to the trough." Dear God, I'm channeling Nan, albeit a little less graphically.

Of course, I don't say that out loud. Instead, I opt for the more passive, "Well, we're all busy now that we're grown-up and moved away from home. It's hard to keep in touch with old *friends*." Please note, "friends" is said with an inflection that suggests nothing of the sort and my mouth might look less like I'm smiling and more like I'm a vicious she-wolf about to rip him to shreds.

Sam clears his throat uncomfortably. "Yeah, I can't believe we haven't seen each other for so long. I thought for sure our paths would have crossed over summer vacations or Christmases, or something."

I don't answer. I merely offer a non-committal, "Mmm." The reason our paths never crossed is because I made darn sure they didn't. I had no intention of laying eyes on Sam Hawking again in this lifetime, and if I allowed myself the fantasy that we did meet, he was usually in a coffin about to be put six feet under.

My parents are finally beginning to glean that their surprise isn't a pleasant one for me. The fact that I get up and walk to the counter, grab a bottle of gin and take a healthy swig straight out of the bottle may be what finally tips them off.

My dad clears his throat and offers, "The Hawkings are joining us for Thanksgiving dinner tomorrow. Isn't that wonderful?"

Wonderful. Like sudden blindness is wonderful. Wonderful, like an itchy yeast infection and running out of toilet paper is wonderful. I have no words. None, zero, zilch. I have to sit down to a holiday dinner with Ethan, his parents, my ne'er-do-well brother, my foul-mouthed grandmother, my clueless parents, and the former love of my life? *Holy hell.* Was I Hitler in a past life? Judas Iscariot? Is that it? It had to have been someone that awful for karma to be gunning for me like this.

I force my mouth to tilt up at the corners, which I'm sure looks like I'm in the throes of major constipation. I don't sit back down with them. Instead, I grab the bottle, a straw, and walk out of the room without even bothering to excuse myself.

As I near the stairway, I hear my mom say, "That went better than I expected."

Boulders from Heaven

If you've never heard pebbles being thrown at a window before, you might mistake the sound for something much more nefarious. Of course, that depends on who's throwing the rocks. Axe murderers generally tend to get your attention in more aggressive ways and don't usually fool around trying to get you to open a window to let them in.

If it sounds like I'm rambling, I am. I look at the clock to see it's two in the morning. My head is more than a little fuzzy from the amount of gin I consumed after Sam left. Note, gin goes down pretty fast with a straw. Not four cases worth, but I can definitely see why my mom bought so much of it. If she has any more surprises planned like last night's, it's going to come in handy.

But rocks at my window, I know this sound. It's a sound I associate with the most intense emotions of my life: anticipation, yearning, love, and to be quite honest, unbridled lust. In other words, it's a sound I associate with Sam Hawking.

I look guiltily across the room to Ethan to make sure the noise hasn't woken him before hurrying to open the window. It's freezing cold out, so I don't want to keep it open for long. I just grab the paper weight sitting right next to the clock and drop it. Then I quickly shut out the arctic blast.

It's my greatest hope the four-pound geode hit Sam directly on top of the head and rendered him unconscious. I'd hate for it to have actually killed him, as I much prefer he lay out in the elements for a few hours, regain consciousness, and maybe require a couple of small amputations—nothing vital, a baby toe or the tip of his pinky finger. Just enough for him to carry the memory of his wrong-doing for the rest of his life.

I wait for three minutes to make sure he's good and passed out before I peek out the window again. Gah! There he is, standing with a smile on his beautiful face, the full moon illuminating him like an angel's halo. He's not in the least bit injured or comatose. In fact, he's tossing the geode up and down like it's a baseball, taunting me with his very being.

I ought to climb back into bed and succumb to the sandman again, but Sam crooks his finger at me in a come-hither kind of way that I'm totally helpless to resist. I grab my robe off the back of the desk chair, put it on, take one more look at a sleeping Ethan, and tiptoe out the door.

When I reach the bottom of the stairs, I rethink going outside for approximately six minutes, hoping the intruder has given up on me and has had the good sense to leave. I look out the peep hole in the front door and realize no such voodoo has occurred. He's standing there with his hands in his pockets and a huge smile on his face, staring right back at me.

Unlocking the deadbolt on the door, which has been painted nearly every color under the sun during my parents' thirty-year tenure in this house, I inhale like it's my last breath on earth and step out into the bracing cold.

Sam steps inward. "Aren't you going to invite me in?"

I push him farther out into the elements. "Why in the world would I do that?"

Batting hypnotic blue eyes at me, he answers, "Because it's freaking cold out here and you've kept me waiting for fifteen minutes."

I've kept *him* waiting? For fifteen minutes? Try fourteen years, buddy! I'm so furious, I briefly contemplate beaning him with one of my dad's spittoons. He notices where my eyes dart to and seems to make a pretty accurate guess at my intentions, which is probably why he reaches out to grab my hands. He doesn't have gloves on, but his hands are still warm, so very warm. Warm enough to trigger flashbacks of happier times that I have no business remembering.

They're bigger than I remember and they totally envelope mine. Tears unconsciously fill my eyes, and I hang my head to try to compose myself. When I finally look up, it's to see Sam staring down at me with such tenderness and yearning that I want to crawl between his arms and sink right into him.

I should not be having these feelings.

Yet, this is the face I'd thought I'd wake up to every morning of my life. This is the face I thought I'd see in my children, the one it took me years to get over. It's the face I currently want to kiss and punch at the same time.

Sam leans in, pulls me tight to him, and releases one word with such longing it's all I can do not to jump him. "Cat." The sound pours over me like warm maple syrup, thick and sweet, full of anticipation and possibility.

I shake my head, trying to free the hold he has over me. "Sam. Why are you here?"

Still clutching me tightly, his eyes plead with mine as he answers, "I'm here to apologize. I'm so sorry about what happened between us. About how it ended. I never thought we'd go this long without seeing each other. I thought I'd be saying this to you years ago."

Note, he doesn't say, "I'm sorry we ended." He says, "I'm sorry about *how* we ended." And of course, he could have said this to me any time in the last decade if he'd ever bothered to pick up the phone.

I don't want his apology, now. And if I did, I'd want him on his knees begging for forgiveness—perhaps with his head covered in honey right next to a swarming hive of bees. I'd want him aching with remorse and regret. I'd want him to feel a thousand times the pain I felt the first two years after he devastated me, and what I felt every single time after that when I recalled any memory of high school. Because he was at the center of every recollection that was worth having.

With a bionic strength that can only be rooted in total devastation and years of heartache, I pull my hands away, square my shoulders and smile, "Thanks for that. I appreciate your coming by." Then I step back.

The look on his face is priceless. I don't know what he was expecting to happen, but this isn't it. And while I'd like nothing more than to march him up to the hay loft and relive some of our more special moments, I force myself to say, "I'll see you later today at Thanksgiving dinner." Then I walk through the front door like some kind of flipping superhero. Wonder Woman has nothing on me.

Sam Hawking is my past. He's had his time in my life and that time is over. I'm not the innocent, naïve girl I once was. I'm a successful, happily engaged woman, who's tougher than she looks. I'm going to show Sam who I am at dinner, and he's going to rue the day he walked away from my awesomeness.

With my resolve firmly in place, I go back up to the room I'm sharing with my fiancé and fall right back to sleep—only to be tortured by dreams of what might have been.

Dreaming of the Devil

"SAM!" I yell out the front door at the top of my lungs. "Catch!" I hurl the popsicle like a torpedo shot out of the business end of a warship. The little league practices are sure coming in handy. No other nine-year-old can throw as fast as I can.

He reaches out and grabs it midair like a pro. "Yum, cherry, my favorite!" While he's tearing the wrapper off, he says, "Hurry up, Cat, I have to go soon. We'll never have time to finish if you don't move it."

We're playing twenty questions and have only gotten to seven. It's just so darn hot out, we needed something to take the edge off. I demand, "Fine, you're twenty years old. Would you rather marry Brittany Stephens or eat a dead frog covered in dung beetles?"

"Can I cook the frog first or do I have to eat it raw?" he asks.

I stare up into the clouds and think for a second before answering, "You can boil it, but you can't grill, and you can't use any barbecue sauce or anything." As an afterthought, I add, "And you have to eat the skin, too." Sam always uses barbecue sauce to cover up the taste of food he doesn't like.

He scratches his head. "Can I use salt?"

I roll my eyes and bite the tip off my popsicle, savoring the sweetness as it drips down the back of my throat. "Nope."

He thinks for a second. By the look on his face, his answer could go either way. Finally, he asks, "Would I have to kiss Brittany?"

"Duh! You'd be married. Of course, you'd have to kiss her."

He licks his popsicle until his lips begin to turn red before answering, "I guess I'd marry Brittany. She's not so bad."

I pick a handful of grass and throw it at him. "Last year you said you'd eat the frog and the dung beetles and you didn't even ask for barbecue sauce." I taunt him, "You loooooooove Brittany. You want to marry her and kiss her ..." I make kissy sounds as I jump up and dance around in circles, "Sam and Brittany sittin' in a tree, K-I-S-S-I-N-G ..."

Before I can finish, Sam leaps at me and tackles me to the ground in punishment for teasing him. "Fine, I'll eat the frog!"

"Too late," I announce. "You love Brittany and I'm going to tell everyone."

He threatens, "You tell anyone, and I'm going to tell them you peed your pants in second grade during our Christmas concert."

I inhale deeply. "No fair! You promised to take that secret to the grave."

He challenges me with his big blue eyes. "Neither one of us says anything, deal?" Then he sticks out his hand for me to shake.

I glare at him for a long minute before licking my hand and shaking his. "Deal. But I'm done playing this stupid game."

"Oh, no!" he declares. "You only answered six questions, and I've answered seven. You've got one more before we're even."

I drop back on the ground, close my eyes, and accept my fate. "Fine, what do you want to know?"

He makes a low humming noise in the back of his throat before he says, "You're sixteen and you've just learned how to drive. You want to go out with Sarah and go cow tipping, but your parents won't let you. Do you steal their keys and go anyway, or do you stay home like a loser and watch TV?"

I scoff, "You suck at this game. First of all, of course I'm gonna go tip cows. But I'm not stupid enough to take my parents' truck without permission. I'm gonna make *you* pick me up."

Sam laughs and slaps his hands on his jeans. "And I will, too. Cause you know I can't wait til we're old enough to go cow tipping."

The memories flood my dreams throughout the night, breaking through like water breaching a dam, wreaking destruction on the low-lying fields. Sam Hawking was my best friend long way before he was my boyfriend. We played together, shared secrets with one another, poured over pictures in the National Geographic we had no business looking at, and always stood up for each other no matter what. All that before we even shared our first kiss. We played twenty questions every year until he broke my heart. He's entwined in my DNA in such a way I'll probably need an exorcism to get rid of him.

In my foggy sleep-brain, I order myself to call Pastor Abernathy in the morning to set it up.

I'm Thankful for Gin

I look at the clock and discover it's already nine. Images of last night with Sam, both in the front yard and in my dreams, fill my mind. Damn that man! Why couldn't he leave well enough alone and stay away from me?

Ethan's bed is already made, so I know he's up and at 'em and ready for another day in bedlam. I hear my mom call up the stairs, "Shake your tail, Cat! We've got loads to do!"

When most people think of Thanksgiving dinner, their minds immediately go to images of the first Thanksgiving, the one they saw illustrations of in history books during elementary school years. The white man and the Native American sharing a feast of corn and brotherhood, side-by-side in harmony, passing the peace pipe.

It might briefly wander to images of a Charlie Brown Thanksgiving with Snoopy serving buttered toast and pretzels, before landing on the scene of a happy family, holding hands, going around the table giving thanks for the bounty in their lives and for the people they're sharing their lives with.

Images of giant turkeys stuffed with sausage and acorn stuffing come to mind. Whipped potatoes, green bean casserole, and pumpkin pies made by loving hands. A fire crackles in the background and classical music fills the pockets of air not already consumed by sheer gratitude. Our celebration is nothing like that.

A Masterton Thanksgiving is more a tribute to our Scottish roots than our American ones. The table is set with our family plaid, instead of the requisite autumnal colors one would expect. My mom adorns it with a very large bucket of fake heather, as the real stuff isn't in bloom in late November. The purple clashes tremendously with our colors of bright gold, green, and red, but no one seems to care.

My dad wears full-chieftain regalia, including a kilt, vest, suit coat, bow tie, knee-socks and feather in his cap. It's worth noting he's been wearing the same outfit since I can remember. As his girth has increased dramatically since my childhood, it's become a bit of challenge for him to get into it. He's taken to squeezing into a man-girdle on these special occasions, if there's even a hope in hell he can get into his kit. Luckily, the kilt is just a long piece of material and can be adjusted accordingly.

The women adorn themselves in long skirts, white blouses, and beanies—I'm not kidding. Nan wears her family's tartan, which is the McTavish plaid. It's predominately light blue, dark blue, and red. I wear the Masterton plaid and my mom has on a combination of both. The whole scene basically looks like Scotland threw up on us.

When we have guests, which is luckily not a frequent occurrence, we have extra plaids for them to wear over the clothes they arrive in. I've warned Ethan of this, and he assures me he'll play along without complaint.

I jump out of bed, grab my robe, and hurry down the stairs, only to run into Ethan. He takes my arms and gives me a sweet kiss, then offers, "I'm thankful for you."

New York Ethan is making an appearance. I kiss him back, "I'm sorry my family is so nuts."

He waves his hand dismissively. "Don't be. Like you said, I'm marrying you, not them." Then he pats my butt and winks. *Ooooh, is it possible he might be relaxing his rule of no hanky-panky in my parents' house?* I look forward to finding out. But there's no time now.

When I get to the kitchen, preparations are in full swing. My mom tends to the Cullen skink, which is a thick haddock soup. Nan works on the tatties, herring, and black pudding. My job is the *clootie dumpling*— essentially, flour, bread crumbs, dried fruit, suet, sugar, spices and milk, all wrapped up and baked in a clootie, or cloth. We work harmoniously as we have been preparing this meal together for close to three decades.

My dad is in the garage practicing his bagpipes, which sounds more like a wild goose massacre than actual music. My brother is probably getting high watching football. All in all, it's like every Thanksgiving that has come before.

Ethan follows me in and offers to help. Nan has yet to have any lengthy interaction with my intended, a happenstance which thrills me beyond words, but at that moment she turns to him and mutters, "Filthy Sassenach."

My intended raises his eyebrows in question, so I push him off to the side. I explain, "Nan's Sassenach is dirty. She's been trying to clean it all morning." I'm hoping he doesn't know that Sassenach is a Scottish word for English person, which of course Ethan is, by blood anyway. I suggest, "Why don't you go entertain your parents while we carry on in pursuit of our dinner."

Once he leaves the room, I turn to Nan and demand, "What was that all about?"

"What?" she asks with big-eyed innocence.

"Why did you just call Ethan a filthy Sassenach?"

She shrugs her shoulders. "I don't know, dear. You know how it is with these strokes. Sometimes words just come out of my mouth and I can't stop them."

What she says is true, but I think, and have thought for some time, that my grandmother uses her strokes as an excuse to blurt out whatever she wants to. Yet, being that she has no reason to dislike Ethan, maybe it wasn't really intended. I suggest she go downstairs and light up a fatty to take the edge off.

Ethan's already left the room in search of sanctuary, so when Nan does the same, I ask my mom, "What do you think of Ethan?"

She hems and haws, "Oh, my, well … he's nice, isn't he?"

Obviously, I think he's nice. I've agreed to be his wife. This isn't quite the reaction I expected from my mother, though.

"Yes, he's nice." I push, "But what do you *think* of him?"

Here's something you should know about Mags, and something I should have thought about before asking this question: my mother doesn't lie. She doesn't believe in it. She feels that if you request her opinion, it's her true feelings you're after. So, don't ever ask her if your butt looks fat in a pair of pants when there's even the slightest chance the answer is yes.

Luckily, the phone rings and I'm spared the answer to my question.

Enya Isn't Scottish

The day passes in a whirlwind of activity. Aside from helping get the meal ready, setting the table, and tidying the house, I take extra pains with my appearance. I like to think I'm doing it out of respect for the holiday, but the ugly truth is I'm not. I want to show Sam what he's missed by rubbing my gorgeousness in his face, as suggestive as that sounds.

Natalie joins me in the dining room as I put the last touches on the table. She visibly startles when she takes in the riot of clashing colors. She's holding a Masterton plaid and looks confused. "You mother was kind enough to give this to me, but I don't know what to do with it."

Ethan's mom is wearing a beautiful, light-pink silk dress, which will look atrocious with the plaid, but that's not the point. The point is, our Thanksgiving table is one of solidarity and everyone who sits at it must be wearing the family colors. "Here, let me help you," I offer.

I fold the fabric lengthwise in half and then drape it across her torso like a sash. She looks like a contestant in the Miss Scotland Pageant. Once that's complete, I fasten both sides together at her hip with a kilt pin. Finally, I splay the fabric open on her shoulder so that it dips half-way down her arm.

She smiles delightedly. "Thank you, dear. Is this how Jason and Ethan should wear theirs, as well?"

I shake my head. "No. They wear theirs like kilts. They can either do that over their pants or without pants. It's their call."

Natalie looks alarmed. "Oh, my. I'm not sure they'll know how to accomplish that on their own."

I respond, "Don't worry. I'll send my dad up to help them."

An hour later, we're all assembled in the living room waiting on Sam and his parents. Both Ethan and his dad have opted to keep their dress slacks on under their plaid. If I'm brutally honest, they look ridiculous. Kilts aren't for everyone, but the only way to wear them properly is to do so fearlessly. You've got to show your knees and carry yourself like a warrior going into battle.

Ethan leans into me and whispers, "This skirt keeps bunching up. I think I have static cling."

"It's not a skirt, it's a kilt," I reply. "And that's what happens when the wool rubs up against another fabric." I instruct, "You need to take your pants off."

He looks appalled, like I've just, well, asked him to take his pants off.

When the doorbell rings, my parents and I jump up to answer it.

I truly am happy to see Sam's mom and dad. Liza and Ned Hawking have been in my life since I was a little girl. They've been devoted friends to my parents and a great supporter of Nan's—especially when she first started going around town offending everyone in her path. They even hired Travis, during his clown phase, to perform at their annual Fourth of July barbecue, which was a weird entertainment fit to say the least.

When Sam and I started dating, they welcomed me into their family like the daughter they'd never had. Liza taught me how to bake pumpernickel bread, and Ned showed me how to ride a motorcycle. They were once threads woven deeply into the fabric of my life.

I've had no contact with them since I left for school, even though they bought me a gift for my college graduation and still send me a Christmas card every year. I've never encouraged contact, but for some reason they haven't been able to shut the door on me. So, when they walk through ours, I hug them like the long-lost friends they are.

Liza holds onto me like a lifeboat in the middle of the ocean during a hurricane. When she finally releases her grip, it's only to look at me from arm's length. "Cat, you're gorgeous! I swear you were the prettiest girl in town, and you're an even more beautiful woman." I could get used to compliments like this.

Ned grabs me, picks me up, and twirls me around. "Kitty Cat, you haven't seen my new chopper! What say we take a ride together later?" Ned's new motorcycle could be seven years old for all I know, but he asks me to go riding with him like no time has passed since our last adventure, leaving me so full of emotion I could choke.

Sam walks in last and greets me like a recalcitrant puppy who got caught chewing his owner's slipper. Good, he's taken my hint from his little middle of the night visit. "Cat, how are you?"

"Tired," I snap.

I lead the way into the living room and everyone follows

behind. I introduce the Hawkings to Ethan's parents. "Liza, Ned, I'd like you to meet Natalie and Jason Crenshaw, my future in-laws."

Natalie and Jason stand up with smiles on their faces and their hands extended in greeting. Liza and Ned don't follow suit. After a long moment, Liza finds her voice and says, "I'm sorry, what?"

"My future mother and father in-law," I enunciate slowly and perhaps a bit too loudly.

Ned looks positively bewildered. "I don't understand."

I feel like I've fallen through a crack into an alternate universe. I'm not quite sure if everyone stopped speaking the language, or perhaps they're stroking out like Nan. So, when Ethan stands up, I explain, "This is Ethan, my fiancé."

That's when Sam decides to join in, exclaiming, "Your what?"

What's wrong with everyone? Have I started speaking Dutch or something. So, I try again, "Liza, Ned, Sam …" I break to make sure they're tracking me. "This …"—I spokesmodel Ethan with big dramatic hand gestures—"is my FIANCÉ." I almost yell the last word.

Liza turns to my dad and asks, "Dougal, what is she talking about?"

My dad looks sheepish and replies, "Did I forget to mention that Cat is engaged?"

What the hell? I stare at my father with an expression that demands explanation. He looks down and starts to wobble nervously from side-to-side. "Well, honey, you've only just gotten engaged. I didn't … um … what I mean is … uhhhhh … well … I guess I just forgot to mention it." I don't remind him I've been engaged for over a year.

Sam runs his hands through his hair like he's trying to wash it or something. Then he looks at me with haunted eyes. "You're engaged?"

I can't help it, I almost yell, "What's wrong with you people? Liza, Ned, Sam …" —break for emphasis—"THIS is the man I'm going to marry and his parents. For the love of God, please say hello to them."

All of a sudden everyone seems to get their bearings and they reach out and clasp hands, pretending this isn't the most awkward scene in the history of the world.

Ethan catches my eye and pulls me off to the side. "Are these people okay?" Then he points to his head and rolls his eyes from side to side. "Or are they a few bricks short of a full load?"

I shake my head. At this moment I feel like we're all a few bricks short of a full load, whatever the hell that means. Ethan pulls a CD out of his suit pocket with a plaid bow on it and says, "I bought this for your grandmother. Would now be a good time to give it to her?"

I shrug my shoulders to indicate now is probably as good a time as any, thinking we could all use a distraction from the weirdness. So, Ethan walks over to Nan, who so far has barely given him the time of day, and hands her his gift.

Nan takes it, looks at it closely, and sees it's an Enya Christmas CD. She audibly scoffs, then hands it back to Ethan and declares, "Enya isn't Scottish."

Make Mine a Double

Nan is so happy to see Sam she's nearly sitting on his lap. She says things like, "There's my fine boy," and "I've missed you so much, lad." Now might be the time to mention that Sam doesn't have slacks on under his kilt and he looks better than I remember—very confident with his manly knees on display. Nan seems to be enjoying them, as well.

Meanwhile, Ethan is standing in the corner pouting, no doubt feeling hurt by the rebuff of his gift. I don't blame him in the least. Not only was Nan exceedingly rude to him, but no one is making an effort to make him feel included in their private little club.

His parents seem to be holding their own though, which is good. My mom has managed to mostly keep herself in the kitchen, so I excuse myself to check on her. Ethan nearly tackles me to the ground as I pass. With panic in his eyes, he begs, "Don't leave me here."

I sigh. "Come with me if you want, but I need to check on the dessert." He sticks to my side like glue.

When we get into the hall, he demands, "What's going on in there? Who are those people and what's wrong with them?"

I shake my head. "They're old friends of my parents. Sam and I used to go to school together. End of story." While not the full truth, no part of my answer is a lie. It just doesn't seem worth going into the whole sordid affair when we're never going to see them again. And believe me, after that circus, we are NEVER going to see them again.

We walk into the kitchen to find my mom sitting on the floor next to the oven like a forgotten rag doll. "Mom, what's going on?"

She startles and looks up. "Nothing, dear. I'm just thinking."

"On the kitchen floor?" Ethan asks. I want to push a button and have this day end. Of course, my mother chooses this time to break with reality. I mean, why wouldn't she? It's not like my fiancé and his family are here or we have guests or it's Thanksgiving.

My mom gestures for Ethan to join her. He looks at me to see what I think he should do, so I say, "Go."

He gingerly sits on the linoleum next to her, and she takes his hand. After several long seconds, where I'm sure Ethan is once again wondering about the sanity of my gene pool, my mom announces, "Sometimes when things don't look right from one perspective, I like to view them from another perspective." Then she turns to him and asks, "Do you know what I'm talking about?"

He shakes his head. "Not even a little bit."

My mom tries again. "The kitchen looks one way when you're on your feet. It looks another way when you're sitting at the table. But when you're on the floor, it's a brand new room altogether."

Ethan looks like he wants to cry. He's clearly not used to the bizarre ponderings of the woman I call "Mom." He asks, "Mrs. Masterton, are you happy on the floor? Do you like the way your kitchen looks from here?"

My mom shakes her head sadly. "I don't."

"Then why are you sitting here?"

She exhales as though unloading all the burdens of the world. "Because I don't like how it looks from *any* vantage point anymore. I stood up, I sat in a chair, and now I'm on my floor. The truth is, I just don't think I like my kitchen anymore."

Ethan is more confused than ever, but I'm not. I know the kitchen is just a metaphor for something else my mom is questioning. Granted she's doing so on the floor, while there's a load of people in the other room waiting for her version of Thanksgiving dinner. It isn't the best time to be having a crisis of faith, but holidays always bring out the best and worst in us. They make us reflect on the past and look to the future. They cast a glaring spotlight on the present, and often force us to see things in a new way we don't always find pleasing.

Thanks Be, Already

My dad stands at the head of the table and holds his hands out, palms up, like that picture of Jesus found in most Sunday-school rooms, except Jesus was never wearing a tartan. He booms, "Some hae meat and cannae eat. Some nae meat but want it. We hae meat and we can eat and sae the Lord be thankit."

Ethan catches my eye as if to ask, "What kind of prayer is that?"

I choose that moment to stand up, which isn't our tradition at all. All eyes turn to me, wondering what I'm up to. I look every single person in the eye, one at a time, with excruciating thoroughness while wearing a borderline psychotic grin on my face. Then I announce, "I'm particularly thankful this year and think this is the perfect time to share my gratitude with my loved ones."

Travis burps in the background, but as I'm not including him in my "loved ones" category, I could care less. "I'm grateful the man I love asked me to marry him." I grace Ethan with a thousand-watt smile. He looks marginally uncomfortable to be the center of attention but seems to appreciate the sentiment.

"Ethan and I have been together for two years." I hold up two fingers high over my head to illustrate my statement. "We've been living in a one-bedroom apartment in New York City for a year." I'm sure this last bit is going beyond the bounds of tastefulness, but I don't care. I want to make it clear that we're together in every sense of the word.

"We read the paper in bed, together." Pointed stare at Nan. "We go for long walks through Central Park and feed the ducks on the boating pond, together." Pointed stare at Sam. "We sit on the kitchen floor and ponder the meaning of life, together." No, we don't, but I stare at my mother while I say this, and she won't meet my gaze.

I clear my throat and continue, "I'm in love with Ethan because he's constant and true. He would never leave me or throw me away. He's my partner and the future father of my children." I smile over at Natalie and Jason when I say this. After all, they're the ones who raised this paragon, and I want to give them a bit of credit during my unorthodox speech. They seem to appreciate it and nod their heads encouragingly, unlike everyone else who looks like they've eaten something that didn't agree with them.

I raise my glass in a toast, "To Ethan!" Then I face him, "Thank you for seeing my value as a woman and partner. Thank you for the life we're building together and for never breaking my heart." Then I take a sip of my wine. Okay fine, maybe I drink three quarters of the glass, but only because I'm so darn thrilled.

Then my mother stands up and takes center stage. *Oh Jesus, God, what have I done?* She picks up her glass and announces, "I'd like to toast my daughter, Cat." Ho-lee crap. It's on.

Facing me, she says, "Cat, I know we've not always been the family you wanted. I know we embarrass you at times and that it's hard for you to accept us as we are. But we've always done our best by you and we always will. We're proud of the woman you've become. We support all of your *good* choices …" —she looks at Sam, of all people, when she says this— "and we hope you understand that our actions are only with your best interests in mind. To Cat!" I have to pour another glass for myself after that one.

I'm sure you're aware that by this point I've unleashed the collective family beast and quite possibly started a dangerous new tradition. Nan pushes herself up next with some difficulty. I'm hoping to hell that when she went downstairs to get her sweater, she rolled a fat one and got higher than a kite, otherwise I have no idea what we're in for. She picks up her wine glass, drinks it down, pours herself another, raises it high in the air, and salutes, "To that bitch Dorcas Abernathy! He may have asked you first, but he was my husband for fifty-one years. Take that, whore!"

We all drink to that one. Not that the Crenshaws know what it's all about, but at this point in the game, everyone understands inebriation is on the menu if we're going to get through the coming meal alive.

Before anyone else can stand up, I move to the sideboard to get the soup tureen. "We don't want the Cullen skink getting cold, now do we?" I look at my mom, "Mags, what do you say, want to help me?"

My mom shakes her head. "We can always heat up the soup, honey. I think we should go around the table and see if there are any other toasts, don't you?" I would rather chew off my own arm, but I suppose I started this, so I might as well suffer through everyone else's feelings.

Ethan senses things aren't quite right, and God bless him and the horse he rode in on, he stands up and raises his glass to my parents. "To our hosts! Thank you for preparing this lovely meal!" We all drink again.

Natalie and Jason pass on the opportunity to add to their son's sentiment, thank God.

Liza stands up next, "I would like to toast common sense." *What the hell?* She looks at Sam and says, "Sometimes in life we make stupid decisions because we're young and don't know any better." Then she looks at me, "And sometimes we make the wrong choices because our feelings are hurt, and pride gets in our way." Then she raises her glass, "To common sense. May we all have it and not be afraid to use it!"

Travis stands up, lets out a loud whoop and adds, "Hell, yeah! Put that in your pipe, Cat!"

I've had three glasses of wine at this point on an empty stomach. I'm no longer tipsy, I'm borderline drunk. Just when I think this meal can't go downhill any farther, flipping Sam stands up.

He raises his glass high and the room is positively vibrating with anticipation. "To first loves!" Everyone but me raises their glass with him. "They are one of the most wonderful gifts in life. May we always be thankful for them. May we always do right by them and may we always cherish the memories if that's all we have left!"

While everyone drinks, I excuse myself from the table and hit the powder room under the back stairs. When I'm done, I yell, "FLUSH!" as loud as I can in critique of Sam's toast.

Feed Me

Mom never does reheat the Cullen skink and it's lukewarm at best by the time it's served, and we finally start to eat. It probably wouldn't matter if it was a solid block of ice. We're all so hungry and drunk we'd undoubtedly bite the head off a live snake if that's all there was.

The tatties and herring are slightly charred by the time they're rescued from the oven and put on the table, and the black pudding is, well, black pudding. In my humble opinion, you can't make that worse than it already is: pig, lamb, and goose blood mixed with assorted ground meats, suet, and spices, stuffed into natural casings—a.k.a animal intestines—and served. Yeah, no thanks.

The meal lasts the better part of seventy-two hours or feels like it does anyway. Hardly anyone speaks during dinner, which is a blessing. There doesn't seem to be anything left to say that we didn't air during our toasting hour. It's just a whole bunch of silverware clanking and chewing sounds.

My bringing Ethan home was all about us sharing our wedding plans with our parents. It was about us uniting our families as one. But now, there's no way we can do that without pulling the pin out of a grenade that's past primed to explode.

I get up and start clearing the dishes when most have finished eating, since I need to get the clootie dumpling, my contribution to the meal. I don't bother scraping and stacking the plates, I just dump them all in the sink for whatever poor sucker gets stuck with cleanup. God knows it isn't going to be me.

I pull the two dumpling cloths out of the oven and plop them on a serving dish, then I grab a bottle of Glenfiddich and head back to the dining room like a condemned prisoner. My mom has stacked a pile of dessert plates at my place.

I know what's coming next, and I'm so full of dread over it, I can barely carry on. But if I leave now, I'll tip my hand to giving a rat's ass about a certain someone sitting at the table, and I absolutely refuse to do that. I cut open the strings on the cloths holding the dumplings. Then I set them on the serving dish and pull the stopper out of the scotch with my teeth before dousing the dessert until it's soaked through.

Finally, I strike a match and set it on fire. My whole family and Sam's have already crossed their arms over their chests and taken the hands of those standing next to them. Ethan and his family follow suit, so it's just me they're waiting on. Finally, I do the same and when the entire table is connected this way, and the fire burns out on the dessert, my dad's deep baritone rings out like the voice of God.

"Should old acquaintance be forgot, and never brought to mind?
Should old acquaintance be forgot, and old lang syne?
For auld lang syne, my dear, for auld lang syne,

We'll take a cup of kindness yet, for auld lang syne.
And surely, you'll buy your pint cup! and surely, I'll buy mine!
And we'll take a cup o' kindness yet, for auld lang syne.

For the next verse he looks between me and Sam as though dedicating it to us.

We two have run about the slopes, and picked the daisies fine;
But we've wandered many a weary foot, since auld lang syne.
We two have paddled in the stream, from morning sun till dine;
But seas between us broad have roared since auld lang syne.
And there's a hand my trusty friend! And give us a hand o' thine!
And we'll take a right good-will draught, for auld lang syne."

"Auld Lang Syne" isn't traditionally a New Year's song, like we've grown to think of it. An old Scotsman gave it to Robert Burns in 1788 to write down and make sure it got passed on. As I look around our Thanksgiving table, there's a lot of "old time sake" to be had, so the song seems more appropriate this year than most, even if it does dredge up a lot of the past that I wish had remained there.

When it's over, and we've unchained ourselves from one another, I serve the pudding and pass the dishes around the table. I take a double helping, because I only get it once a year and I made it so, why the heck shouldn't I?

My dad pours everyone a wee dram of the Glenfiddich and gives our traditional toast. "To old times and new times, to old friends and new! May we live long enough to sing about our new adventures as old. *A h-uile la sona dhuibh's gun la idir dona dhuibh. Slàinte mhòr agus a h-uile beannachd duibh!*"

The last bit means, "May all your days be happy ones. Great health and every good blessing to you!"

The atmosphere finally picks up over dessert, almost like we've all gotten some much needed perspective on this gathering. The past lives on, but it isn't our present. I can surely get through this one meal and then hopefully, I won't have to see Sam and his family for at least another fourteen years, even though a part of me can't bear to think of such an absence again.

It's a Party, Dammit!

While everyone finishes their clootie, my dad gets up and retrieves his instrument. I grew up listening to bagpipes, and I love the sound of them, just not when my father plays them. There are some things that are so wrong they should be illegal and we're about to experience one of them.

Dad stands at the head of the table like he's ready to march our clan into war. All eyes are on him as he announces, "I have a confession to make!" Oh, good Lord, may it not be anything too shocking. The last time he bared his soul at a gathering, was to tell everyone that he didn't wear underwear beneath his kilt to honor our ancestors *and* to let his boys roam free. I do not think the Crenshaws need to know that much about him quite yet.

He clears his throat before saying, "I'm not a very good bagpipe player." Well, duh. Does he really think this is something we haven't already figured out for ourselves? He continues, "And surprisingly, I've discovered my son, Travis, has a real knack for it. So, I'm retiring the pipes and passing them down." Say what?

He motions for Travis to stand up and join him at the head of the table, which my brother does while simultaneously giving himself a good scratch. Once he gets there, my father hands over the pipes and my brother gets suited up. What happens next is one of the great wonders of life, right up there with Stonehenge and Old Faithful.

Travis begins the opening strains of "Scotland the Brave," and chills race through my body, causing the hair on my arms to stand straight up. The notes are textbook perfect, the emotion is spot on. My idiot, stoner, loser of a brother is something of a musical savant!

My dad motions for us all to get up and follow him into the living room, where the furniture has been preemptively pushed to the side. Then he stands in the middle of the room and signals for Travis to move on to a reel. He, my mom, Liza, and Ned stand in position and wait for the right moment to break into dance. They're a pure delight to watch.

When my dad signals the rest of us to join in, Ethan and his parents pass, but I can't. I've been doing this my whole life and it's a tradition I love. I expect my mom to sit out, so I can partner with my dad, but that's not what happens. Sam stands up and joins the line with his eyes trained on mine the whole time.

Oh, my sweet, ever-loving Lord. I don't want to dance with him. The memory of the night we taught him how comes back like a flood of biblical proportion. It was right after Sam's metamorphosis from mere mortal to Greek god, making it the tenth grade. It was October and we had a bonfire going out back.

Dad had brought out his pipes and announced, "Sam, my boy. It's time you learn what being a Masterton is all about!"

My mom had stood across from him and positioned herself in the opening pose, with her feet together, pointed forward, and her hands on her hips. She instructed, "Just follow me and do the same thing I do."

He had immediately copied her. When my dad began to play, Sam kicked into gear, hopping and twirling and kicking like he was born to it.

Nan had clapped her hands and whistled until my grandfather stood before her with his hand out. They joined in that magical night like there was nowhere on earth they'd rather be than in each other's arms, dancing the reel. The memory leaves me weak in the knees.

I stare at Sam over fifteen years later offering me his hand in dance and feel like I'm about to cheat on Ethan right in front of him. Yet, I'm helpless to stop myself.

Sam and I dance like we were only meant to do so with each other. We spin and turn like we've been practicing for weeks. Somewhere along the line, our parents sit down and it's just the two of us swinging wider and spinning faster. When the song finally ends, we break apart with laughter and pure joy. Holy crap.

Everyone in the room claps and cheers for us, even Ethan's parents. My fiancé, however, does not look overly pleased. And who can blame him, really? I've just been having the time of my life with a man who isn't him.

When I return to his side, he suggests, "Why don't you sit the next one out."

Sit the next one out? I get to dance like this maybe twice a year if I'm lucky. I counter, "Why don't you stand up and let me teach you the native dance of your future wife's people?"

He shakes his head declining my magnanimous offer. That's

when I start to wonder if I'm supposed to give this tradition up because he won't join in. While everyone moves on to the next song, I motion for him to follow me into the kitchen, which he does.

When we arrive, I smile kindly and ask, "Why won't you let me teach you how to dance the reel?"

He replies, "Catriona, you know I don't dance."

"But why won't you learn?" I demand. "This is a tradition I want to pass down to our children someday."

He shakes his head. "Statistically, there's a forty-seven percent heightened risk of pulling a muscle or worse when dancing and the odds only increase with the more rigorous varieties."

What? I mean, I know Ethan can be a bit of a bore with his statistics. For example, he refuses to ride a bike in New York City because of the thirty-four percent increased chance of head injury, but refusing to learn how to do the Scottish reel? Seriously? I just shake my head.

"Ethan, you've got to lighten up and live a little. So what if you pull a muscle, if you do it while you're having fun? Muscles heal."

"Perhaps, but this isn't my idea of fun. I guess I don't mind if you do it though, so go ahead and carry on without me."

He doesn't mind if I dance? I should just carry on? Well, you know what? I think I will. After surviving this horrendous day, I deserve a fun night cutting loose and having fun with my family. So, while Ethan excuses himself to get some fresh air, I go back to the living room, prepared to show everyone how to really cut a rug.

Timber!

After the seventh song, Travis declares, "I need a break." He puts the pipes down in favor of the bottle of Glenfiddich, which he drinks straight out of the bottle. The rest of us collapse in exhausted heaps, while sweat drips off us.

That's when I notice none of the Crenshaws are in the room. I get up and start to look around the house, but I don't see them anywhere. I climb the stairs to find the door to Nan's room closed and assume Natalie and Jason have gone to bed. Then I see the door to my room is shut, as well. I open it and discover Ethan sound asleep. How can any of them sleep with the sounds of such gaiety going on? Who does that?

That's when it hits me. My future family are a bunch of party poopers. While it makes me feel a bit sad, I also realize it's been a long day and since this isn't their tradition, they aren't as invested in it as I am. So instead of shaking them awake and making them come back downstairs with me—something I'm truly tempted to do—I opt to kiss Ethan on the cheek and return to the living room, alone.

When I walk in, I discover the furniture has been restored to its normal location and everyone is draped across it willy nilly.

Darn, I think this means we're done dancing.

I look at the clock and see that it's after eleven. My mom yawns. "That was fun!" Once upon a time, Sam and I couldn't wait for this time of night. As soon as our parents went to bed and we promised to be good and not stay up past midnight, we used to sneak off and explore the raptures of teenage hormones to their fullest.

Sam catches my eye, and I realize he's thinking the same thing. I look away like I've just been caught with my hand in the cookie jar.

Liza stands up and declares, "This was our best Thanksgiving ever, but I'm bushed."

Ned joins her and wraps his arm around her. "Me, too. I think it's time we get ourselves on home."

That's when we hear it. A creaking that sounds like the jolly green giant walking across rickety old floorboards, followed by a crash and crunch so loud it makes the hair on the back of my neck stand on end. What just happened?

We all rush to the front door and open it, only to discover one of the big oak trees in front of our house laying across the Hawkings' car. In all the noise we were making dancing the reel, we didn't even notice the winter storm going on right outside the window. It doesn't look like anyone is going anywhere.

My mom and Liza pull out the sleeper sofa in the family room, and I go up to the linen closet to get sheets and towels for our unexpected overnight guests. Nan and Travis retire downstairs, while the men go outside and check out the damage.

I should really hit the hay too, but I don't want to leave my mom with all the cleanup. My mood has come full circle from earlier in the evening, and I'm no longer mad at everyone. So, when my dad comes in, I say, "Why don't you two go off to bed? I'll get to work washing up."

They smile gratefully and head up the stairs. We used the good china tonight, which means it has to be handwashed.

Sam, whose bed has been set up on the couch in the living room, comes in and joins me, "Hey."

"Hey," I barely manage. "Why aren't you asleep?"

"I'm not going to sleep and leave you with all this mess by yourself."

I throw him a dishtowel. "Fine. I'll wash, you dry."

We work in companionable silence for several moments before he utters, "So, you're engaged."

I nod my head. "Yup. Surely that's not such a hard thing for you to believe."

I sneak a look in his direction. "God, no. Not hard at all. In fact, I'm surprised you aren't already married with a few kids."

I can't help myself. I answer, "I might have been, had things turned out differently."

He shakes his head sadly and puts down the dish he's holding. Then he turns to me and pleads, "Cat, I'm such an idiot." He's got that right. "I loved you so much, I really did. I just got scared. We'd been living in this little town our whole lives and I just, I don't know, I guess I wondered if there was more out there than what we had."

Even though I didn't agree with him at the time, I truly can understand what he's saying. If he and I had gone off to college together, and gotten married like we'd planned, we both would have had very different lives. At this point, I can't say that would have been better or worse. I sure as heck would have never moved to New York and gone to work with Jazz. I wouldn't have met Ethan. It would have been a very different existence without them. I ask, "Was there more out there for you? Did you find what you were looking for?"

He sighs deeply. "There's no easy answer to that. There was a lot out there, but was it better than what might have been? I don't know. I can tell you this, though, I've never loved another woman as much as I loved you."

He's staring at me so intently, I feel like we're somehow fusing together, which is not okay. I force my gaze away from his and back to the sink full of dishes. "Sam, it's all water under the bridge at this point. What's done is done and we aren't those same people anymore."

He reaches for my hands. "But why can't we be them again?"

I pull away. "Well, for starters, I'm engaged to another man. And secondly, wait, forget secondly. I'm off the market, Sam. I'm taken."

"You're not married yet, Cat. Are you sure you love Ethan? Are you sure he's the one for you?"

Fury boils in my blood. "How dare you ask me that? How dare you waltz back into my life without even a phone call in fourteen years and think I'm going to drop everything I've built and run back to you!"

I take a breath, but I'm in no way done with him. "You walked out on me, Sam Hawking. You dumped me and went after whatever else you were searching for. Maybe you found it, maybe you didn't. Either way, it doesn't affect me. I'm not yours anymore. I'm never going to be yours again."

I can't look at him for another second. I just drop my washcloth into the sink and storm out of the kitchen, away from the man who's making me feel things I have no right feeling.

The Morning After

I stay in bed the next morning and listen to chain saws cutting down our old tree. I know I'm being a coward by not getting up and facing everyone, but I just can't bring myself to do it. I have zero interest in seeing Sam again, and I'm not getting out of this bed until I know he's gone, even if it means faking sleep like I've done for the past two hours.

Somewhere along the line, I must really pass out though, because when Ethan wakes me with a gentle nudge to the shoulder, I jump a mile. "What time is it?" I croak.

"Eleven thirty, sleepyhead. Breakfast is already cleared, but your mom left you a stack of pancakes, if you're interested."

I salivate at the thought. There's still enough alcohol in my system that I could definitely use a good pancake sponge to soak up. I ask, "Have the Hawkings left?"

Ethan nods. "Yeah, they got up early and moved the tree before the tow truck came. Your dad is taking them home now."

I can see he wants to say something else, but doesn't, thank god. I jump out of bed, put on my robe, and announce, "I'm starved. Come keep me company while I eat?"

We sit companionably over a stack of blueberry pancakes,

neither of us saying anything until Ethan breaks the silence. "Last night was something, huh?"

He could be referring to any number of things, but it's my guess he's speaking of my dancing with Sam. I don't want him unduly concerned as I put Sam in his place after he went to bed, and my ex is no threat to Ethan.

"Was it a typical Thanksgiving?" he asks.

I shrug my shoulders. "In some respects. We always eat the same food and dance the reel. It's normally not so tense, if that's what you're referring to. I think everyone was just buckling under the pressure of a new dynamic." Not to mention the subterfuge, bad manners, and false hopes.

Nan walks in and sits down next to us. She greets, "Morning, Cat." Then she looks at Ethan and adds, "Sassenach."

Ethan forces a smile and stands up to pull my grandmother's chair out for her. "Good morning, Nan. How did you sleep?" He wants to connect with some member of my family and wrongly assumes Nan is the way to go.

She sits down and shrugs her aging shoulders. "As well as I ever sleep. Getting old is a bitch. I don't recommend it." Then she reaches out and pours herself a glass of orange juice.

Ethan clearly doesn't realize he's just been dismissed and pursues, "Can I ask you a question, Nan?"

She efficiently nods her head once. So, he continues, "Why don't you like me?"

Oh, no, he didn't. Has he learned nothing during this visit? You do not, under any circumstances go looking for honest answers in my family, because you WILL get them.

Nan puts her juice glass down and looks Ethan square in the

eye as she answers, "It's not so much that I dislike you or mind you sharing the same planet with me, it's just that you're not right for Cat. She's too much woman for you."

Oh. My. God. I turn to my grandmother and gasp, "How dare you? How dare you say that to him? Who do you think you are to know what or who is right for me?"

She points a gnarly finger in my direction. "Listen here, young lady. He asked me, so I told him. What was I supposed to do, lie?"

"Yes, dammit, that's exactly what you're supposed to do! Why is lying such a foreign concept to you people?" Why can't my family understand the truth is not some sacred thing that they must uphold 'til the death? Everyone lies. It's part of living in a civilized world where people aren't bent on ripping each other apart with the truth.

Ethan intervenes. "I appreciate your honesty, Nan. I really do. But I hope you'll understand that I love your granddaughter and plan on making a life with her. I hope you can accept that."

"Screw it," Nan says. "You'll do what you'll do. It's not up to me. I just hope you lighten up and learn to have some fun or you're going to crush all the happiness out of my little girl here."

We have only been home for two days and it feels like a year. I'm so worn out by all the emotional upheaval and drama of the last forty-eight hours I could spit. Seeing Sam again, and dancing with him, have certainly muddied the waters. While part of me wishes I hadn't come home at all, a bigger part of me is glad I did. The whole situation has left me riddled with confusion, not to mention guilt.

FLUSH!

Other than Natalie thinking she has second degree burns on her scalp, everything is moving along like a typical day after a holiday. Apparently, before I woke up, Ethan flushed the toilet, without warning, while his mom was in the shower. The result was her standing under scalding hot water and not getting out in time to avoid disaster. She's currently not speaking more than monosyllables to her son.

My brother announces, "Nan and I are going out to the back porch."

My grandmother's eyes are tellingly glazed over. "We want to enjoy the pristine blanket of fresh snow." Being stoners has turned them into poets.

Mom bangs around the kitchen and warns, "Be careful you don't slip and fall." She's making dinner because unlike traditional Thanksgiving, the only leftover we ever have is black pudding, and let's face it, we make that more out of habit than enjoyment.

Ethan and his dad are in the living room reading *The Economist* together. Yes, I know, I'm kind of yawning at how dull that is, too. But at least they're having fun, and no one is insulting them or telling them how boring they are to their faces. So that's a plus, right?

Dad is out in the barn dressing his field mice for Christmas. This is one of his oddities that really defines him as the eccentric he is. The day after Thanksgiving, all twenty-eight of his taxidermied pets get rigged out in various holiday gear, from Robert the Bruce to Sir Walter Scott to Santa Claus. He'll bring them in when he's done and randomly decorate the house with them.

I go upstairs to my room and pull out an old box from my closet. It's the "Sam" box. The one where I've stored things from our childhood. I unearth it with the intention of looking at everything one last time before throwing it out and closing that chapter of my life forever.

I open the photo album, and the first picture I see causes such a tidal wave of emotion that I can barely breathe. My chest constricts to the point of physical pain.

There we are, two little kids covered in mud wearing the biggest smiles you've ever seen. The only parts not covered are the whites of our eyes and our teeth. You can't even discern what color our hair is, white-blonde in my case, and medium brown in Sam's.

Our moms were busy playing cards with their friends, so we decided to go out back and entertain ourselves. We found a garden hose and the rest is history. It's a memory so deeply ingrained in my brain, I remember everything about that day. I know we had ham sandwiches for lunch, with the potato chips from a can. I recall the air smelled like star jasmine and a warm breeze was blowing. That was the day Sam explained sex to me.

A boy and girl, who like each other a lot, play a game called sex and they make a baby. It's a card game, so we better stop playing cards together, just in case.

Damn, I'm not throwing this box away today. It contains as much of my life as it does his, and even though I don't currently like him, I'm a big fan of me. I don't have the energy to keep looking through it though, so I stash it back in the closet.

I pick up the phone and call Sarah. "You wanna do something?"

She squeals, "Really? Can you get away for a couple of hours?"

"Everyone's busy doing their own thing," I answer. "I'll just tell them I'm running out to the store. They'll never know I'm gone." I could really use a sounding board right now and Sarah is the only person I can think of that's far enough removed from the drama to offer unbiased insights.

We make a plan to meet at the diner in town and I hurry to get changed into some warm clothes. Even though we get winter in New York City, it's nothing compared to the brutal cold of farm country in the Midwest. There are no buildings to block the wind and no subway heating the ground from below. It's one hundred percent frigid.

When I get into town and park, I spot my friend standing in front of the diner. She's covered head to toe in a snowsuit, with an earflap hat that looks like it once belonged to Elmer Fudd. I giggle, "You look like Nanook of the North."

"I brought the snowmobile. With my parents in Florida, I didn't want to face clearing the driveway alone," she replies.

"Your parents are in Florida? Why didn't you tell me? You could have had Thanksgiving dinner with us!"

She stamps the snow off her boots and scoffs, "There is no

part of your Scottish ritual that doesn't contain animal sacrifice. Even your dessert is full of suet." I can see where a confirmed vegetarian might find it a difficult meal to enjoy.

"You've got me there, but if I recall correctly, before you gave up meat, you used to love it."

Sarah opens her wallet, "I will give you cold, hard cash if you promise to forget that and never speak of it again." We laugh and walk inside to grab a table. It's blissfully empty as most of the town is probably still stuffed from yesterday's holiday meal.

After we order two slices of apple pie, I confess, "I need you to tell me the truth about something."

She looks up alarmed. "I know how you feel about the truth, Cat. No good can come from it." It's true. I've felt this way for ages, but sometimes you just need someone to give it to you straight.

"Please," I beg. "I swear I'll listen to whatever you have to say, and if I don't like the answer we'll agree right here and now to never to speak of it again. Okay?"

She shakes her head. "Our friendship means too much to me to play Russian roulette with it like that."

"Sar, I've got you and I've got Jazz. I'm in business with Jazz, as well as being her friend, so I just can't go there. Please. It's important."

"Grrrrrrrr," she growls. "Fine, what's so important you need to hear the truth about it?"

"Ethan," I answer. "What do you think of him?"

She shakes her head. "Nope, not doing it. Look, my first impression at the airport wasn't great, so my whole opinion is tarnished. I'm not answering." Except she just did.

"What do you think about us as a couple? We're a good fit, right?" It's clear where my family stands on this issue and I'm hoping my friend feels differently.

"Catriona Fiona Masterton, you don't play fair! How can I say if you guys are a fit? I've seen you together for a grand total of three hours, and not even in your own habitat. There is no way for me to answer that question." Except she just did, again.

I explain, "When we left your house the other day, my parents surprised me with Sam. He was in our kitchen drinking coffee, acting very happy to see me."

My friend releases a low whistle. "Wow. That must have knocked you off your game."

"You could say that. But that wasn't the real surprise. Turns out, Mags and Dougal invited his whole family to join us for Thanksgiving dinner."

Sarah's eyes pop open even wider. "How did that go?"

Rolling my head from side-to-side, in a vain attempt to release some of the accumulated tension, I answer, "Horribly. My dad didn't tell them I was engaged, so Ethan and his parents came as quite a shock. The Hawkings were positively rude to them." I continue, "After dinner we danced."

"You and Ethan?" she asks.

I shake my head. "Me and Sam."

She leans across the table totally fixated on me. I confide, "The chemistry was intense."

"Wowza! What are you going to do?"

"The only thing I can do," I reply. "Never see him again."

"That's not your only option, Cat."

"Sarah, I purposefully found a man like Ethan because I don't want to lose my heart to someone like Sam again. It took me years to recover from our breakup. What kind of idiot would I be to want to be with him after that?"

"Love doesn't play by any rules," she answers.

"I love Ethan," I retaliate.

My childhood friend reaches across the table and takes my hands. "Kitty Cat, life is about feeling. It's about the ride. Do you want to be on a merry-go-round your whole life, just traveling in the same circle over and over again? Or do you want to risk it all and hit the roller coaster, where you're going to feel all the highs and lows that come with the journey?"

Tears fill my eyes of their own accord. "I know what you think I should want. I'm just not sure I have the strength to want it for myself."

When Everything Changes

I think about what Sarah said the whole drive home, and I keep coming back to the same thing. I have two years of adult life invested in Ethan. We live together, for heaven's sakes! We're completely entwined in each other's lives, we get along beautifully, and last but not least, we're engaged to be married.

Before this weekend, I hadn't even seen Sam in fourteen years. I thought we had our lives planned out to the nth degree. But then he broke up with me and went a completely different direction. I thought I knew him, but it turns out I didn't.

If you consider all of that, what kind of idiot would I be to even think being with Sam is a viable option? After all, it's his fault I am who I am today. If you follow that line of reasoning to its logical conclusion, he's responsible for me being with Ethan.

I pull into the driveway more resolved than ever to stop thinking about Sam Hawking and what might have been. I can't wait to leave Gelson, go back to New York with Ethan, and forget this weekend ever happened.

I pull into the driveway to discover an ambulance with the back doors wide open. Fear courses through me like food poisoning. My stomach is rolling over and I definitely have the urge to throw up. I run inside as fast as I can and find the house in turmoil. My parents are in the living room, and Nan is being strapped onto a gurney at their feet. "What happened?" I demand.

My mom flutters around like a moth on a string. She finally stops moving when she sees me and answers, "Oh, my god, honey, we don't know. She was out back with Travis when she complained about a pain in her head. She came in to get an aspirin and then just started weaving all around. I put her on the couch before going to call the doctor, and when I came back she was lying on the floor."

I look at the EMT who's taking her blood pressure and ask, "Is she going to be okay?"

He looks young, but remarkably competent. While reading the dial, he answers, "We don't know, yet. All we can do is stabilize her and get her to the hospital." Everything feels surreal, like it does in a dream—disconnected, yet oddly hyper-focused.

My mom says, "I'm riding in the ambulance with Nan." Then she turns at me and adds, "Bring your dad, but don't bring Travis." She leans in and confides, "He's toasted and I don't want his drug use coming up."

"My grandmother has been smoking pot today to help with her neurological symptoms," I explain to the paramedic.

My mom's eyes bug out and she whisper/yells, "Why did you just tell him that?"

"Because, Mom, I want them to know everything going on, so they know how to help her."

She nods her head vigorously. "Okay, right, good thinking."

She adds, "Nan had a toaster strudel for breakfast and a cup of coffee with one sugar." How that's going to help, I have no idea, but my mom is clearly not coping well at the moment.

After Mom and Nan are loaded into the ambulance, I go inside and hurry my dad along. He's putting on a flannel shirt over his t-shirt. It's mis-buttoned but I don't comment on it. Instead, I say, "Let me just go find Ethan and tell him what's going on, and I'll be right down to drive us over to the hospital." All of sudden my dad looks really old. He's only sixty, but the fear and uncertainty on his face make him look about a hundred.

I run upstairs and find Ethan lying in bed with headphones on. No wonder he wasn't downstairs with everyone else. He's probably listening to an audio book. He's recently gotten hooked on some historical series he keeps trying to get me to listen to.

I shake his arm, and say, "Ethan, can you hear me?"

His eyes pop open and he sees my concern, "Catriona. What's wrong? What do you need?"

"Nan just left for the hospital in an ambulance. My mom is with her. We don't know what's wrong yet, but I'm taking my dad over right now."

He sits up quickly and throws his legs over the side of the bed. "Just let me get my sweater on and I'll go with you."

I love him so much for that. Ethan is in his element in a crisis. He will immediately jump in and do whatever needs to be done. I sit down next to him and give him a big hug. "Thank you for being you. But, I think it's best if you stay here with your parents. We're probably not going to know what's wrong with Nan until they run a bunch of tests. Just keep your phone on and I'll update you when we know something."

"Are you sure? I'm happy to come along."

I nod my head. "I'm sure, but I better get going. My mom's a little freaked out right now."

He stands up and walks me downstairs and repeats, "Make sure to call if you need anything."

My dad and I walk out the door together. Nothing feels like it did the last time I did this only a few short hours ago. I was trying to escape my family then. Now I wish I'd never left.

In the car I ask my dad, "How's Nan been feeling lately? Any problems?"

His hands fidget like a nervous bride as his eyes stare out the window. "No, nothing out of the ordinary. Just the same old feisty Nan."

There doesn't seem to be anything else to say. We drive the three miles in silence, both of us lost in our own thoughts. I drop my dad off at the emergency room entrance to meet my mom and promise to join him as soon as I park the car.

After I find a space, I turn off the ignition and just sit there. I should be rushing out the door to be with my parents, but I'm not. All I can think is how I'm not ready to lose my grandmother. She's eighty. She's lived a long life. She's struggled with health issues and has been a widow for nine years. I should be willing to let her go if it's her time, but I don't want to.

I want my grandmother to be at my wedding, even though she's made it clear she doesn't think the groom is the man for me. I want her to meet her great-grandchildren. I don't want my last words to her to have been angry ones.

Dear God, give us more time. I know I'm not the only one to ask for a reprieve, but I promise if you come through for me, I'll be a better person. I'll try to appreciate my family more and I'll do my best to come home more often. Just please, please don't let this be it.

So, What Do you Do?

When you see a friend you haven't seen in a long time, you normally ask them a number of questions. I have a list. "What do you do? Are you married?" If yes, "Do you have kids? Where do you live?" Then I wrap it up with something like, "You look great! Let's stay in touch." I'm sure these are pretty typical things most people say.

So why in the world, when I saw Sam after fourteen years, didn't it occur to me to ask any of my go-to questions? I presumed he wasn't married with children, due to the lack of wedding ring and his clear interest in me. I assumed he was visiting his family for Thanksgiving because, well, that's what I was doing. As far as where he lived and what he did for a living—never crossed my mind.

That's why I'm completely, and I mean totally, shocked to walk into the emergency room and see Sam talking to my parents. That would be Dr. Samuel Hawking, according to his name tag. You might be wondering why Mags and Dougal never mentioned this to me, because I sure am. I'm also wondering why Sarah never said anything. I mean, yes, I've forbidden them to ever speak my ex-boyfriend's name, but I don't know, this seems like something they might have found a way to mention.

I reach my parents in time to hear Sam say, "We've already drawn blood and are sending it to the lab. I've ordered a CT scan and depending on what we find, we'll know if it was another stroke and whether or not we need more tests to determine our next course of action."

When he sees me, he acknowledges me by only saying, "Cat." That's it, nothing more. Of course, I don't want him to stand around and chit chat while my grandmother needs him, but I require something else here. I turn to my parents, "Why didn't either of you tell me that Sam was a doctor and worked here in town?"

My mom looks confused. "Because you told us we were never allowed to say his name to you."

I fling my hands up in the air in a very Italian gesture. "Yet, you somehow think setting us up to have dinner together with my fiancé and his parents is within in the bounds of acceptable behavior?"

"You never said we couldn't do that," my dad answers.

Oh. My. God. "Did I ever tell you that you should never mess with me or I'll go crazy on you? Did I ever do that?"

My mom shakes her head. "Not that I recall."

I scream, literally scream at them, regardless of any audience we might have. "Well, I'm telling you now! Stop messing with me!!!"

They both look totally taken aback, like I should have stated this dictate long before now. I just shake my head, turn around, and go sit down. Who are these people? They aren't right in the head. Nothing about them makes sense. In a world full of relatively normal human beings, the fact that they found each other and fell in love should be in some kind of record book. The fact that they're able to function in society is simply amazing to me.

My dad offers to get us a cup of coffee. I pass, but my mom says, "I'd love a great big one with lots of sugar and any kind of fancy creamer they have. Hazelnut, if that's an option."

I want to stay mad at her, but she looks so fragile at the moment, I just can't. I reach out and take her hand. "How are you doing?"

With tears trickling down her face, she answers, "I'm only fifty-nine. I'm too young to be an orphan."

"Oh, Mom." I pull her into my arms. This crazy, frustrating, lunatic of a woman, who has spent my entire life vexing me, looks so vulnerable and lost right now. I'm supposed to go home with Ethan tomorrow, but I know in this moment I'm going to stay here as long as my family needs me.

I pick up my phone and text Jazz.

Nan is in the hospital. Don't know what's wrong yet. Not coming home tomorrow as planned.

She texts back immediately.

OMG, sending BIG love! Don't worry—the girls and I can cover everything on the books. Let me know what I can do. XOXOXOX

Then I call Ethan, because right now I really want to hear his voice. "Hey."

"How's your grandmother?" he asks.

"We don't know anything yet. They're still doing tests."

"How are you?"

I think of the possibility of losing Nan and recall the shock of seeing Sam. I'm not good, but I don't say that. Instead, I go with, "I'm okay."

"Are you sure you don't want me to come over?"

"It's not that I don't want you here. I just think you're more help holding down the fort at home." The truth is, I can't imagine how my fiancé would react to seeing Sam again. Ethan never let on that he knew Sam was my ex at Thanksgiving. Even though he knew my heart had been broken in high school, I never mentioned names. Instead, I referred to my first boyfriend as "the one who must not be named." But after watching us dance, he'd have to be a total idiot not to have gathered the relationship was deeper than what I'd copped to.

"Okay. I'm here if you need me."

"I'm not going home with you tomorrow," I tell him. "I need to be here for my parents."

"I'd stay too, but I have a big meeting on Tuesday. I can't miss it."

I understand and am actually glad he won't be here. I need this time with my family. "I don't know how long I'll be here, but I'm guessing it'll be at least a week."

We say goodnight and suddenly I feel very alone. Ethan doesn't even like my parents, let alone consider them his family. My parents obviously feel the same way. Then there's Sam. I feel like a circus monkey is banging symbols on either side of my head and is determined to get them to collide regardless of the fact that my cranium is in the way.

A Tough Nut

Sam informs us, "Nan has a brain aneurysm that burst. This means she's bleeding into her brain until we can go in and tie off the bleed." He imparts, "This isn't an operation most small-town hospitals are known for performing, unless it's an extreme emergency."

"If you can't do it, who can?" I demand. "And is it safe to move her?"

"We've got a call out to the surgical neurology team at the university hospital to try to get one of their surgeons here, ASAP. Moving her would be too big a risk."

I don't feel particularly comforted by this news, so I ask, "Who does the surgery if you can't get one of them here?"

"Doc Fischer," he responds. Doc Fischer is a good guy, but he's almost seventy and wears glasses as thick as my forearm. I might trust him to take out an appendix or tonsils, but I cannot imagine ever handing him a saw and letting him operate on a person's brain. Sweet Lord, what now?

"Why don't you come back and spend some time with Nan?" Sam suggests. The look he gives me over my parents bowed heads suggests this might be our last opportunity while she still draws breath.

"Is she awake?" my mom asks.

Sam shakes his head. "No, Maggie, she's not. And I wouldn't expect her to wake up for at least a day after the surgery." The great question mark hanging in the air is, will she even get through surgery?

My dad has his arm around my mom and gently leads her back to pre-op. They both look shorter and older to me, like they've aged twenty years in the last thirty minutes.

No one ever wakes up one morning and says, "You know what? Everything's going so smoothly in my life right now. Work is great, my house is clean, and I've never felt better. It would be a great day for somebody I love to die, because I think I could handle it, today."

I'm thirty-one years old. I should be able to face the thought of losing Nan. Gramps died when I was only twenty-two, and I seem to have survived that just fine. Granted, I was a senior in college and deep into a pretty selfish phase in my life, but I remember thinking I was lucky to have had him for so long. A lot of my friends lost their grandparents when they were still in elementary school.

The difference is, the last words I said to Gramps were not angry ones. I don't remember exactly what they were, but they were probably along the lines of, "Mark my words, the Cubs are going all the way this year!" or "You don't have to keep giving me money when I go back to school. I promise I'm not starving."

My last exchange with Nan was to yell at her for telling Ethan he wasn't man enough for me. I can't live with that. I walk behind the privacy screen sectioning off her bed from the others. When I see her lying there looking so helpless, it's all I can do not to throw myself at her and beg her forgiveness, even though she has no idea I'm here.

My mom sits on one side of her and holds her hand, and my dad sits on the other. I motion for Sam to follow me back out into the hallway. When we get there, I look up into his very worried blue eyes and demand, "What are the chances she'll survive surgery?"

He looks grim, like he doesn't want to be the one to answer my question. After several moments, he exhales and answers, "For an average adult in fairly good health, I'd say fifty-fifty."

"But Nan isn't your average adult in good health, is she? She's an eighty-year-old woman with a history of multiple strokes."

Sam nods. "But she's tougher than any other person I've ever met. She's not someone I'd bet against in a street fight."

I laugh in spite of my current mood. Nan *is* tough. She's been through a lot in her life and has always come out on top. If anyone can survive what's ahead, she can. Before I have an opportunity to say anything else, Sam gets a page. "It's the head of neurology at the university hospital. I'll come in and let you know what he says as soon as I'm off the phone with him."

I watched a documentary once on death and grieving. It talked about the difference between chronos time and kairos time. Chronos time is when time passes sequentially. You wake up, have breakfast, take a shower, go to work—basically just plod through life as expected, totally connected to the timeline.

Kairos time is an indeterminate period in which everything seemingly happens at once. It's what occurs during times of exceptional crisis and excitement. Two hours or ten days can pass, and your brain doesn't process the passage of time the same way it would if it were just a normal phase of life. I have a conscious realization that as of this moment, my family is hitting the pause button on the timeline. We're hanging in suspended animation waiting for news that will either keep us there or drop us back into the land of the living. It's excruciating.

The Beat Goes On

I call Ethan to let him know what's happening. He asks, "Are you sure you don't want me to come to the hospital?"

"I'm sure," I answer. Between you, me, and the fence post, the real reason I don't want him to come is because of how Nan feels about him. My ornery grandmother does not like Ethan. He's too buttoned-up and controlled for her tastes. I don't want him here because truthfully, I don't think Nan would want him here.

"Please tell Travis what's happening and make sure your parents get dinner. I don't know what Mom was making, but I'm sure you can do something with what she started."

"Don't worry about us," he replies. "I've already taken care of my parents. I'll go find Travis right away and update him."

When we say goodbye, I experience a strange moment like I've been shot out of my body and am staring down at all of us like we're in a movie.

I can see myself sitting in the hospital waiting room looking, quite frankly, pathetic. I appear deflated and small in my oversized sweater and winter boots. My hair hangs lank and lifeless by the sides of my face. I look like I'm melting and all

117

that's left is a pile of winter clothes.

I see my parents sitting with my grandmother. Mom's head is resting on her mother's shoulder and she's crying. My dad is across the bed from her, holding Nan's hand like she's a child, and he's trying to will his vitality into her body to keep her going.

I see Ethan standing in the kitchen staring out onto the snow-covered backyard with the phone six inches from his ear, lest he increase his odds of cancer by putting it closer and receiving more radiation than he feels is prudent. He looks helpless too, just like we all are.

I even see Travis sitting on the couch in the basement cradling his head in his hands. My brother is lost in more ways than one. He's a twelve-year-old boy imprisoned in a man's body. He's surrounded by a bag of pot, a bong, bottles of pills, and a pile of dirty clothes. The vision is so clear, I can even see which clothes they are.

Then before I know it, Poof! I'm back in my own skin and feeling the weight of dread sucking me down. When I hang up with Ethan, I'm not sure what to do with myself.

Sam eventually finds me and takes my hand. He walks me into the room with my parents and explains, "We're going to get Nan ready. The surgeon will be here within the half hour."

He looks very serious, but adds, "This is good news. It's Nan's best chance of making it. I'm going to need you all to step out for a bit, while we get her prepped. You can come back in about fifteen minutes."

My mom gently kisses her mother on the head before Dad pulls her into his arms. They walk past me out the door. I approach the bed, not sure what to do. I finally sit next to Nan and put my hands gently on top of hers. I beg, "Please don't die. I think you're pig-headed, stubborn, and borderline mean at times, but I also think you're the best person I know. I love you with my whole heart."

Then I stand up and add, "Dorcas Abernathy is a complete whore and Gramps is lucky she didn't marry him. He got the better end of that stick, let me tell you."

The Waiting Game

Sam comes out every hour to update us on how Nan is doing. He's not part of the surgical team. He's there to be our eyes and ears and to hold my grandmother's hand. I'm so grateful she has a loved one with her.

The first time he visits us in the waiting room, he assures, "Nan is doing great. They've located the bleed and have started the process of isolating it." He instructs, "Why don't you all try to close your eyes? I'll be back out soon."

My mom comes over to sit next to me. "Will you play hangman with me?"

I snort in response. My mom loves to play hangman, but no one will ever play with her because she always chooses words and phrases the common man has never heard of. A small example of her questionable vocabulary includes words like, limerence, nudiustertian, pulveratricious, scopperloit, and floccinaucinihilipilification. Yet I don't have the heart to deny her right now.

She writes _'_ _ _ _ _ _ _ on the back of an outdated *People* magazine. It takes me all of two minutes to solve her puzzle. "I'm scared."

I assure her, "Me, too, Mom. Me, too."

During hour three of surgery, Travis walks into the waiting room. He's clean, his hair has been combed, and his clothes are pressed—as in ironed. At first, I don't know who he is. He sits down next to Mom. She doesn't so much as do a double-take; she recognizes him immediately.

I move next to my brother and put my hand on his arm. "How are you doing?"

He looks haunted as he answers, "This is all my fault."

"I don't think so, Trav." Then I confide, "The last time I talked to Nan, I yelled at her for not liking Ethan. If anything, I'm the one who upset her."

We sit silently offering each other our support. That's when I realize a family is like a stew. We're all just a bunch of ingredients, simple items on our own. Then we get thrown into the stewpot and start to blend together. Our edges soften as we mix with the other ingredients in such a way that it's hard to recognize what we were before becoming part of the whole.

I'm either getting totally deep and profound here or I'm losing it altogether. But it occurs to me that maybe that's Travis's problem. He never identified what ingredient he was before becoming part of the family stew. I think he needs to step away from the pot (I mean that both literally and figuratively) and find out who he is before he can add anything of real value to either himself or our family.

The fifth time Sam updates us, he announces, "Nan is being closed up. Dr. Philmore will be out to talk to you as soon as he's done and she's in post-op." I look over at the clock and see that it's already midnight. It could as easily be ten in the morning, as time simply doesn't make any sense right now.

We wait, staring off into space, full of relief that she's still with us. When the surgeon joins us, we nearly maul him with our combined presence. He explains, "The aneurysm was significant. We can't know the amount of damage that was done until she regains consciousness and can answer some questions."

He addresses my mom, "That won't be for at least twenty-four hours. Why don't you go home and get some rest before coming back in the morning?" He says, "There's nothing more you can do for your mother right now."

My mom doesn't want to leave, but I assure her, "I'll be right in her room the whole night. I promise to call you if she so much as twitches her little finger."

"Come on, Mags," my dad encourages. "You need some rest. I'll bring you back as soon as you wake up in the morning." My mom looks like a lost little girl as she ultimately lets my dad lead her away. Travis follows along like a stray dog.

When everyone's gone, a nurse takes me to the room assigned to my grandmother to await her arrival in ICU. She announces, "Normally, visitors aren't allowed to stay overnight in intensive care. Dr. Sam said we could make an exception for you." I don't like being in Sam's debt, but at the moment I don't care. I need to be with Nan for both my sake and my mom's.

The nurse hands me a pillow, a blanket, and travel-sized toiletries. She smiles kindly. "If you need anything else, just ring."

I take a minute to wash my face and brush my teeth. My eyes look like something out of Night of the Living Dead. They're bloodshot and drooping like they've decided a trip south is in order.

When I come out of the bathroom, Sam is sitting on my makeshift bed. He opens his arms to me and I don't hesitate. I run toward him like his embrace is the only place that makes any sense for me to be. I clear my mind of all thoughts that I'm betraying Ethan. I need comfort right now, too. Which is why I let Sam hold me and rock me until I fall asleep. I don't remember anything else until the morning light pours into the room to signal the start of a new day.

A New Day

When I wake up, the first thing I do is look over at my grandmother. She looks like a corpse lying there so still and unanimated. In addition to having a breathing tube and being hooked up to all kinds of monitors, she's wearing a bandage wrapped around her entire head, that makes it look like she's got on an old-fashioned swimming cap. I immediately feel like it should be adorned with a giant plastic flower to jazz it up a bit.

Sam walks in carrying a large coffee and a banana. He hands them over before sitting down next to me. I'm sure my hair looks like something you'd pull out of a drain and my breath could probably kill a small animal, but he doesn't seem to care.

I take the lid off the coffee and indulge in a huge gulp. It's pure heaven and I finish half of it before I peel the banana. We don't say a word to each other. We just sit with our auras bumping up against each other in silence.

Nan's machines are whirring and ticking and filling the atmosphere. Sam gets up to check a readout from one of them, then he changes a bag of saline dripping into her arm. When he's done, he sits on the chair next to my grandmother and says, "Nan has been closer to me than my own grandmother ever was."

I nod my head. I know this. His grandmother lived in Washington and he only saw her for one week out of the summer when his family went to visit. She never came to see them, and she didn't like to talk on the phone, so it was hard for Sam to really get to know her. His other grandmother died before he was born.

He offers, "I'm off for the next two days, but I plan to be here with Nan. I'm not going anywhere."

I nod my head. "Do you think she's going to wake up today?"

"No, probably not until tomorrow or the next day. There's a lot of swelling with brain surgery, and it needs to come down before she can be conscious and alert."

"Would you mind if I ran home and showered? Ethan and his family are leaving this afternoon, and I'd like to spend a little time with them before they go."

"About Ethan …" he starts to say.

I cut him off, "No, Sam. Nothing about Ethan. Nothing that is happening right now is about him. And it's only about you and me insofar as we both love Nan and she loves us. There's no Cat and Ethan or Cat and Sam right now. None of that matters at the present."

"I was only going to say I'm sorry."

I turn on him like a wild animal. "You're not sorry. You're not sorry at all. You're only saying that because Nan could be at death's door and you don't want me to be mad at you. You don't want to feel uncomfortable around me while we wait to see what's going to happen."

"Kitty Cat, you misunderstand. I'm not sorry I said anything to you. I'm only sorry that it upset you."

My hands start to tremble. "You're sorry it upset me? What did you think it would do saying that stuff to me? Ethan's my fiancé! How was I supposed to react when you asked if I really loved him? Do you think so little of my ability to love that I'd accept his marriage proposal without feeling deeply for him?"

He shakes his head sadly. "Cat, I've never forgotten what we had. I've never gone a day where I haven't thought of you. Everywhere I go in this town, I run into the ghosts of our younger selves, and I want to stop and warn them to never let each other go. I can't go anywhere without seeing *us* having some adventure, and it breaks my heart."

"Why in God's name did you ever come back here?" I demand. "Why didn't you just move to Chicago like you'd planned and lose yourself in the big city where there are no memories?" I don't add, because you wouldn't stay with me long enough to make them.

"I came back because it's the only way I ever thought I'd see you again. I didn't plan on being a small-town doctor. I'd always planned to work at a big hospital, but if I didn't move home, how was I ever going to run into you?"

I want to throw my remaining coffee at him. "How dare you put this on me? You could have called me and apologized anytime in the last fourteen years. You could have found out a long time ago that I moved on from you. Don't tell me you've been alone all these years pining away for me, because I don't believe it."

"No, I haven't been alone. In fact, I was with a woman throughout medical school, a perfectly lovely woman whom I lived with."

Ah, a plot twist. Saint Sam of the broken-hearted hasn't been self-flagellating every minute since he walked away from me. "What happened to her?"

"She wanted to get married."

I scoff, "Psh, yeah. Why do you think she was living with you all that time? Because she wanted to do your laundry?"

Sam gets up and turns to look out the window. "No, Cat. I get that she wanted a long-term future with me. I thought I saw one with her too, until the time came to make it official. When I thought of buying an engagement ring, I couldn't envision giving it to her. Your finger is the only one I could imagine putting a ring on."

"Samuel Davis Hawking, you are the devil! You have no right to say that to me. You don't even know me. You know nothing about the adult me. You don't know what experiences I've had that have shaped me and made me who I am today. You're in love with a memory, that's all. And you need to wake up and get a life, because I did, and you're not in it."

I grab my purse and slam out of the room before he has a chance to say another word. Because so help me, I'm ready to tear his head off and feed it to the wolves.

Goodbyes

When I walk through the front door of my parents' house, Ethan is standing there with two suitcases in his hands. He puts them down and I fly into his arms. He holds me while I unleash a hurricane of tears all over him. After several long moments, he asks, "Is it your grandmother? Did she ... not make it?"

"No, she's still with us, just not conscious." I inadvertently get snot all over his shoulder when I try to dry my eyes.

Ethan takes my hand and leads me into the living room. We sit together on the couch. I'm actually more on his lap than on the couch. I have my head resting against his shoulder. He asks, "What do the doctors say?"

I don't mention Sam by name, I merely answer, "They think she might regain consciousness today or tomorrow. But, they won't even begin to know if she's going to be okay until she can breathe on her own. Then they'll check her motor responses and reflexes. Only when she regains consciousness will they be able to ascertain whether or not there's been any brain damage."

He exhales loudly. "Did you know that only one out of every ten thousand people will suffer from a brain aneurysm in their lifetime? The majority of those happen between the ages of thirty-five and sixty, so already Nan is quite exceptional." He continues to ramble, "Fifteen percent die before even reaching the hospital, and four out of seven who recover wind up having disabilities."

Ethan and his statistics. I have no doubt that he didn't even have to look any of this up. Information like this just lives in his brain. I reply, "That's not very reassuring."

"I-I-I'm sorry," he stutters. "I was just trying to inform you. I didn't mean to upset you."

I know that, but still, I wonder if Ethan was born with an impaired sensitivity gene. "That's okay."

"Do you have any idea how long you'll be here?" he asks.

"Not until Nan wakes up. I'm guessing it'll be at least a week though, if not longer." Then I apologize, "I'm sorry this trip hasn't been the best for you. I mean, my family is so abnormal and well, quite frankly, rude."

He releases a half-hearted laugh. "They *are* quite different from what I expected. I mean, you're so sound and grounded. They're a bit more unpredictable, aren't they?"

"You could say that." But in this moment, I realize that even though I've fought against the craziness of my clan my whole life, I do love them and I'm not quite sure I'd want them to be anything other than what they are. I ask, "Have my parents left for the hospital yet?"

Ethan scoots me off his lap. "About five minutes before you got back. Listen," he says, "I have no idea why, but my mom was hoping to talk to you before we leave"—he looks at his watch— "which we should be doing in about forty minutes. Would you mind if I got her?"

I try to work out Ethan's timeline in my head. Three hours to get to O'Hare (even though it should only take two), one hour to return the car (it should take half that time), one hour to check in luggage and get to the gate (which it probably will) and what, another three in case of alien invasion? I wish he'd spend his emergency buffer time here with me and not sitting at the airport, but I guess I can't blame him. It's how Ethan is wired. So, I say, "Sure, I'd be happy to talk to her."

I wait in the living room while he goes to find Natalie. When she comes into the room, she's wearing her winter coat and hat. "I thought we could take a walk."

Okay, then. I get up, and put my coat back on, and walk out the door. I offer, "I'm sorry about all the chaos." I don't know what exactly I'm apologizing for: the unorthodox Thanksgiving, the upheaval with Nan's aneurysm, the burnt scalp, the shuck and chuck—maybe all of it.

Natalie leads the way across the front yard, crunching across the snow. She finally stops next to a low fence in front of the barn. "Catriona, you have nothing to apologize for. Your family have been lovely hosts, and we've thoroughly enjoyed getting to meet them."

I grin painfully in response. Ethan's mom must either be completely dense, or an award-winning actress. My family have been lovely hosts like rabid bats are sweet little birds. That's not to say they can't be lovely, but from Natalie's perspective I can't see how that's her take-away.

I don't know what to say, so I just wait for her to get on with whatever she wants to talk to me about. The next two minutes of silence feel long enough to have a root canal. She finally announces, "I want to tell you a story about my life."

At my expectant and somewhat frightened look, she continues, "Ethan's dad, Jason, was not the first man I loved."

Oh, my god, please don't let this story be as awkward as I predict it's going to be. She says, "I was in love with a boy in college, and we were pretty serious. Everyone thought we were going to get married."

I don't really want to know anymore, but I can hardly not ask, "What happened?" I'm hoping she says he got hit by a bus, then she met Jason and there you have it, story's over. But no, that would be too easy.

She smiles. "He asked me to marry him, and I said yes. His name was Jacob, and he was an adventurer. He wanted us to see the world together and live in far-off lands and build huts and experience things we've never experienced before."

Before I can stop myself, I exclaim, "That sounds wonderful!" Note to self: there's a reason they didn't get married, Cat. Don't make it sound like you think he's the perfect man.

Natalie grimaces. "It was a wonderful dream, for him. It just wasn't my idea of happily-ever-after."

Because I don't know when to leave well enough alone, I ask, "Couldn't you have compromised?"

She shakes her head. "Only if living in Cambodia half of the time and Westchester the other half was something we could have both agreed to. For me, that wasn't an option. Even though I loved him, I didn't want what he wanted. I only wished him the best, but I knew I couldn't make a life with him that would fulfill both of us."

I don't have to be a rocket scientist to know where she's going with this story. "Natalie," I say, "I love Ethan and we're very happy together." Trying for levity, I add, "And neither one of us wants to live in Cambodia."

She puts out her hand to stop me. "Catriona, it doesn't have to be something that extreme. My son is like me. He's not a compromiser on the big things. He wants what he wants, how he wants it."

"I want the same things he does," I assure her. "I want a family and security and stability. I want to plan and prepare and know what's coming next. Truly, put your mind at ease. We're totally on the same page."

She looks at me with haunted eyes, "Cat." Uh-oh, she's never used my nickname before. "Make sure of it before you marry him. Ethan is not going to turn into someone more flexible and open. If anything, he's going to get more set in his ways. Please, take this time while you're here to really think about what I've said."

I'm not sure I can handle much more drama right now. I don't know what to tell her, except to say that I'll consider her advice. She smiles at me sadly, reaches out to hug me, and then leaves me behind as she walks back to the house.

Not only does my family question whether I should be with Ethan, but apparently his parents are doing so, as well. Sarah's on the same page even though she won't come right out and say it. Ethan and I are the only ones who think we should still be together and to be quite honest, it's a lonely feeling.

Truce

After Ethan and his parents leave, I head upstairs and draw myself a bubble bath. I use the hottest water I can stand and then climb in with every intention of spending an hour soaking away my cares. Not that they'll be that easy to shake, but I'm going to give it a shot. My brain is so full I don't know how to begin to process everything running through it.

I only last twenty minutes before the water starts to get cold. I hurriedly wash my hair and shave my legs before rinsing off in the shower. Then I wrap up in the plushest towel I can find before crawling into bed. I lay there for about an hour contemplating how nice life would have been had I not come home for Thanksgiving. Somehow, I blame myself for Nan's burst aneurysm and decide she would have never had it, had I not upset everyone's apple cart by bringing Ethan home.

At eleven o'clock, I finally pull myself out of bed and dry my hair. I even put on some makeup in hopes of feeling a little perkier. After making a sandwich, I go down to the basement to find my brother to see how he's doing.

Travis is sitting on the couch wearing the same clothes he had on at the hospital last night. I sit next to him and ask, "How are you holding up?"

His eyes look haunted and I briefly wonder if he's slept at all. He shakes his head. "I'm not good, Cat."

"Is there something I can do?" I've barely spoken to him since we've become adults. As much as I've kept my distance though, I find that I miss him. I've missed getting to know him. But how could I when he doesn't even know himself?

"Nah, there's nothing you can do," he answers.

I know exactly how off kilter he feels because I feel the same way. I say, "I'm heading over to the hospital if you want to come along."

He turns his head and stares into my eyes. "I appreciate it, but I have some things I need to take care of. If Nan comes to, tell her that I love her. Tell her I'm ready to make some changes."

I reach out and hug my brother. "Okay, kid, I'll do it. Let me know if you need anything."

He holds on for a moment longer before releasing me. "You're a good sister, Cat."

Before I leave for the hospital, I fire off another text to Jazz to let her know not to expect me home for a while, then I head out the door. I stop by the bakery to get a box of sticky buns and then swing by the craft store to find a pink daisy to stick to Nan's bandaged head. I won't put it on without the doctor's approval, but I thought it would cheer her up to see it when she wakes up and asks for a mirror, which she's bound to do.

I run into Sam as soon as I get off the elevator on Nan's floor. Literally, I run into him. I get knocked back a couple of steps and after he helps steady me, he takes the box of buns out of my hands. I ask, "Is she awake yet?"

"Not yet. I was just on my way to the cafeteria to get your folks a bite to eat." Lifting the pink bakery box a few inches, he says, "I'm guessing you bought something better than we could ever hope to get there. Let's go take these in."

I follow behind like his shadow. "Sam," I say. He stops in his tracks. "I meant everything I said to you this morning." He nods his head in understanding, so I continue, "But I don't want to fight with you."

"I don't want to fight with you, either. Where does that leave us?"

I shrug my shoulders. "I guess it leaves us being civil to one another as long as neither of us"—pointed glare— "steps out of line."

"Civil?" he asks. "Or friendly?"

"Is there a difference?"

"Yes, there's a difference. Civil is for strangers, and friendly is for friends. The question you have to ask yourself is, can you be my friend?"

I quickly fire back, "I think the more accurate question is, can *you* be *my* friend? Nothing more, just my friend?"

He sighs. "If that's all you're offering, then yes. So long as you're in my life in some capacity."

I grab the pastry box back from him and dismissively start walking. Over my shoulder, I order, "Okay, friend, I want hot tea to go with my sticky bun. I'm sure you wouldn't mind getting that for me."

I hear him laugh as he turns around and heads back in the direction of the cafeteria.

Navel Gazing

In some ways, Nan's still being unconscious is a gift. For instance, if she's going to die and we don't know it yet, I'd much rather be anxiously wondering about her outcome than planning her funeral.

I'd rather not know if she's going to be in a coma for a month or wind up a vegetable. There's an odd comfort sitting in her room with my parents, expectantly hoping for the best, with the worst nothing more than a looming possibility.

There's also a tangible sense of relief that Ethan and his parents have gone home. Our dysfunctional family holiday is officially over. We've all survived the first meeting, and while it was not a Hallmark movie ideal, no one is dead, yet.

I'm not sure how I expected the weekend to go. I knew my parents weren't going to suddenly turn into the consummate sitcom family, whose quirks were mild at best. Dad was always going to force his guests to spit nut shells across the room. He was always going to dress up dead mice and wear a skirt. It's who he is.

Nan was destined to be rude, and my mother was always going to be disappointed my intended wasn't Sam.

In the deepest corner of my brain, I suppose I was hoping Ethan would somehow react differently than he did. Like, all he needed was the right push to loosen up a little before falling in love with spittoons and starting a collection of his own.

Perhaps he might have discovered swearing was fun. Maybe he could have developed a fondness for dead mice. That would have certainly gone a long way in my dad's book.

I've always known Natalie and Jason were a couple of duds, but I'd hoped being around my family would have loosened them up a bit. Had the Crenshaws only jumped on board with the shuck and chuck the first night, things could have been so different. In retrospect, I suppose my parents did welcome Ethan and his parents with open arms, but simply put, felt rejected by them. No one responds well to rejection. Ask me how I know.

I think about Natalie's and my conversation and let the question of whether Ethan and I are really meant to be enter my brain. How will he act in five years or ten? What will happen if my mom and dad need to move in with us in twenty years, due to health issues? How will he handle that?

He'd probably just push to have them put into a nursing home, so they didn't upset our lives. Could I let my parents be shoved into a home just so they didn't cause my husband any upset? What about our children? Would we be raising mini-Ethans, always afraid to try something new for fear of pulling a muscle?

Damn Natalie and her story. Why hadn't Ethan and I just stayed in New York City and watched the Thanksgiving Day Parade on television? I know full well we would have never gone in person, even though it's just a few blocks from our apartment.

Even I know there's a nineteen percent greater risk of personal injury attending a parade. Not to mention the three percent increased chance of a broken bone.

I try to imagine what it would have been like for Ethan to meet my family for the first time at our wedding. That would have been a disaster, as well. I could just see my dad insisting on walking me down the aisle while playing "The Flowers of Scotland" on his bagpipes, tripping on the runner, and flashing his bare bum to the entire congregation.

Nan would have probably stood up and objected when the minister asked if anyone had just cause why we shouldn't marry. Travis would have stayed in front of the church toking for all he was worth. I think my mom would have actually tried to suck it up and be good, but there would be no light in her eyes. No joy at her only daughter's wedding.

I try to visualize the event now that they've all met and the only image that comes to mind is bleak. Everyone striving hard to be on their best behavior. No one having fun for fear of upsetting the bride and groom. Is that what I want my wedding to be like? Is that what I want all future contact with my parents to be like? Maybe we should just elope.

I have a lot to think about, but for the time being, I'm going to hit the pause button on all decisions and stop navel gazing. Right now, I'm going to sit at Nan's bedside with my parents and eat a sticky bun.

No Place Like Home

Liza and Ned show up to check on us. I smile when I see their arms laden down with food. They bring sandwiches and cookies to help sustain life in our time of need. In New York City, my friends bring flowers when they visit loved ones in the hospital. But in the Midwest, we like to say, "Every crisis is cause for a casserole." *Casserole* being any food we happen to bring.

I leave my parents and decide to head outside for a jolt of fresh air. The streets are still being plowed from the Thanksgiving storm. Six-foot piles of snow form as the roadways get cleared. I watch as children bring out their sleds hoping for a little excitement from the makeshift hills.

Growing up in this little town was ideal, like living in a Norman Rockwell painting. It was a safe and secure environment where kids could roam free and explore without getting into too much trouble. I appreciate that now. As a kid though, I couldn't wait to get out of Dodge and make my mark on the world.

I try to evaluate if I've done that. I moved to New York right after college and have been there for nearly eleven years. I love the Big Apple, but wonder how much longer it will be the life for me. Ethan and I have talked about leaving the city when we have children. He thinks we should head to Westchester.

I like his suburban hometown, but since it's only forty miles from the city, it's still close enough to the action that kids grow up quicker than I did here in rural Illinois. Ethan's job is in the city, so he'd have to commute. Heck, my job is in the city. I'd have to commute, too. Party planners are probably not in great demand in little towns like Gelson.

I don't see Sam until he's nearly on top of me. He greets, "Heya, Miss Kitty, it's pretty cold out here." He rubs his hands up and down the arms of his doctor's coat.

I turn to him and press my nostrils tightly together for a few seconds before releasing them. When they stick together, I answer, "Looks like it."

"Remember that big storm in nineteen ninety-nine that closed school down for ten days?"

I do remember. It was wonderful and scary and so cold I nearly got frostbite. "My dad opened the front door the morning after it started and there was a five-foot snow drift blocking us in. I couldn't even see above it."

Sam smiles. "Remember how he shoveled through it and made a tunnel to the driveway?" It's just one of a million memories Sam and I share. For too long when I thought of Sam, I only remembered the day he broke up with me. This trip is definitely bringing back some of the good times.

I cock my head and look at him closely. "Do you like living here?"

He thinks for a moment before answering, "Yeah. I went to med school in Chicago and loved it. I stayed there through my residency and have only been back in Gelson for two years, but

I really do like it here. I like that it's quiet and familiar."

We're silent for several moments before he adds, "It's home. All the best stuff that ever happened in my life happened here and I like being surrounded by those memories."

"Not much of a night life, I'm guessing."

He flashes some jazz hands. "I don't know about that. Bingo night at the Catholic church can turn pretty wild, especially if Nan wins."

"Please don't tell me you go to bingo night!"

He barks with laughter, "Why? Would you be jealous of all those old ladies trying to set me up with their granddaughters?"

He's only partially joking. I know Sam and he's not going to let our friendship truce get in his way of pushing for something more. So, I tease back, "Nope. Been there, done that. I'm good with sharing you."

Of course, that's not what he wants to hear, and he looks temporarily hurt, but he brushes it off pretty quickly. "I came out to let you know that Nan moved her fingers a couple of times. It looks like she could be coming to any time now."

Suddenly, everything feels right with my world. If Nan comes out of this all okay, then there's nothing I can't face. There's nothing like a little burst brain aneurysm to gain perspective.

She's Baaack

When we walk back into my grandmother's room, Dr. Philmore is standing over her looking into her eyes with a penlight. Sam asks, "How's she doing?"

The surgeon, a distinguished looking man about my father's age, puts the torch back into his breast pocket. "She's looking good. I'm a little surprised by how good, actually. I'm cautiously optimistic."

When he steps aside, I can see Nan's eyes are still open and she's staring at us in moderate confusion. She croaks, "We havin' a party?"

And with that, a collective cheer goes up. "Nan!"

My mom rushes to her side. "How are you feeling, Mom? Are you okay?"

I move to the other side. "You scared us to death!"

We buzz around like a hive of hyperactive bees until Dr. Philmore suggests, "Why don't you all step out for a few minutes so as not to overexcite the patient. I'll just ask her a few questions and then come talk to you."

Why don't we all step out? Clearly this man doesn't know us. Stepping out in the face of such good news isn't our way. Yet somehow, Sam gets behind our group and pushes us through the door without any fuss.

In the hallway, my mom bursts into tears of joy, then she nearly collapses on my dad. "Thank you, God … thank you, God … thank you, God!"

I couldn't agree more. Turning to Sam, I ask, "Does this mean she's going to be okay?"

He shakes his head slightly. "It's a good first step, but there are a lot more until we can conclude she's out of the woods."

"I'm just so relieved that crazy old bird is still alive, I don't quite know what to do with myself," my dad interjects.

And in that moment, I realize I can never see Ethan saying the same thing about either of my parents, let alone Nan. I want to be married to a man who loves my family, who will miss them when they're gone and pray they don't go too quickly because of the void they'd leave in his life.

It's like the heavens have opened up and dropped a load of bricks on my head. I stagger under the weight of my epiphany, but I can't address it at this moment.

When Dr. Philmore comes out, he announces, "You can go in, one at a time, until she falls asleep. I don't want her overstimulated."

"Will she be okay?" my mom asks.

The surgeon smiles. "If I were a betting man, I'd say she has a better than average shot at recovery. But truthfully, only time will tell." Then he adds, "Don't expect her to be leaving the hospital for at least a couple of weeks. She's had a serious brain trauma and we'll need to keep a close watch over her."

I sag against Sam in such relief I feel like my bones have

melted. This is the best news, ever. He puts his arms around me, not only to hold me up, but to hold me close, as well. I stay still, reasoning that friends are allowed to hug each other.

My mom goes in first, followed by my dad. When it's my turn, Nan has already fallen asleep, so I just sit and hold her hand, grateful she's still with us.

Life is a roller-coaster, and for the moment I'm comfortable with that. The highs are so very high, they just might make the lows worth the journey.

Crickets and Apologies

The next day starts the beginning of a comfortable pattern. I wake up early, put on a pot of coffee, and then drink the first cup while sitting at the kitchen table. This is the time I use to recap what happened the day before.

I take the next cup out to the front porch and stare at the barn. It's such a peaceful view. The trees are covered in snow and look like they're wearing furry white coats. These same trees will bud and burst forth with new life in the spring. But right now, they're resting, gaining their strength for a new season. Hopefully, that's what Nan is doing.

Everywhere I look, I remember my childhood. Travis and I used to climb the wooden fence separating the grassy front yard from the edge of the field. Once we reached the top, we'd jump down, pretending we were bailing out of an airplane that had just been shot down. When I look at the fence now, it doesn't seem that intimidating, but to my child eyes, I might as well have been jumping off the top of the barn.

My dad comes out in his robe to join me. "This place has sure hosted a lot of living, hasn't it?"

"I was just thinking how much fun Trav and I used to have

out here. I used to think I'd live here forever."

My dad smiles. "You know the old saying—man plans and God laughs. I've always thought the bigger purpose in our lives was kept from us, so we could enjoy the journey. If we knew how it was going to turn out right from the start, we wouldn't have as much fun reaching our destination."

"If I recall, thinking like that led to some pretty interesting family vacations. Like the summer you pulled out a map, blindfolded us all and made us play pin the tail on the United States. Then we played poker to decide which of the destinations we'd travel to that summer."

My dad jokes, "Hey, I always wanted to see Fidget River, Arkansas."

I add, "Best pulled pork sandwiches, ever. Scariest people though. Remember the guy with no teeth who followed us around town spitting out tobacco and yelling, 'Yankees aren't welcome?'"

My dad grimaces, "I forgot about that. Remember how the motel room filled up with crickets every night and the front desk clerk had to come in and vacuum them out before we could go to sleep?"

My whole body shudders. "Sleep? Did you actually sleep that weekend? I swear I went seventy-two hours straight without closing my eyes longer than it took to blink."

"We would have been better off just going to Hawaii like your mom wanted. Not that it would have been as much fun as Fidget River," he jokes.

"Yeah, luaus, body surfing in the Pacific Ocean, climbing volcanos … sounds like a real snore."

My dad exhales deeply. "I'm glad you're here, Cat. Your mom and I are so worried about Nan. Having you with us is a real comfort. Thank you."

"I wouldn't be anywhere else, Dad. Plus, it's been a long time since I've been home longer than a couple of days. I forget how much I love this old place." Then I wink at him, "And the people in it."

"You know, we were pretty surprised when you moved to New York City after college."

I drink down the last sip of my coffee, which has turned icy cold. "I guess I needed to get away and Chicago just didn't seem far enough."

"Running from Sam, huh?"

I nod my head. "Yeah, that was most of it. Once college ended, I was pretty much over him, I just didn't want to see him before I could prove how well I'd done without him."

My dad snorts. "You kids. Mags used to think you'd come home and bump into him and then the two of you would pick right up where you left off after high school, but that never happened."

"Is that what Thanksgiving was all about? You wanted to throw us in each other's paths to see if there was still a chance?"

"I guess so. I know it wasn't a nice thing to do to Ethan, but we were running out of time to see if that was still a possibility. I'm sorry, Cat. I hope you can forgive us."

"I forgive you, Dad." I know they didn't mean any harm and if I was truthful, I'd say I'm glad it happened. Not having Sam in my life has been a real void. I'd like to think we can find a way to be friends again, for all our sakes. I just don't quite know how to accomplish that.

Zombies, Vampires, and Aliens, Oh My!

The day after Nan regains consciousness, I start spending most of my days with her. She doesn't have the attention span to read or play games, and she barely has any interest in television. Although the nurse did turn on the Santa Clarita Diet for her for background noise sometime before I showed up this morning. Nan seems to have paid some attention to it because she greets me with, "You know, I think there are more zombies out there than people let on."

I take my coat off, adjust the flowers by her bedside, and tidy up her breakfast dishes. "I wasn't aware there were any zombies."

She shoots me a look. "How can there be vampires and no zombies? That doesn't make any sense."

I don't know if Nan is just being her peculiar self or if she's coming back from surgery a little weirder than she went in. "Nan, there're no such things as vampires. That's what you always used to tell me when I was growing up." I try reminding her that she didn't believe in them either.

"Well of course I told you that. I didn't want you to go

around worrying Dracula was going to carry you off. But you're grown up now, Cat. You should have figured that out on your own."

Okay, so this bizarre thinking, is in fact, a pre-existing condition. I ask, "How was I supposed to have figured that out? Where do you meet vampires? And if had met them, how would I know they were the living dead, short of them biting me?"

Nan closes her eyes. "Catriona Fiona, don't get fresh with me. It's a simple line of reasoning. If aliens exist, then vampires certainly exist, then it's just a short leap to zombies."

"Aliens exist?" I ask. "When did you come to that conclusion?"

Without missing a beat, she answers, "Nineteen seventy-four. I was thirty-six and your grandfather came running in through the back door to tell me a flying saucer had landed in the corn field."

"I'm sorry, what did you say?"

She waggles an arthritic finger at me. "You heard me. I was shucking corn when it happened. I was wearing my favorite apron with the roosters on it. You know, the one that says, 'Don't Let the Cock Doodle You'?"

I nod my head. How could I forget that apron? I encourage, "Go on."

"I dropped that corn right in the garbage can and ran out the door after him. When we got out to where he saw the spaceship land, there wasn't any sign of them, but there was one of those crop circles everyone's talking about nowadays."

"You're kidding? Why have I never head this story before?"

She shrugs her shoulders. "You weren't even born, so it's not like I could have told you at the time. When we found the second circle, you were only four and we didn't want to scare you."

I decide to placate my grandmother and play along. "So, there were two of them?"

"Yup."

"But you never saw a spaceship or aliens?"

"That's correct," she answers.

"But because you saw what you think were crop circles, you started to believe in aliens?" I'm going to try to figure out her reasoning if it kills me. And at the rate we're going, it just might.

She nods her head. "That's right."

"And because you believe in aliens, you figure vampires are a sure thing?"

She shrugs her shoulders. "I wasn't convinced until I started reading that Anne Rice. No one can make up stories that good unless they're true."

I roll my eyes. "And as of this morning, you now believe in zombies."

"Drew Barrymore is very believable. Her poor daughter, though. Having a zombie for a mother must be a horrible cross to bear."

The only way I'm going to get this conversation to end is to agree with her. "It makes you grateful for the life you have, doesn't it?"

She motions me over to sit by her. Once I'm perched on her bedside, she says, "I'm grateful for you, Kitty Cat. Thank you for staying once I went and burst my head."

I stare down at my very frail-looking grandmother and send God a psychic message that I owe him big for letting her live. "You're welcome, Nan. I'm just relieved you're doing better. The doctor says they'll probably discharge you sometime next week." But by the time I finish talking, her eyes are closed, and she appears to have dozed off.

Sam walks in a short while later to check on Nan. When he sees she's sleeping, he announces, "I have time to run to the cafeteria for some coffee, if you'd like to join me."

I figure there's no harm. He's certainly gone out of his way for my family and it's been a great source of comfort knowing he's here keeping an eye on Nan. The least I can do is have a cup of coffee with him.

Coffee or Tea, Not Me

I admire Sam's good looks as we walk through the sterile hospital hallways. His dark hair is thick and wavy, his eyes are twinkling and happy, and he smells like a spicy aftershave I've always associated with him. Everything about him is familiar and inviting. How did I ever go fourteen years without seeing him?

When we get to the cafeteria, I look around the ancient dining room and wonder when the last time they updated the décor was. I'm pretty sure mauve and chrome were all eighties. And I can't imagine that look ever making a comeback. "Coffee or tea?" Sam asks.

"Peppermint tea. I've had enough coffee in the last week to keep the Navy awake for a year."

He studies me closely and reaches out to a strand of hair that's dangling in my eyes. "Poor you. You've been under a lot of stress lately." Then he orders our drinks. While he pays for them, he asks, "Are you planning on staying in town for a while?"

"No. I'm actually going back to New York in a couple of days." The sides of his mouth droop as low as a depressed hound dog. I should just leave it like that and let him think I'm walking out of his life again, but I don't. I add, "I'll be back in plenty of time for Christmas."

"That's wonderful! I hope we can get together when you come back." The smile on his face could resuscitate a dead heart.

We sit at a table for four by a window overlooking the parking lot. I shrug my shoulders. "Maybe. But what's the point? I mean, I'm engaged to Ethan."

"You said we could be friends," he pouts.

"I know. But is that going to be enough for you? Answer honestly."

He opens a prepackaged creamer pod and pours it into his coffee. "I told you before, I'd make do with any part of yourself you're willing to share. If friendship is all you're offering, I'll be fine with that."

"Should I invite you to my wedding?" I ask.

"I wouldn't miss it for the world," he replies.

I taunt, "I'm getting married in New York."

"I know how to get to the airport."

The thought of Sam as a guest at my wedding to Ethan eats a pit in my stomach the size of the Grand Canyon. Nothing about that scenario seems right. I decide to change the subject. "Nan believes in aliens."

He looks briefly confused by the change of topic. "Well, yeah. I mean ever since the crop circles, anyway."

"You know about the crop circles?" I demand.

"She told me about them while we were in high school."

"Why didn't you tell me?"

He shrugs his shoulders. "She made me promise I wouldn't. She didn't want to give you nightmares, and she wanted to make sure I knew so I could protect you if they ever came back."

"It would explain a lot, you know."

"What?" he looks up over his coffee cup. His blue eyes sparkling with curiosity.

I giggle. "Maybe my whole family has been abducted and partially lobotomized in the name of Martian science."

He laughs. "I can see where that might make sense." Then he gets serious. "Cat, you can never walk out of my life again, okay?" I don't point out that I never did. He was the one that pushed me out.

I don't know what to say. Can I have Sam in my life as just a friend? It's such a foreign concept. What would we do, call each other on the phone and talk about our lives? Have lunch when I'm in town like I do with Sarah? How can I go back to that after I thought we'd spend forever together?

I don't answer.

"Stop thinking so hard. You're going to hurt yourself," he says.

"I'm just trying to imagine what friendship with you would be like. Would we recommend books to each other? Talk about moisturizers, what?"

"We were friends long before we were anything else, Cat. We certainly can be again."

What he's saying makes sense. Sam was like a brother to me for most of my life until he became more. I need to ask myself if that's enough. Could I listen to him tell me about his girlfriends? Could I go to *his* wedding? I have a lot of thinking to do, and I know I'm not going to be able to do it here in Gelson. The sooner I get back to New York, the better.

After we finish our beverages, Sam walks me back to Nan's room before going on his rounds. I continue to ponder what I'm going to do with him. It would be so much easier if I walk away and never spare him another thought. I'm just not sure I can. Sam Hawking is like french fries. One encounter is never enough.

Time to Go

My thoughts are full of Sam and Ethan. Hardly a minute goes by where I'm not thinking of one of them and wondering what I should do. I don't talk to anyone else though. My family and Sarah have made it clear they think I belong with Sam. While I have my concerns about Ethan, I've decided to go back to New York and see how I feel in our home together. I'm going to return to my old life for a full week before entertaining any notions about our future. I owe it to him. I owe it to us.

The more I think about it, I realize Ethan is a good fit for my New York persona. It's just with Nan's scare, and everything else, I'm reminded there's more to me than just who I am in Manhattan. There's a whole history, a whole family who are part of my make up that I've been ignoring.

My mom sits on my bed while I pack. "I don't know what we would have done without you here."

"Come on, Mom. You would have been just fine. You're tougher than you think you are."

"I miss you, Cat. I miss being a part of your everyday life."

I know what she means. There's a special something that happens with a parent/child relationship when it evolves into a friendship. I left home to start my own life before that could ever develop with my mom and dad.

This is the longest I've been home since the summer after college. It turns out it takes more than four days of togetherness to break down old dynamics and connect in a new way. Who knew?

My dad pops his head in the door. "Sarah's here. She's waiting in the living room." My friend and I have had precious little time together and an O'Hare run will give us some quality moments to talk.

Nan is doing well, but they're going to keep her in the hospital for at least five more days. She'll either come home or enter a short-term care facility, depending on what her rehab needs are. Either way, she should be back in the house by Christmas.

As I walk down the stairs, I spy several field mice dressed like they're going to visit the queen's court. I can't imagine how my dad gets knee breeches and ruffled shirts on such tiny rodents. I know he's taken to sewing some of their outfits onto them, so they look more realistic. More realistic for an ecstasy-induced rave, maybe.

Speaking of drugs, I run into my brother at the bottom of the stairs. He takes my arm and asks, "Can I talk to you for a minute?"

I let him lead me into the dining room. "What's up?"

"I wanted you to know I've thrown away all my pot. I feel like I'm responsible for what happened to Nan. I'm going to clean up my act." His head hangs low in contrition.

I sigh. "Marijuana didn't create her aneurysm, Travis. But

I'm glad you're going to turn over a new leaf. It's time you start to live your life and quit hiding from it." At this moment I feel like I'm connecting with my brother for the first time since we've become adults.

He leans in to embrace me and declares, "I love you, Cat. I promise, I'm going to change."

I hug him back. "I love you, too, Trav. I believe in you. It's time you believed in yourself."

He nods his head. "Thanks, sis." Then he walks away with a purposeful stride I don't think I've ever seen before.

I kiss my parents before hugging the life out of them. I try to convey everything I'm feeling in that embrace. *I love you. I accept you. We've faced death and won. Things are going to be different. And most of all, thank you.*

When I wave goodbye as my friend's pickup pulls out of the driveway, I don't feel the normal sense of relief I've felt in the past. I feel longing and sadness. I feel a strong desire to turn around and go back and never leave again.

Follow the Yellow Brick Road

There's one runway at LaGuardia Airport that has me on pins and needles, negotiating with God, every time I land there. It ends right at the edge of the East River and every single time, it feels like we're going to miss it and crash into the water. Guess where I land today?

When the plane stops at the gate, and my stomach finally drops out of my throat, I grab my overhead bag and make my way out into the melee toward the Uber stand. It's only two in the afternoon, so hopefully I won't be sitting on the Triborough Bridge for an hour. I purposely arrived at this time to try to avoid that treat.

The added bonus is that I'll be back in the apartment before Ethan gets home from work. I want some time by myself to form my own opinion on whether it still feels like my home.

I love driving into Manhattan. The skyline is thrilling to me. It's like the yellow brick road leading into Oz. I just know magic awaits in one form or another. Today's entrance inspires the same nostalgia, but it's not quite as intense as it usually is.

When the Uber pulls up in front of my apartment building, I get out slowly, as if seeing it for the first time. I smile at the doorman when he holds the door for me. I like Edgar. For having such a short stature, he commands an authoritative presence. Though I'm several inches taller, and I'm no Amazon, I don't doubt his abilities to protect our domain. He's one of the interesting characters that's a part of my life here.

The lobby smells like matzo ball soup, so Mrs. Fein must be working her magic. I wonder if she's noticed that most of the times I stop to see her are when she's making it. Note to self: stop to see Mrs. Fein, soon.

When I get to the twelfth floor, I hesitate before stepping off the elevator. Somehow, I know things will be different the moment I cross the threshold, and I'm not sure I'm ready for that. I try to convince myself that I'm being ridiculous, but a full minute lapses before I step out.

When Ethan and I decided to move in together, we opted for his apartment because he owned it. Mine was bigger, but going back to paying rent once you've bought into Manhattan real-estate is a giant step backwards.

The prospect of gaining a life partner seemed a fair exchange for my single-girl-in-the-city furniture. Stability in the form of blah-beige couches and sensible matching end tables. I reasoned we wouldn't be living in his apartment for too many years before we bought something else that suited a growing family. My decorating style could certainly sit on the back burner until then.

So, when I walk into to 12B, it feels like I'm entering a good friend's domain. It's familiar and nice feeling, but not like I can't wait to settle in and start nesting. This is Ethan's home, not mine.

The apartment is unchanged. Extremely tidy, with everything in its place. The narrow, glass-topped trestle table to the left of the front door is fingerprint free, but the basket of Russian nesting dolls I keep there is nowhere to be found.

The pile of papers I'm perpetually sorting on the kitchen counter top is also missing. I walk into the living room and discover my red cashmere afghan is not on the back of the couch where I keep it. The few items that show I live here are absent.

Without my strategically placed pops of color, the monotony of Ethan's boringness screams at me. Brightly painted matryoshka dolls, a deep red afghan, a royal blue vase, and wicker basket full of green and gold mosaic tile ornaments really made something out of this place.

I find the vase in the pantry along with the dolls. The basket of ornaments is where it always is except it's covered by a beige tea-towel, and the afghan is in the linen closet. The whole scene kind of takes my breath away. Apparently, when I'm not here, Ethan obliterates all traces of me. What in the actual hell?

I continue to walk around and inspect everything like an anthropologist studying an extinct civilization. Perusal of the kitchen indicates Ethan has switched the silverware drawer and the gadget drawers back to how he had them before I moved in. I changed it out of necessity. With me doing most of the cooking, I needed an efficient way that made sense to me.

This alerts me to look in the dish cabinet. Sure enough, he's moved the dinner plates to the second shelf and put the salad plates on the first shelf. Who does that? Every sane person in this world knows the heavier plates go on the bottom and ascend accordingly.

Suddenly, I don't want to be here by myself. I'm not quite

sure where to go, but I don't feel like I belong here anymore. I grab my purse and coat and walk out the front door. I briefly toy with the idea of stopping in on Mrs. Fein, but I don't particularly feel up to small talk, even though a bowl of matzo ball soup would really hit the spot.

I walk out onto Columbus Circle and cross the street to Central Park West, which will take me to my perfect thinking location. I stroll for several blocks until I get to Strawberry Fields, where I grab a spot on one of the park benches. I sit and watch people go by—except I'm not really watching them. It's more like they become blurred distractions, fading into each other.

I try to talk myself down and ask why I care if Ethan doesn't like my knickknacks. I reason it's because those things represent me and my taste. They're my contribution to our home. By hiding them away when I'm not there it's like he's hiding me away. I had concerns coming home, but now they're magnified significantly.

A half hour passes, and I wonder if I'm making too much of this. Maybe I'm overreacting because of all the upheaval at home with Nan. Maybe this is no big deal and I'm just emotionally overwrought. Maybe one of Nan's flying saucers will drop out of the sky and take me away from all this.

I stop and pick up our favorite Chinese takeout on the way home. I promised myself I would come back to New York and live for an entire week before making any decisions. In order to do that, I need to put my irritation on the back-burner.

The Master of the House

When I get to the apartment, I leave the food on the countertop to microwave later. I set about unpacking before Ethan comes home, but I don't bring my decorative touches out of hiding. I leave them where the master of the house has put them, wondering if he'll return them to their proper place now that I'm back.

Ethan is always home by six, so at six thirty I begin to worry about him. I fire off a quick text, but he doesn't return it. At seven, I microwave some lo mein and steamed veggies and pour myself another glass of wine.

When I check my texts, I find that I have two. One from my mom and one from Sam, both wanting to make sure I got in okay. It's nice to know someone cares. After eating, I pick up the phone to call Jazz. I haven't heard her voice in a week and I miss her.

When she answers, she nearly breaks my eardrum screaming into the receiver. "YOU'RE HOME!"

"Sweet God, woman, I think I'm deaf. Don't yell at me."

I hear her say something to Dylan in the background, before she focuses on me. "I want to hear every detail of your trip, but

I only have five minutes. What are you doing right now?"

"I'm waiting for Ethan to come home. He's late."

"He's never late," my best friend replies.

"Well, he's late tonight. I just took a bath and poured myself some wine. I'm torn between cranking up some vintage Foo Fighters or watching Jane the Virgin on Netflix."

Jazz votes, "Go with the V. That chick has got it made in the shade. In the first season alone, she falls passionately in love with two dudes, gives birth, and somehow stays a virgin. Oh, and let's not forget graduate school. Life in a telenovela rocks!"

Meanwhile, I'm not in a love triangle because I'm being faithful and monogamous to the man I've committed to share my life with. A man who hides my afghan. One who's afraid of taking a cruise because he dreads a horrendous salmonella outbreak and refuses to consider camping because ticks live in the great outdoors and he doesn't want to contract Lyme disease. No one is ever going to turn my life into a television series.

"What are you doing tonight?" I ask my friend.

"Sex date," she answers.

"Wow, talk about a lot of information. I hope it's with Dylan."

She laughs. "Totes. You know how it is during the holiday season. We're both so busy we have to schedule every encounter." She whispers, "Uh-oh, gotta go. He's started doing a striptease in the hallway. That's my cue."

"Happy hunting," I offer. Although I don't think her prey is going to put up a fight.

I fall asleep on the couch. When Ethan finally walks through the front door, I open my eyes just enough to make out what he's doing through my still intertwined lashes. According to the clock in the stove, it's ten. I observe my fiancé as he puts the mail in the mail holder and hangs his keys on the middle of three hooks located to the right of the can opener. Then he takes his shoes off and puts them in the front closet—all before flipping on the light.

When he turns around and sees me, he jumps and borderline screams like a little girl. "Catriona! What are you doing here?"

I sit up and for a split-second experience a very strange feeling—like I've traveled back in time and don't live here yet. Ethan seems that surprised to see me. "I came home today." Then I remind him, "We've been texting about it."

"Is today Wednesday, already?"

"Ethan, why don't you know what day it is? Didn't you go to work today? Didn't you happen to discover it was Wednesday when you ordered your Wednesday lunch at the deli?" He always has the turkey breast on white bread, dry, with one slice of cheddar cheese and a lettuce leaf on Wednesday. Dear God, just thinking about it is enough to make me want to punch him. How in the world did his crazy routine ever make me feel comfort?

He continues to look befuddled. "I didn't go to the office this week. I went home to see my parents."

Now I'm completely confused. "Why? You just spent four days over Thanksgiving with them." He normally only sees his folks once a month. I can't imagine they had anything left to say to each other.

Ethan continues to just stand there. "My mom had something very important she wanted to talk to me about. She said it couldn't wait."

Icy fingers of dread crawl up my spine into the base of my neck. Is that flipping busybody planting seeds of doubt in her son's head about me? I've done nothing for her to question my commitment to him. Nothing. I finally manage to ask, "And what did she have to say?"

He shakes his head. "I'm really not sure I can explain it properly. But the long and short of it is she's leaving my father."

"What?! Where in the world did that come from?" After my conversation with Natalie, I had the feeling she was holding her relationship up as the model of what a healthy marriage looked like. Now she's leaving Jason? It makes no sense.

Ethan finally walks over and sits down on the couch next to me. He answers, "I don't know. She talked about traveling a lot and said she's been thinking that maybe she should have done more of it in her life. She says she wants to try to be adventurous."

I feel as shell-shocked as Ethan. "Can't she do those things with your dad?"

He shrugs his shoulders. "I asked her the same question and she says she doesn't want to. She said my father has never wanted to travel farther than the grocery store and while she used to feel the same way, she doesn't want to die without having discovered who she might have been had she made different choices in her life."

Holy crap. "Did your mom say where she wanted to go?"

Ethan looks like a lost little boy when he answers. "Cambodia."

Where Do I Start?

I get up this morning and nearly run into work. When I see Jazz, I push her into our office and shut the door. "OMG, you're never going to believe what Ethan told me last night!"

"What?" she demands.

"I don't know where to start. I mean I have to tell you about the trip before I tell you what Ethan said or it won't make sense," I say.

"So tell me, already!"

When I get to the part about the shuck and chuck, Jazz holds her sides in laughter while I try to adequately explain the expression on the Crenshaws' faces when I taught them how it was done. She gasps for air, "OMG, I know Natalie and Jason, and cannot for the life of me imagine their horror at being asked to perform such an act."

Then she blows on her fingernails and rubs them on her shirt as though shining them. "I, on the other hand, have aim so pristine I almost took the crown from your dad."

"You're the ultimate renaissance woman," I tease.

I gloss over some of the other highlights from Thanksgiving in hell, so I can hurry up and get to the part where Natalie warned me away from marrying her son. Then I dive right into the news that she's decided to leave her husband.

"You're kidding? It sounds like talking to you inspired a change in attitude about her own marriage. I wonder if she's going to look up her old college flame."

I startle at the thought. "Do you think so? She told me all about him and used her experience with him as the model for why I shouldn't marry Ethan. I never thought she'd start pining for what she passed up. She sounded like she was perfectly content with her choices."

"What do you make of her warning?" Jazz asks. "Have you reconsidered your engagement?"

I look up sheepishly. "I haven't made any final decisions yet, but she's got me thinking." Then I recount my discoveries of Ethan's removal of my possessions from plain sight.

"Cat, you know I love you, right?" After I nod my head, she continues, "Because I love you so much, I'm about to lay some truth on you, even though you think that particular kind of thing is overrated." I nod again, only slower.

"Neither Dylan nor I have ever been able to figure out what you're doing with Ethan." At my crestfallen expressions, she adds, "He's just so different from you." She's says "different" in the same way you'd say "alien" or "in need of a mental help."

"But Dylan and Ethan have been friends since they were little boys." I insist, "Dylan has to like him!"

My friend takes my hand like she's trying to keep me from freaking out. "Yeah, he likes him. He likes him because they have a history together. But he also thinks he's OCD to the extreme and must be a real pain in the ass to live with."

I'm speechless. I always thought my friends were thrilled Ethan and I were together. I had no idea they'd been questioning the sanity of my choice. It hurts my feelings. It also makes me want to yell at Jazz and ask why she didn't say something sooner.

"So, you don't think I should marry him?"

"Do you love him?" she asks.

"Of course, I love him. I'm living with him, aren't I?"

Jazz looks deeply into my eyes. I expect her to say, *you're getting very sleepy.* Instead she goes with, "But are you *in* love with him?"

I shrug my shoulders. "I don't know. Maybe I am and we're just wearing into the groove of being together. We've been a couple for two years. Even I know the fireworks don't last that long."

Her mouth hangs open in shock. "Cat, I've been with Dylan for four years and every time he kisses me, my knees go weak."

Clearly, I've been reading the wrong magazines. "Really? After four years?"

She nods her head slowly. "Yeah. When did the fireworks start to fizzle between you and Ethan?"

I think it was around the third month, but I can't possibly say that out loud and maintain even a shred of self-respect. I'd always assumed Sam and I had such a strong chemistry because we were teenagers with raging hormones. I never expected to find that kind of sizzle again. I thought it was biologically impossible.

My head is so full of questions, it feels like it's about to explode. But the one thing I keep coming back to is, how can I break things off with Ethan now that he's mourning the death of his parents' marriage. Wouldn't that be the ultimate cruelty?

The Masterton of the House

Jazz has made me realize I shouldn't wait a full week before making changes. I need to take control of my life in a way I haven't done since moving in with Ethan. I have to see if he can live with me, the way I am. Because I've discovered I can't put myself in the backseat of this relationship any longer. I'm starting to question everything about us.

Amazingly, we don't have a big party tonight, so my partner and I hand off the two small cocktail receptions to our staff. When I get home, I pull my red afghan out of the closet, retrieve my blue vase and Russian dolls from the cabinet, and pull the dishtowel off my glass ornaments. I even switch the dishes and silverware back to what I consider their proper place, but I don't stop there.

In the bathroom, I squeeze a glob of toothpaste on the counter, before running my hands under water and flinging them at the mirror. I don't leave until I mess up the bath towels and drop my razor into the middle of the tub.

My phone rings and I look at the display and see it's Jazz. I answer, "What do you want?"

"You're mad at me, aren't you?" She doesn't let me answer,

she just barrels ahead, "You hardly spoke a word to me all day after I told you what we thought about Ethan. Cat, if you stay with him, I promise I'll never mention it again."

When I don't answer right away, she asks, "What are you doing?"

I growl, "I'm currently trashing my apartment to see what His Highness does when he gets home. What do you think of that?"

"I think it's a great idea. I mean, let's face it, your Buddha-nature isn't to be anally retentive. I bet it feels good to mess the place up a bit."

"It does," I confess. Jazz knows my tendencies well, as we lived together for several years before she met Dylan.

"Make sure to throw some clothes around and short sheet the bed," she suggests.

I take in my handiwork. "The place actually feels like it's mine this way."

"Feed his low-fat cheese to the garbage disposal while you're at it. If he can survive all of that, then maybe there's a chance for you, after all."

I promise to give her a blow-by-blow in the morning. I tell her, "I have to go. I want to sit and contemplate my situation in quiet for a while."

She signs off with, "I love you, Cat. Be strong."

I sit on the couch in the near dark and stare at the boringness of the space around me. Except for the splashes of color I've introduced, everything looks bland like it was decorated by a robot.

Ethan doesn't come home on time for the second night in a row. It's eight seventeen before the front door opens. Once again, he slides the mail into the mail holder, hangs his keys, and positions his shoes in the front closet before he seems to realize where he is. Then, without even seeing me, he goes into hyperdrive and starts cleaning up the apartment. He puts the leftover Chinese food back into the refrigerator, but not before transferring it to a proper Tupperware, with a sealed lid. It's a testament to how rattled he was that he didn't do that last night.

When he starts to unload the dishwasher and notices the plates have been switched in the cupboard, he changes them back to the way he likes them. He doesn't seem angry, just extremely focused. When he spies my decorating touches are back where they belong, he seems to vacillate between picking them up to hide again and leaving them where they are. I can see an old-fashioned scale in his head, each side moving up and down until he finds equilibrium.

When he finally notices me, he comes over and sits down. "How was your day?"

How was my day? I want to scream "freak!" at him and physically shake him. Has Ethan always been this nuts? How could I have missed that?

"It was pretty good," I answer. "We booked three more parties the week of Christmas, and we promoted Jen to vice-president." Then I ask, "How was your day?"

With a vacant look on his face, he responds, "Did you know there are a hundred and sixty-nine volcanos in the United States?"

Um, no, I did not know that. "Really? That seems like a high number."

"None of them are in New York," he assures me.

I nod my head. "Good to know." Then he turns and really looks at me closely and announces, "I hate that afghan."

"I'm starting to realize that. Why do you think that is?"

"The color for one. It's so startling. I mean red? A blanket should be a soothing color, don't you think?"

Clearly, I don't agree as I'm the one who bought it. "What else?"

"Well, the tassels for another. They just hang everywhere. So, disorderly."

"Ethan," I ask, "Are you happy?"

He looks startled. "What do mean by that?"

"I mean what you think I mean. Are you happy? Do you like your job, your home, me? Do you wake up in the morning and think happy thoughts? Are *you* happy?"

"Catriona, that's a ridiculous question. I'm comfortable with my life. I feel a sense of accomplishment in my job. Is that what you're asking?"

I shake my head. "No. I'm asking if you ever feel joy."

He looks at me like I'm the crazy one. "Yes, I enjoy things."

"Gah, Ethan! I didn't ask if you enjoyed things. I asked if you ever feel joy." Then I switch topics. "Do you love me?"

"Of course, I love you. I asked you to marry me, didn't I? What kind of question is that?" He continues, "We fit together nicely, don't you think?"

"I don't think we do. When I came home, everything of mine was hidden away like I don't even live here. How does that say 'fit' to you?"

He looks at the afghan and then at me. "But you've put them back, so everything's okay, right?"

"When's the last time we made love?"

He looks as uncomfortable as he would have if I had just asked him to defecate on the coffee table. "Why does that matter?"

"Because that's part of loving someone."

"Look, Catriona, this is a very difficult time in my life, with my parents breaking up and everything. Why can't we just go back to the way we were and stop trying to dissect every aspect of our lives together?"

"Because, Ethan, I do feel joy. I'd like to feel joy with you. I'd like to go away and not have you hide my things because they make you feel uncomfortable. *I* shouldn't make you feel uncomfortable."

He looks so completely lost, I can't help but feel sorry for him. He finally looks me in the eye and says, "If you're not happy with me or us anymore, I don't think we should be getting married."

"I agree."

He stands up. "Okay, then, I guess you should start looking for somewhere else to live."

I nod my head and my eyes fill with tears. This isn't the way things were supposed to go. Ethan was supposed to fight for me. He was supposed to tell me that he loved me and would do whatever it took to make us work. He wasn't supposed to wash his hands of me the minute I challenged him in any way.

Tears start to run down my face. Our relationship was nothing like I thought it was. Was my only value to Ethan to support his life? Didn't he care about sharing mine? With my heart fracturing in two, I have no idea where I belong.

Mistress of the Couch

I sleep on the couch because Ethan goes into the bedroom and brings out my pillow. Wow. He really has washed his hands of me. Which, as you know, I've been thinking of doing with him. The difference is, I was willing to give us a fighting chance in deference to our history. He seems to have dropped the idea of "us" like a hot potato.

What in the hell just happened? How is it possible to break up with someone and show no emotion? One minute we're engaged and talking, and the next I'm moving out? No tears, no negotiating, nothing.

It takes me ages to finally fall asleep. When I wake up, he's already left for the day. There's not even a note. He just walked out the door like nothing earth-shattering ever happened last night.

I stumble into the bathroom and see Ethan's already filled a box with my toiletries. I look around in shock before catching a glimpse in the mirror. That haunted looking blonde woman in the mirror can't be me. Yet, when I splash my face with water, she does the same.

In the closet I find two more boxes already assembled, waiting for my clothes. From the looks of it, he expects me gone by the time he gets home. Suddenly, I'm very happy to accommodate him.

I call Jazz and announce, "Ethan and I broke up last night."

She sighs deeply before answering, "I know. He called Dylan and told him. How are you doing?"

"I'm not sure. I feel like I've just fallen from a ten-story building and had the wind knocked so far out of me, it might as well be in New Jersey. I don't know what to do or where to go."

"Don't come into work. Just pack up and go to my place." My best friend announces, "Dylan's already put sheets on the couch for you and you know where everything else is. He'll go home at noon to let you in."

"Thanks, Jazz. I promise I won't be there for long."

"As long as you're out by the time our first kid comes along, you're okay. If you need anything, call me and I'll come right home."

I thank her and then spend a couple hours packing. I lovingly wrap my trinkets in tissue paper, the same ones Ethan can't stand. I promise them when I unwrap them, I'll put them in a place of honor, so they can boldly proclaim their existence, with no judgment.

I pack a suitcase with enough jeans and sweaters for the next few days and fill two more boxes with the rest of my clothes. I take my books off the shelves, which take another two boxes. Then I pull more out of the front closet that are already packed from when I moved in. They contain framed photos and other personal touches Ethan claimed we didn't have room to display. I realize now, I should have pushed the issue.

By the time I'm done, all of my adult possessions stand before me in a meager stack. Eight boxes. I suddenly realize just how much of myself I've given up to be with Ethan. Eight boxes shouldn't be enough for my shoes, let alone my whole life.

When I'm done, the apartment looks like the same old boring place I moved into a year ago. There are no traces of me anywhere. I put my engagement ring on the counter next to the mail holder, where it will be easily discovered, and call downstairs to ask the doorman to get me a car. Twenty minutes later I schlepp my belongings to the elevator. I don't pass any other tenants. I do not pass go. I do not collect two hundred dollars. I just walk away from the last two years of my life like they never even happened.

Edgar helps me load my worldly possessions into the Uber. He can obviously see I'm moving out, but he doesn't ask any questions. He just says, "It's been a pleasure knowing you, ma'am."

The doorman's been part of my periphery for a year. I feel like I should thank him for all of the doors he's opened for me, or at the very least offer to take him to coffee, but I don't. I just reply, "Thank you, Edgar. It's been a pleasure knowing you, as well."

Habib, the driver, smiles at me with great big white Chiclet teeth, "Where to?"

"461 Central Park West. It's on the north side of the street."

I watch as the park streaks by. At 106th Street, we bang a U-turn. Jazz and Dylan don't have a doorman, so I buzz up to let Dylan know I'm here. My best friend's husband comes right down to help me with my things.

Moments later, he's standing in front of me in his navy-blue lawyer suit looking like a GQ model. He takes the box out of my hands, puts it on the ground next to him, and pulls me in for a great big hug. He doesn't ask how I'm doing, he just declares, "You're better off without him."

With my face pressed to his chest, I manage to ask, "Do you even like him?"

He shrugs his shoulders. "He's like a distant relative who's been in my family for so long, he's just kind of there. I've seen more of him in the last two years, since you guys have been together, than I saw him in the ten years before that."

I push out of his embrace and smile, "So, I was the draw, not Ethan?"

"Hell, yeah! You're the vivacious, fun little sister who's the life of the party. He's the crazy old uncle you hide in the attic."

How in the world did I ever wind up with the crazy old uncle? I need to think long and hard about the choices I've made in my life. What exactly brought me to a place where I would settle for that? Yet there were so many sweet times, like doing the New York Times crossword puzzle together, feeding the ducks on the boating pond, and strolling through Central Park. Ethan may not be quite normal, but there is an awful lot of good in him.

Once my things are safely re-homed in apartment 4E, I assure Dylan I'll be fine and send him packing back to work. Then I sit down and start to rifle through my memories to see if I can figure out exactly where I went wrong.

Distinguished Guests,
Families, and Friends ...

My college graduation ceremony was the final hurdle for me to get out of Illinois. My parents and grandparents were there, but Travis wasn't. If you can believe it, he was at an all-state track meet, competing in the high jump. Somewhere along the line, he quit jumping and just kept getting high.

As the valedictorian started her speech, "*Distinguished guests, families, and friends ...* "I passed out. Not only was the day hotter than Hades and as humid as a Turkish bath, but I was wearing a lovely polyester graduation gown to seal in the enjoyment.

Yet, the heat wasn't the reason I fainted. Heck, everyone else was in the same boat I was in, and I was the only one to go over like a house of cards in a wind storm. I was sitting there waiting for my name to be called when I flashed back to my high school graduation, the day, that up until that point, had been both the best and worst of my life.

It was mostly the best because it signified a huge accomplishment and the beginning of my adult life. Sam and I were going away to college together after the summer and

179

everything would change for us. I couldn't wait.

Then came that night. After our graduation party, we lay out under the stars on a Masterton plaid picnic blanket. "Time of Your Life" by Green Day came on the radio and we held hands and listened to it. I loved that song. It made me feel all kinds of things: pensive, hopeful, content.

When they sang the chorus, I thought, *Not only have I had the time of my life, but it's only going to get better.* I was with my soulmate and our lives were about to take off. I couldn't imagine a better outcome.

Then Sam turned to me and said, "Kitty Cat, we need to talk."

I turned my face up to stare at him and positively melted into those blue eyes of his. I could look at them forever. I responded, "What would you like to talk about? The perfection of this day or our amazing future?"

His face grew serious and he sat up, disconnecting himself from me. "Cat, remember that scholarship offer I got from Northwestern?"

I smiled obliviously. "Sure, but you turned it down, so we could go to the U of I together."

He shook his head slowly. "No, I didn't."

"Didn't what? Turn it down?" He nodded his head in affirmation. I managed to say, "I don't understand." And I didn't. Our whole lives were plotted out and his going to a different school from me was not in our plan.

Reaching out to take my hands in his, he explained, "I want to go there, Cat. I want to get out of the middle of this state and stretch my wings. There's a big world out there and I want to see what it has to offer."

As my life hit the toilet, I bolted upright and pathetically replied, "But I didn't apply there. There's no chance I can get in this fall."

"I know," he says regretfully.

I was crazy hurt, but offered, "Maybe I can transfer sophomore year. We can still see each other most weekends. I guess if that's where you want to go, we'll just have to find a way to make it work."

Sam reached for both of my hands and squeezed them like he was sending me a message in Morse code. "Cat, I think we should both go to college, unencumbered, and see what the future has in store for us."

And then, like a clap of thunder and a bolt of lightning at the same time, I understood what he was saying. "You're breaking up with me. Now? Before the summer even starts?"

He made a strangled sound deep in his throat. "I'm leaving next week."

"What?!"

"I'm going to physics camp at MIT. I'll be gone most of the summer."

That's when I realized he'd been planning this for a long time. I never knew about camp, and I sure as hell never knew about Northwestern. He'd let me blather on all senior year about our future and never once thought to correct me or inform me of the program change. It was like being stabbed in the heart.

"I love you, Cat. I really, truly do. I just want to go off and experience college fresh. I want to meet new people and have new adventures. I just don't want ..."

I interrupted him. "Me around. You just don't want me around." And while that may not have been the way he wanted to say it, it's exactly what he meant.

"We still have a week before I go."

That's when I positively flipped my biscuit. "For what? You can't possibly think I want to see you again before you leave. In fact, Sam Hawking, I never want to see you again. Forget you know me. Forget where I live. Go have your wonderful new life with all those exciting, new people. Just get the hell out of my sight!"

And he did. He walked out of my life and I made sure I never saw him again. I had a great college experience. I made friends and joined a sorority and did all the things I was supposed to do. I even spent a semester at the University of Edinburgh, but I did all of those things without Sam.

The Spoiled Apple

At some point in my recollections, I get up and raid Jazz's refrigerator. While she has actual foodstuffs in there, I ignore them in favor of a jar of maraschino cherries, a can of spray whipped cream, and a container of blue cheese-stuffed Spanish olives. Stressful times always require my own special salty/sweet therapy. I'm sure Ethan never approved, although he wisely kept his opinions to himself.

I've had a lot of fun in New York. In fact, there have been way more good times than bad. It's just that during a rough period, like breaking up with your fiancé, the positive adventures aren't the ones that jump to the forefront of your mind.

In deference to the good times, I've had experiences here I never would have had otherwise, like planning parties for celebrities and going to movie openings. We have a client who hosts an amazing Halloween blowout every year at whatever night club is *the* place to be seen, and he always invites us as guests, along with his friends Eddie Vedder and Adele.

There have been perks, like the diamond earrings from Tiffany's. Another regular client loaned us his yacht for a week, along with his crew. We took it to Barbados. I would have never been privy to adventures like these had I not lived here.

I continue to sift through the rubble of my thoughts while eating nine olives and six cherries. I'm currently spraying whipped cream directly into my mouth when my phone pings with a new text. I look down and it says, *I know I said I wouldn't call, but you never got back to me to let me know you got to NYC safely. X Sam*

I text him back, *Safe.*

The phone doesn't beep again. Instead, two minutes later, it rings. When I see the 217-area code, I know it must be him. So, I answer, "What?"

"That's it? You know, in civilized countries most people find a greeting a more appropriate way to start a conversation."

"I don't want to talk to you."

"Would you want to talk to me if I had news about Nan?"

He has my full interest. "Fine. Hello, Sam. How are you? Do you have news about my grandmother you'd like to share?"

He chuckles. "Hello to you too, Kitty Cat. I'm doing great. Thank you for the courtesy of asking after my well-being. I thought I'd call and let you know Nan is being released to the nursing home tomorrow morning. We don't anticipate she'll be there for longer than a week."

I'm so relieved I feel like I could float to the ceiling. I reply very sincerely, "Thank you for calling to tell me."

"Anytime, Cat." He continues, "I'm amazed by how well she's doing. She appears to be making a full recovery. I haven't heard her swear once. Although she did tell her surgeon that he had the yummiest butt she'd seen in a coon's age and she asked him out on a date when she was recovered."

I let out a bark of laughter. "She didn't! What did her doctor say?"

"He said if she's well enough to leave the care facility by the fifteenth, he'd invite her to the holiday party he hosts at his house. I think Nan has sufficient motivation to get better, fast."

Leave it to my grandmother. I love that old woman so much it hurts. I want to spend as much time as I can with her before she checks out of this life for good.

Before I hang up with Sam, I assure him, "I'll let you know when I get home for Christmas."

"Will Ethan be joining you?" he tentatively asks.

"He will not." I don't say anything more on the topic. I just hang up.

In that moment, I wonder what I'm doing sitting here on Jazz and Dylan's couch devouring their condiments. I no longer have an apartment or a fiancé. I have no interest in working. I pick up my phone and text Jazz:

I want you to buy me out.

She writes back immediately.

What are you talking about? Did you fall and hit your head? We've been building this business for years!

I quickly respond.

I want to go home.

Her only response is:

We'll talk more tonight.

When I put my phone down, I realize how true that really is. I built a life in New York. It was exciting and adventurous on a business level and often disappointing on a personal one. My job doesn't define me. The people I love define me. And if Nan's aneurysm taught me one thing, it's that those people are getting older, and their lives are getting shorter. I don't want to be a full day's journey away from them. I want to make the most of our time together and enjoy the absolute crap out of them while I have the chance.

I spend the afternoon taking my boxed-up life to the post office and shipping it back to my parents' house. All that I have left is a carry-on bag with my essentials for the next few days. I don't know where I'll live or what I'll do, I just know I took my bite out of the Big Apple and now it's time to spit it out. I'm ready for this chapter to end. If only the new one wasn't filled with such uncertainty.

Gathering Stones

When I tell her I've already shipped my stuff home, Jazz screeches, "You can't make a decision like this on the fly! You certainly can't do it in the middle of an emotional shit-storm."

I pick up my margarita and take a sip. "I feel calmer and surer about this than I have about anything in a very long time."

She draws a frowny face in the condensation on her mineral water bottle. "But what about us?" she begs.

"Jazzy, I'm not breaking up with you, I'm just moving home."

She shakes her head like she's playing a maraca. "No, no, no, no, no. You *are* breaking up with me. You want me to buy you out, so you'll never work with me again."

I shrug. "Yes, I'd like you to buy me out, but that doesn't mean we won't still be besties. I just don't want to live in New York anymore. I promise it has nothing to do with you. Nan's aneurysm really shook me up. It made me realize my parents are going to be next, and I don't know, I need to spend more time with them."

She sighs mightily. "I thought they drove you crazy. I thought you couldn't wait to get away from them."

"I thought so, too. But things are different now. I feel driven to do this, Jazz. I need to do it."

"Fine, go. Stay as long as you want, but I'm not buying your half of the business for six months. I'll keep depositing your share of the profits into your bank account, but I won't make it final until I know you're serious about this and it's not just some knee-jerk reaction to breaking up with Rain Man."

"Rain Man? Oh, my God, you can see how mentally unsound my decisions have been living here. Clearly, I need to get out and figure out where I went wrong."

She still looks concerned. "Are you going back for Sam?"

"No! I just told you, I'm going back to spend time with my parents and Nan. Be forewarned, I'll be practicing the shuck and chuck every night, so when you come to visit, I'm going to take back the crown."

Jazz doesn't believe me. "I think part of you is going back for Sam."

I shake my head, "I don't even know if I've forgiven him for breaking up with me."

"But if he didn't break up with you, you would have never moved to New York and we would have never met," she points out.

I really think about what she says. "I suppose when you put it that way, I *have* to forgive him. Just know that if I do spend time with Sam, I'm going to take it slow. I haven't really known him for fourteen years." *How in the world has so much time passed?*

Then my best friend bursts into tears. It's the full-blown ugly cry. She's sobbing and hiccuping and falling to pieces. "Jazzy, what's wrong?"

She's more strung out than I've ever seen her. "Cat, I'm pregnant. I just finished my first trimester. I didn't tell you before because of the two miscarriages. I figured if I waited until the pregnancy was safe, we wouldn't both have to go through another loss if it didn't take."

My heart hits my feet. Jazz and Dylan are having a baby. It's the best news! I throw my arms around my friend's neck and tease, "Of course, you're going to name her Cat, and I'll be her godmother, and I'll spoil her absolutely stinking rotten, and I'll visit her all the time."

She sniffles in response. "But it won't be the same. I won't see you every day. You won't be here with me through my pregnancy. You won't be around to babysit and change dirty diapers."

"Call me the very second your water breaks and I'm on the next plane. I'll be there, Jazz. You can drop her off at my house every summer and I'll watch her while you and Dylan vacation in Europe. We'll call it Cat Camp!"

"Last night I laid in bed reliving all of our best memories. You're the sister I never had, Cat. You mean the world to me," she sobs.

"Jazzy, I'm distraught to be leaving you, especially now that you're pregnant. But you're a rock star and you're going to do great. I've had one foot on a banana peel for too long in New York. It's time to say goodbye."

That verse from Ecclesiastes comes to mind:

For everything there is a season, and a time for every purpose under heaven: a time to be born and a time to die; a time to plant, and a time to reap; a time to kill, and a time to heal; a time to break down, and a time to build up; a time to weep, and a time to laugh; a time to mourn, and a time to dance; a time to throw away stones, and a time to gather your stones together.

That verse is so universally relatable. It's the whole human journey wrapped up into one gigantic run-on sentence. I feel like I've lived it all in the last week, except for the last part. That's why I'm going home. It's time to gather my stones together.

Releasing

After breakfast, Jazz and I walk to our office like we've done a hundred times before. I feel like I'm floating above myself, like I'm a puppet and some force, other than my own, is propelling me forward.

Our new VP, Jennifer, greets us when we walk in. "Thank God you're here! I've been on the phone with Mrs. Cleave three times already this morning. She wants to fire the caterer and cancel the tulip order. There's no way we'll get other flowers in time for her daughter's wedding!"

Jazz waves her hand dismissively. "Do whatever you have to do. Just deal with it."

Jen looks like she's going to vomit. This is a situation one of us would have normally scooped up and run with in the past. And by "in the past," I mean yesterday.

Our employee reacts like a chicken with its head cut off. There's some jerky circular movement before she finds traction and goes. I kind of feel sorry for her, but I also know trial by fire is the best way to gather valuable experience.

When we get to the oversized office we share, my friend and I quietly sit on the couch side-by-side. Words aren't necessary.

Our communication runs deeper than that. Five minutes pass, then ten, before Jazz says, "Thank you, for everything, Cat."

We sit hand in hand with tears streaming down our faces. "Thank *you*, Jazzy. All my best adult memories have you in them. You're my best friend and no amount of distance can change that."

"We'll talk on the phone every day."

"I'm coming back for the birth of my goddaughter," I promise.

"You'd better!" Then she adds, "If Gelson isn't everything you expect it be, you always have a home with me."

Oh, my God, we're turning into the sappiest movie ever made. I can count on one hand the number of moments that have changed the course of my life and three of them have occurred in the last week. This is one of them.

"Are you going straight to the airport from here?" she asks.

I shake my head, "I have one last spot to visit first."

She knows where I'm going. "Do you want me to come with you?"

"I'm good, thanks. I'd rather say goodbye to you right here, at the little empire we've built."

My friend nods her head and stands up. "Okay then, give me a hug and get out of here. One of us needs to keep this ship afloat."

Jazz is such an Amazon, especially in her heels, she nearly lifts me right off the ground. "I love you. I'll call as soon as I get settled."

"You'll do no such thing!" she exclaims. "You'll call as soon the plane's wheels touch down, then you'll call as soon as you rent your car, and you'll call again, as soon as you drive into that blip of a town you call home."

I promise her. "Okay, you're on. But you have to promise me that *you'll* call every time you throw up, the very minute you feel little Cat move for the first time, and the second you go into labor. I don't want to miss any part of your pregnancy."

I know Jazz wants to yell at me to stay, but she seems to finally understand how important this next part of my journey is to me. She responds, "I'll report every hemorrhoid, cramp, and craving I get. You just go home and take care of yourself."

We continue to hold each other for a few more moments until I can compose myself enough to walk away.

My last stop in New York is the same as my first, eleven years ago. I take the subway downtown to Battery Park and walk to the ferry. When I first moved to Manhattan, I took the guided four-hour tour of the Statue of Liberty on Ellis Island. It's the place where all my ancestors first stepped foot in their new country.

Nan and her family arrived on February 4, 1942. Pearl Harbor had been bombed fewer than two months earlier and World War II was in full swing. Italians, Germans and Japanese were no longer allowed to immigrate to the US. But no such restrictions were placed on the Scottish.

My grandmother was only three years old when she came to America. I get a thrill thinking of her as a little girl staring up at Lady Liberty. I haven't been there in years, but it somehow feels like the appropriate place to go to say goodbye to this part of my life.

I don't have time for the full tour. In fact, I only have time to take the ferry out and back. I won't even get off. As the boat pulls away from the dock, I stare ahead. The air is freezing cold, but it's also invigorating. It's the perfect day to end this chapter in my life.

I feel the same way I felt when I first saw the Statue of Liberty from this vantage point, totally in love. Eleven years ago, I was so young and eager and ready to grow up I could hardly stand it. I just knew New York would change my life, that wonderful adventure awaited me here. All of that was true. This town scared, nurtured, and pushed me into adulthood.

In New York I discovered I was a strong woman. I learned I was more capable than I thought possible. Unstoppable. In the fifteen minutes it takes to get to Ellis Island, I remember it all.

My first apartment was no bigger than a walk-in closet, and not a large one, either. The building was full of the sketchiest human element you could imagine, but still, I met interesting people there. Sure, I had to do my laundry while carrying a baseball bat for protection, but that kind of excitement builds backbone. It creates confidence.

My first job was waitressing at a restaurant on the East Side. It afforded me enough money to live, barely. It also led to my becoming a party planner. So much of my life has been lived on this seven-mile island. I'll always be grateful for my time here, but as the ferry pulls into the slip to let passengers out to explore, I fully grasp that it is over.

I came, I saw, I occasionally got kicked in the teeth and dragged over rough pavement. But isn't that what growing up is like for everyone? No one escapes the ravages of personal evolution. Even if I'd never come here, it would have happened somewhere else in some other way.

New York City just made the journey more amplified. The highs may have been higher and the lows possibly lower, but at the end of the day, I grew up like everyone else does, one day at a time.

On the way back into Manhattan, I bask in the skyline of the city I will always love. In this moment I feel totally content with my decision to leave. This big, beautiful, exciting town has given me her best, and I thank her for it, but it's time to go.

I feel the finality of my decision in the back of a Lyft heading over the bridge, away from New York. This is the first time, in over a decade, I've made this journey without a round trip ticket. A small pit begins to develop in my stomach as I wonder what's in store for me. But regardless of what's ahead, I do not turn back.

Home

Once I board the plane and find my seat, I start to second guess what I'm doing. I remind myself what I told Jazz. If I can move out of New York so effortlessly, I can certainly come back with the same ease.

After I land in Chicago, I rent a car for a full month. That should be enough time to know if this plan of mine is temporary insanity or something more substantial, like total insanity. To save pennies, I get an economy car. It's banana yellow, a color so intense, I almost upgrade to mid-size to avoid the embarrassment of driving it.

It's four o'clock by the time I'm on the road. I should be home by suppertime as long as traffic moves along. Which, of course, it doesn't because I forgot to factor in rush-hour around the city. As I nudge closer and closer to the country, I begin to relax and enjoy the journey, and consider various possibilities for my future.

Maybe I'll stay home for a month and then move to Chicago to start a party planning business there. I'll be close enough to see my family every weekend if I want. Although, I'll have to make time to date if I don't want to end up alone.

I think about Sam and consider whether or not there might really be a future for us. How weird would that be? His breaking up with me has been such a motivating force in my life. Every success I've had was me proving to the world what a loser he was for walking away from me. Would getting back together with him somehow be going backwards?

By the time I turn off onto Highway 47, I'm only thirty minutes from home. Snow covered farmland is all I see. Grain silos, barns, and small towns are the skyline here. It's dark outside, making it almost seem like I'm in the midst of a particularly vivid dream.

I cross the railroad track into town, passing a sign that says, "Welcome to Gelson, Population 3241." My hometown has gotten smaller since I was a kid, which is probably why they made sure to tack on those forty-one people. No sense rounding to the nearest hundred when the numbers aren't in favor of making you look more impressive.

When I finally pull into my parents' driveway, my tires crunch on the packed snow. The exterior lights aren't on. I'm assuming it's because everyone is tucked safely inside, not expecting visitors. I turn my headlights off, so I don't alert them to my presence. I don't know why, but I still want to keep my arrival a secret.

I park in front of the garage and close my door quietly. Resting by the side of the house are two pairs of ski poles, just like I'd expected to see when I brought Ethan and his family home. My dad also has a selection by the front door for everyone to use to gain traction and retain balance when walking to and from their vehicles. This is, of course, in deference to the fact that he doesn't believe in shoveling.

When I get to the front porch, I peek in the window like a peeping Tom. My parents are on the couch in front of a roaring fire. They're sharing a plaid for extra warmth and they're talking. My mom is lying down while my dad sits up and rubs her feet.

Dad lets out a big boom of laughter at something she just said to him. I'm positively mesmerized. My parents still look totally in love with each other after nearly forty years together. I know this is who they really are because they have no idea they're being observed.

A thought hits me in that moment. It's something I've know my whole life but am only now consciously realizing. My family doesn't pretend or put on airs for anyone. They are who they are, no pretensions, no false fronts. What a refreshing way to live life.

I eventually knock on the door, not because I tire of watching the peaceful tableau through the window, but because I'm ready to be part of it. After more than a decade, I'm finally home.

Reunion

My dad opens the door and lets out a whoop loud enough to be heard in the next county. My mom calls from the other room, "Dougal, we'd better be under attack. You scared me so much I need to change my underwear!"

My dad hauls me into his arms and shouts back, "This surprise is worth a new pair of drawers, trust me." I take that as the ultimate compliment.

When my mom sees me, she pushes my dad out of the way and nearly wrestles me to the ground. "Cat, you're home! Why didn't you tell us you were coming?"

"I wanted to surprise you. Did it work?"

My mom pulls me back into the living room with them and pushes me down on the couch. She orders, "Dougal, honey, put more wood on the fire." Then to me she instructs, "You can rub my feet while you tell us how long you're home for."

Rubbing feet is a favorite pastime in my family. When I was growing up, we'd all sit in a circle rubbing each other's while recapping our day for one another. My mom used to say, "If world leaders did this, there'd never be war."

I'm not so sure I buy that, but the thought has made me smile on more than one occasion over the years. I answer, "I'm home for as long as you want me here. But I promise to leave before I turn into Travis."

My parents exchange a meaningful look. "What about Ethan?" Mom asks.

I shrug. "What about him?"

"Are you still together, honey?" my dad inquires.

I spill the whole story, how Ethan hid my things while I was away, how regimented he is, how he considered our life fine the way it is. How I worried he'd never let my family in and treat them like his own.

I cry while I share all the thoughts and worries bubbling through me. Then I confess, "My worldly possessions should be arriving next week."

I've rendered them speechless. I feel like I should jump up and write this date down in my diary or something. *Today my parents were at a loss for words. Hell is quite possibly freezing over. At the minimum, somewhere on the planet a pig has sprouted wings and started to fly.*

My mom finally picks up the ball and runs with it. "I'm only sorry if you're sad, Kitty Cat. But the truth is, I'm so delighted for us I don't quite know what to say, except, my baby is home. If this isn't a Christmas miracle, I don't know what is."

"What about Sam? Does he know you're back?" my dad asks.

I shake my head. "I haven't been keeping in touch with him. I don't know what's going to happen between us, if anything. But I'll tell you this. I'm here for me, not him. This is about my journey. Sam Hawking lost his place in my life fourteen years ago, and it's not going to be easy for him to earn my trust back."

I further quantify, "He didn't play any role in my decision."

I'm not sure they believe me. In fact, my mom keeps eyeing her cell phone like she can't wait to pick it up and call Liza. So, I say, "I'd like to keep my arrival quiet, if you don't mind. Let everyone find out when they find out."

Mags looks like a baby who's just dropped her binky. "What about Nan? You can't surprise her or she's liable to drop dead from the shock."

"I'll tell Nan, but that's it." With a pointed look, I demand, "Promise me, both of you."

I eventually get a couple of noncommittal grunts, but I don't think either one of them is going to risk crossing me, especially after the Thanksgiving fiasco. After an hour, my mom gets up and heats up some leftover tuna noodle casserole and my dad pours me a wee dram to welcome me home.

In this moment, I feel so loved and cared for, so wanted, it's almost like the last decade never happened. It's almost like I never left, except I now have so much more appreciation for what's here than I ever did before.

A New Beginning

As soon as I wake up and have a cup of coffee, I call Nan. Her first words are, "Can you be here by ten? The Catholic ladies are having a bingo game. With two of us in on it, I'm pretty sure we can take them for everything they're worth."

"Nan, why would you assume I'm home?" Although I know the answer to that. Get ready for it, my family is about to get even more interesting.

"Catriona Fiona Masterton, I've only been telling you your whole life, but if you're going to pretend you don't remember, I'll tell you again. I have the sight and you know it."

What she means is that somehow her brain is one of the few that hasn't glommed onto reality and she claims she can see things that are happening in other places, as they're happening. She even brags that she can occasionally see into the future. Except for the time she saw Dorcas Abernathy fall into the Grand Canyon while on vacation. We've chalked that one up to more wishful thinking than anything psychic.

I laugh. "Okay, you mystical wonder, I'll be there by ten. Do you want me to stop and get anything for you?" She gives me a list and I write it down. There is no wrath quite like Nan's when she asks you for something and you forget.

My parents let me go to the care facility by myself. I stop by the drug store on my way and pick up a pack of my grandmother's favorite gum, a bottle of ginger ale (non-diet, made with real ginger), a box of tissue with the lotion built in, and a *People Magazine* (but only if that yummy boy from *Outlander* is in it—which happily, he is). Oh, and one historical romance that's set in the Highlands of Scotland, *and the boy on the cover better have good knees,* or she won't read it.

When I get to the nursing home, I collect my purchases and my purse and get out of the banana mobile. I check in with the front desk on my way in and am told Nan is in the recreation room.

When I get there, I stand in the doorway to locate her. I finally spot her, but she's not the first person I see. Sam is. He's sitting next to Nan, whispering something in her ear and she's cackling like he's just told her the best joke ever.

Sam has been regaling my grandmother with jokes for as long as I can remember. The first one was when we were fifteen. I think that was the day my grandmother fell in love with him as much I had. It went like this:

Jock was out working the field when a barnstormer landed.

"I'll give you an airplane ride for £5," said the pilot.

"Sorry, cannae afford it," replied Jock.

"Tell you what," said the pilot, "I'll give you and your wife a free ride if you promise not to yell. Otherwise it'll be £10."

So up they went, and the pilot rolled, looped, stalled, and did all he could to scare Jock. Nothing worked, and the defeated pilot finally landed the plane. Turning around to the rear seat he said, "Gotta hand it to you. For country folk, you sure are brave!"

"Aye," said Jock, "But ye nearly had me there when the wife fell oot!"

I can only imagine the anecdotes have gotten more interesting over the years. I cross the room to their table. Sam jumps up like someone's thrown a cup of ice water on him. "Cat, what are you doing here?"

I ignore him and look at Nan. "You didn't tell him I was coming?"

"Nah," she replies. "I wanted to see his reaction, firsthand."

"Thanks a lot, Nan. I thought you liked me," Sam accuses.

She cackles, "I do, lad, I do. In fact, I love you and you know it. But old ladies don't get a lot of fun in their lives and I wanted to give myself a little gift."

"So, no Catholic ladies? No bingo game?" I ask.

Nan shakes her head, "Even the Catholic ladies are boring in here. I can't wait 'til you spring me and take me home."

I sit down while Sam stares at me like I'm an apparition. I finally ask, "When *do* I get to take Nan home?"

He pulls himself together and manages, "In the next few days, I should think. She won't be completely herself for quite a while, but we'll have a nurse come out to the house to check on her regularly. She might even recover more quickly in her own environment."

Nan smiles up at Sam. "Come back at five and bring a pizza with extra pepperoni and root beer. Make sure you get one big enough for the three of us." Then she winks at me.

"N-n-nan, I don't think that's a good idea," I stutter.

So, she looks at Sam and amends, "Bring her salad, she doesn't want pizza."

That's not what I was saying, and she knows it. She's purposefully steamrolling me. I realize I'd better get used to it. This old lady is sure to be one of the more frustrating parts of being home. So, I look over at Sam and add, "Ranch dressing on the side, if you don't mind."

Fistbla

My grandmother takes the top off the lid to a Scrabble that's sitting on the table in front of her. "Let's play!"

"Your rules or the real ones?" I ask.

"Real rules, bah. I only play those if I want to be bored to death."

Nan's Scrabble rules are as follows: You can't use any real words. You have to be able to pronounce them *and* have a definition for them, if challenged. If you wait longer than five seconds to define your word or if you laugh while doing so, you forfeit your next turn.

After we pick out our tiles, she goes first. Her first word is "fistbla." As it's a seven-letter word on a double word score, I challenge her. Within two seconds she responds, "Fistbla, a soft punch that does no damage."

"Good one, Nan." So, I play off her "b" with another seven-letter word. "Bloxzapa, the art of blocking a fistbla."

"So, you've come home for good, have you?" Nan asks.

"You've talked to Mom!" I accuse.

"I have not." She makes another play. "Psyquin, the ability to see things for what they really are, often confused with psychic phenomenon."

"Polstot," I retaliate. "A place to land in between destinations."

We continue to converse like this for some time. Nan takes her turn, "Stayput, the place you're destined to be."

I lay down, "Nanfers, grandmotherly interference."

We continue to play right through lunch creating such words as sexping, wingdog, fagino, and pustong. I have more fun than I've had in years.

After a lunch of the worst food imaginable—I think it was supposed to be pot roast—I take Nan back to her room. I crowd into her twin bed with her and we snuggle up and take a nap. When we wake up an hour later, she asks, "Will you help me shower?"

Once she's dressed in a clean nightgown and robe, she wants me to put some makeup on her. She's says, "After all, I've got a dinner date to impress."

"Why do you have to impress Sam?"

"A girl always likes to look her best," she informs me.

We take two of the flower arrangements by her bedside and weave them into a crown to disguise her bandage. I declare, "You'll be the most beautiful girl at the ball."

Nan seems so happy and content spending this time together. I'm not hurrying to fit as much as I can into my four days at home, we're just taking each moment as we find it. As I help her back into bed, she says, "Cat, I have a confession to make."

When my eyebrows arch in question, she continues, "But if you tell anyone, I'll deny it to the death, and I'll never play Scrabble with you again."

I nod my head in understanding of the harsh punishment ahead if I betray her trust. She continues, "I've had strokes, but they aren't responsible for my lapses in manners."

I tilt my head to the side and nod once. "Interesting. Are you by chance saying you have control over your mouth and simply choose not to use it?"

She looks shame-faced. "That's what I'm saying."

"And when you called Ethan a filthy Sassenach?"

"I meant every word of it, and I wanted him to know."

The origin of her "illness" is hanging in the air like a heavy storm cloud. I finally can't take it anymore and inquire, "And that Easter Sunday when you called Mrs. Abernathy a, ahem, twat?"

She takes a moment and puts her head in her hands before looking up. "I could have called her worse, you know."

"Really? I think the word you used was quite sufficient being that it was said in church for everyone in attendance to hear, don't you?"

"Maybe." Then she divulges, "Cat, getting old stinks. I went from being a young vibrant woman to a dried-up old shell. People once cared what I had to say and then one day, bam! It's like I was no longer visible. I decided it was time to make sure they saw me again, you know?"

I sit down next to her and take her hand. "Aw, Nan. I think I get it. It's kind of like what happened with me and Ethan. Before him, people looked at me one way, and after him, I just became an extension of his boringness."

Nan is not only honoring me with her trust, she's warning me to make the most of my time right now, while people can still see me. I plan on doing just that.

Pizza Party

I don't dress up for Sam like Nan does. I don't even brush my hair or put on lipstick. If he's going to try to noodle his way back into my life, it's going to be with no encouragement from me.

Nan and I are sitting in the dining hall holding a table, when she whispers, "I don't want that nosy Elvira Stimpson horning in on my special night. Don't let any of those old biddies sit down with us." My grandmother looks like the May Queen with her wreath of flowers around her head. The makeup brightens her face, making her look ten years younger.

"What's so important about tonight?" I look around the nursing home dining hall, and trust me, nothing looks overly special.

Before she can answer, Sam strolls into the room, carrying a load of take-out bags and a pizza box from our favorite local parlor. He leans down to kiss Nan's cheek before turning to me. With a gleam in his eye, he asks, "Anything you want kissed?"

I tamp down the temptation to give him a sarcastic response. "I think I'll pass, but thanks for the offer."

He lays paper plates and plastic silverware out for us before opening the pizza box. He bows to my grandmother. "Just as the lady likes it, half meatballs and anchovies for you, and half extra pepperoni for me."

Nan giggles like a school girl. "If you put any anchovies on this pie, boy, they're all yours. I'm never going to put one of those disgusting things into my mouth."

He looks at me and sighs. "Says the lady who eats sheep guts and calls it a Scottish delicacy."

Nan smacks his hand. "It's a personal preference. You don't know what you're missing."

Sam jokes, "May I never know what I'm missing. But you're in luck, they accidentally made the whole pizza extra pepperoni." He reaches inside one of the bags and pulls out an extra-large salad. Then he sets out a variety of dressings.

"You do realize I'm always eating when I'm with you," I observe.

"Ah, but only because you claim you *have* to eat and you won't spend any time with me when you aren't doing so."

He has a point. I might have to start accepting his invitations to go for a walk or bowling, something that doesn't involve me shoving food into my mouth. Either that or I'm going to need a new wardrobe.

"Sam graduated medical school with honors," Nan announces over dinner.

I nod my head in response. "How nice."

"Your whole family was good enough to attend my graduation," he shares.

My eyes pop open wide in surprise. "Why in the world would they do that?"

Nan smacks my hand. "Because we love him. I even took the

train to Chicago twice a year and stayed at a hotel, just so Sam and I could eat pizza together."

"We dined at every pizza parlor in the loop before declaring Giordano's spinach pie the best," Sam adds.

"We had to give it up though because it gave me gas," Nan explains.

Sam unsuccessfully tries to stifle a laugh. "We also went to the Annual Scottish Festival and Highland Games, hosted by the Chicago Scots, every year. Nan and I danced the reel, and your dad and I lost at the caber toss." He smiles at Nan, fondly. "We've had a lot of good times, haven't we?"

I turn to my grandmother, somewhat hurt by what I perceive as a betrayal. "Why did you carry on so much at Thanksgiving dinner about how happy you were to see Sam? You made it sound like you hadn't seen him in years."

"Well, it had to have been nearly three weeks," Nan exclaims. "That's a long time considering he and I normally get together at least twice a month."

"Whose grandmother are you?" I demand.

She taps my arm. "Don't be jealous, Cat. You were away living in that great big shiny apple of yours and Sam was right here wanting to spend time with me. You can't expect me to have passed that up."

"But he, he ..." I want to say broke my heart, tossed me aside, and treated me like dirt. But I don't have to because we're all thinking it. So instead, I turn to my first boyfriend and offer, "Thank you. Thank you for being there for Nan when I wasn't."

Sam reaches his hand under the table and takes my hand. He squeezes it, but he doesn't let it go.

Early to Bed

As soon as she's eaten her slice of pizza and salad, Nan fake yawns so loudly, people turn around to stare. To give you an idea just how noisy it is, half of the folks in the room are nearly deaf. "Lordy, I'm tired. I hope you children will excuse me while I take myself off to bed."

As far as performances go, it's not a good one. Nan is obviously trying to turn this little get-together into a date. Sam stands up and pulls out my grandmother's chair and asks, "Would you like me to escort you to your room?"

She smacks his hand playfully. "Fresh. Don't be silly. I can make my way there just fine on my own."

I stand up and give Nan a proper hug and kiss goodbye and promise to be back tomorrow. For kicks, I add, "But only if you think you'll be up to it and aren't too tired from all your exertions tonight."

She doesn't even pretend to be chastised. She just gives me a big wink and does a little shimmy like she can't contain her excitement.

Once she's gone, Sam begins to clean up the remnants of our dinner. "What do you say we take a walk and burn off some of these carbs?"

I smile sweetly. "I didn't have any carbs. I ate salad."

"In that case …" he suggests with a wink of his own, "let's walk down the street and get some ice-cream."

"How can I resist such a tempting offer?" I reason that at least we'll be exercising before indulging.

When we step out into the cold December night, Sam reaches for my hand again, and I let him take it. We walk for half a block in silence when I realize how natural this feels, almost like we've never been apart.

Ethan did not like to hold hands in public. He felt it compromised his ability to defend us if we were set upon by thugs. At the time, I thought it sweet. In retrospect, I wonder at his ability to defend us with both hands at his disposal. I mean, what if the mugger was wearing red?

I haven't had a chance to mourn my relationship with Ethan. Everything happened so quickly, and I haven't stood still long enough to feel the impact of it. I know he and I weren't right for each other, but we did share two years. We had hopes and dreams, however misguided. We shared a home, such as it was. There are feelings there that I need to sort through before letting myself get too carried away by the man buying me ice cream.

Sam holds the door for me as we walk into *I Scream*, our old high-school hangout. I order a cup of rum raisin and he gets an entire banana split. When we sit down at one of the cast-iron tables with the pink and white striped chairs, I comment, "This place hasn't changed since we were in high school."

He shakes his head. "You're wrong. They carry coffee flavored ice-cream now, which they never did when we were kids."

"Why do you know that? Did you want coffee flavored ice-cream when we were in high school?"

"Nope. I'm just observant like that. You want to know something else I've noticed?"

I'm not sure I do, but I nod my head anyway. "I've noticed that a particular girl I used to love very much, is no longer wearing an engagement ring."

Oh, man, chills the size of small icebergs pop up on my arms. He reaches out and strokes my bare ring finger in an almost indecent way. Yet, I don't stop him. I merely reply, "That's very observant of you."

"Would you like to tell me about it?"

"I don't think so. I think for now it's enough you know there's no ring there. We'll see if, and when, you earn more of my trust."

He stares at me so hard it's like he's trying to look inside my brain. If he only knew he was already there. "Fair enough, Miss Kitty. But just so you know, I'm not the same stupid boy I once was. I'm a grown man and I'm no longer questioning what I want. I know what I want."

I'm pretty sure I need to get outside, quickly. I'm heating up at a rapid degree and short of a cold shower, I need a cold something to keep me in check. In order to break the tension, I say, "Tell me about the woman you didn't marry."

He startles. "Talk about a buzzkill. Why do you want to hear about that?"

"Because I want to get to know you better. I want to know how you've changed."

He shakes his head. "Nope. You want to pry into my past life

214

which doesn't even matter anymore. That's all water under the bridge. How about this?" he asks. "How about I don't ask any questions about what happened with Ethan and you don't ask any questions about my past? We'll just get to know each other fresh, starting today. How does that sound?"

"I can live with that." I reach my hand out to shake his. "Name's Cat. Pleased to meet you."

He takes my hand and doesn't let it go. He just asks, "Did you know I once dated the most beautiful girl in the world named Cat?"

"I thought we weren't going to talk about past relationships?" I tease.

"I'll try not to, but I've never been able to get that girl out of my head. So, it's going to be hard."

Oh, my God, what am I going to do with this man? Several ideas pop into my mind, but you know what they say, "Once bitten, twice shy." He's still got a way to go to prove himself to me.

M.I.A.

My brother, Travis, is apparently missing in action. He disappeared two days before I came home, leaving a note behind telling my parents not to worry, that he had a line on a job. So, while they're strangely not worried, I still have a hard time foregoing concern.

My mom and I are doing dishes, when I suggest, "Travis is like a housecat out in the wild. There's no telling what's happened to him."

When I share this observation, she scoffs, "Don't be silly. Your brother's fine. He's just decided it's time to start his life."

"But he has no life skills. He's never even lived on his own before. What if he's dead in a ditch?"

"Catriona, don't talk like that! Travis just needed some time to find himself."

"Mom, I'm as hopeful as you are that's what he's doing. I'm just suggesting we hang some posters on telephone poles in case he's wandering around dazed and confused."

Mags starts laughing. "I never took you for a drama queen, Cat, but that's pretty funny."

I stack the juice glasses the way my mom likes them. "What

ever happened to Travis? He used to be so involved and present when he was in high school. Did college ruin him, somehow?"

"I don't know if it was one particular thing. I just know life has a way of knocking some of us off track. As long as we find our way back, that's all that matters, right?"

"So, I can live in the basement for the next eight years and get high and you won't try to stop me," I deduce.

"Oh, I'd stop you all right. I know your strengths. Unfortunately, your brother hasn't had the same path." Then she says, "But you *are* entitled to a break. I'll give you three months before I start pushing you."

I can't imagine not having any direction for three whole months. I'd go insane.

As it is, I woke up this morning, only my second one here, wondering what to do with myself. So, I suggest, "Why don't we have a Christmas party?"

My mom's eyes light up. "Really? I'd love that!" Then she runs to get a pad of paper and asks, "Who should we invite?" She has fifty names on her list before I even say a word.

I love that she's so enthusiastic. I propose, "Since the number is so high, I think we should either do an open house, to stagger arrival times, or have a cocktail party and serve drinks, hors d'oeuvres, and finger desserts."

My mom claps her hands together. "I want a cocktail party! I haven't been to one of those in years and it's been even longer since I've had one. But Cat, I warn you, I'm not very organized when it comes to this kind of thing."

I smile assuredly. "Yes, but I am. It's what I do."

Mags is so excited she's positively vibrating. "I can bring out my box full of Christmas recipes and we can decide what to make! Let me just go get it."

She makes three trips back and forth to the attic. When she finally settles down, there are three Bankers Boxes in front of her, full of recipes torn out of magazines. I stare with my mouth wide open, "What are all these?"

"Recipes!" she declares clapping her hands together. "I've been cutting them out for years. Every time I see one that I like, I just snip it out and add it to the appropriate box. I have them for every major holiday and season, as well."

I don't know what to say, so I ask, "How many of them do you have?"

"Fifteen," she answers proudly.

"Fifteen? Where did you get enough recipes to fill fifteen boxes?"

"Oh, you know, I buy them or tear them out from magazines at the doctor's office. Sometimes I go to the library and snag a few. Just random places."

"How did I not know this about you?"

My mom raises her eyebrows. "You don't know everything about me, Cat. I do have some secrets, you know."

God forbid. I always thought my mom was an open book. If she's got other secrets, and they're anything like her mysterious recipe fetish, we're in trouble. I decide at this moment I can't handle any more, so I change the subject. "How about you go through your recipes and pick one drink, two passed hors d'oeuvres, and one dessert. I'll decide on the rest from ones Jazz and I have used at some of our holiday functions."

My mom immediately takes the lids off all three boxes and

dumps their entire contents onto the kitchen table. She looks like she wants to roll in them or toss them up in the air like they're hundred-dollar bills. I simply walk out the door so I don't have to witness it.

Party Planning in Alaska

I smile when I hear the rocks at my window. I look at the clock and see it's only ten thirty. I happily put on my robe and run downstairs. When I open the front door, Sam is standing there holding a poinsettia. "I was going to get you cut flowers, but I remember you telling me what a waste it was to kill a flower, when all you had to do was buy the whole plant and it could live forever."

"You remember that, huh?" I remember, too. I used to think I'd take all the flowers Sam bought me and plant them in the yard, and then every time I went outside I'd be surrounded by his love for me. Once upon a time, I lived on the fantasies of my future.

I take the plant and let Sam in. "Thank you, it's gorgeous. Mom will be thrilled, too. She's decided to have a Christmas party this year and she loves poinsettias."

Sam takes his coat off and hangs it in the closet by the front door. "Want to go sit in the living room with me?"

I follow him in. "To what do I owe the honor of this visit?"

"I missed seeing you today when you went to see Nan, and I didn't want the whole day to go by without saying hello."

"You just saw me last night."

He gives me puppy eyes. "That was twenty-four hours ago."

I smile. "Hello, then." I push him onto the couch and sit next to him. He puts his arm around me and I lay my head on his shoulder. I finally say, "Remember my cat, Maeve?"

"Brown tabby with gorgeous green eyes and white spot on the tip of her nose?"

"That's her. I always wanted to get another cat, but I never got around to it."

He asks, "Why don't you get one now?"

"Maybe once I figure out where I'm going to land."

"What do mean by that?"

I think hard about how much I'm going to say next. I finally confess, "I moved out of my apartment with Ethan, and I don't know where I'm going."

"But you're here, now."

"Yes," I answer. "In fact, I've shipped my stuff here. I'm going to take a little time to see what direction life pulls me in."

"So, you don't live in New York City anymore?"

I shake my head.

"I better cancel my interview with Lenox Hill, then."

"Excuse me? You're interviewing for a job at a hospital in New York. Why?"

He nudges my arm playfully. "I have a friend who used to live there. I wanted to spend some time with her."

"You were moving there for me?" I'm so shocked I can't process it.

"How do you know I was talking about you?" he teases. Then he seriously adds, "Cat, we're almost thirty-two years old. I, for one, know I've never been happier than when I was with you. I want to explore us."

"What about Ethan?" I demand. "You were going to move to Manhattan while I was engaged to another man? "Why didn't you come sooner before you knew about him?"

"I guess it just took me a while to build up my courage. I knew I never ran into you in Gelson because you made sure of it. I was afraid you'd reject me outright." He adds, "But if I've learned anything from hanging out with Nan, it's that when a Highlander wants something, they'll go to any length to stake their claim."

"You were going to stake your claim? What does that even mean?"

He pulls me onto his lap, and for some crazy reason, I let him. He answers, "First off, I was going to follow you and find out where you had coffee in the morning and then I was going to start bumping into you."

"That sounds an awful lot like stalking."

He shakes his head. "Nope, not stalking. Staking."

"What were you going to do with Ethan, hire a hit?"

"No, again." He smiles playfully. "I was going to stand next to him and look as virile as I possibly could, so you would see I was the better choice."

"That's pretty cocky of you. What if it didn't work?"

"I was going to wear a kilt, so you could see my manly knees. Nan assures me that's the best way to a Scottish lass's heart."

"I see. And now you're going to cancel your interview because I don't live there anymore."

He nods. "Exactly."

"What if I move to Alaska?"

He laughs, "You want to be a party planner in Alaska?"

"Maybe."

"Well, then I'd just have to find out if any hospitals in Alaska are hiring."

"I have a red afghan. Is that a deal breaker?"

Sam looks at me like I'm off my nut. "Nooooooooo. Why would it be?"

"Just checking." Then I stand up. "In that case, why don't you take me out tomorrow night? Maybe we can do a little Christmas shopping for our families together."

"You've got yourself a date, Kitty Cat."

When we walk to the front door, he takes my hand and brings it to his lips before giving it the most delicious kiss. Then he says, "I'll be at the nursing home at ten in the morning in case you can't wait until tomorrow night to see me."

He walks into the darkness like he was never here, and it was all just a sweet dream. I'm going to have to watch my heart with this one. I know what it's like to lose it to him, and I do not want to have to recover from that again.

Painful Afghans

Sarah is back from Florida where she was taking a pre-holiday break from EatMeOrganic. Her parents have a timeshare. She's not staying with them for Christmas, though. Oddly, her B&B is full during the holidays. Her first guest arrives the night of our party, so I tell her to bring him along. The more the merrier, right?

As soon as I fire off my last text to her, my phone rings. It's Ethan. My stomach does a somersault and perhaps a double full layout or two (Gymnastics is my favorite Olympic event, if you couldn't guess.) Why in the world is he calling? I guess there's only one way to know the answer to that question.

"Hello?" I cautiously answer.

"Catriona, how are you?" His voice is tentative.

"I'm fine, Ethan. Why are you calling?" I discard the customary, *how are you*, normally asked in return. I'm still smarting at the way he so easily dismissed our life together.

"I miss you."

I sincerely wonder, "Why? I mean the second you're alone in our apartment, you apparently hide everything that reminds you of me. That doesn't seem like the actions of a man who would miss me."

His slow reply takes me off guard by how sincere it sounds. "Because I love you."

I sigh tremendously in return. "You could have fooled me. The minute I challenged you, you threw a pillow at me and told me to find somewhere else to live. Call me crazy, but those don't sound like the actions of a man in love."

"I'd just come from my parents' home where I'd spent three days listening to my mother tell me she was doubting her life with my dad," he explains. "Which meant she was doubting her life with me. I've never felt so vulnerable. I guess I just panicked and thought if you were having doubts before the wedding, it was better for you to leave sooner rather than later."

"You didn't even fight for me, Ethan. We'd been together for two years, living together for one. If you love someone for that much time, you don't just let them walk away." I clarify, "You don't push them out of your life."

"That's why I'm calling now," he says, his voice full on anguish. "I'm fighting for you, now."

"I've already shipped all of my things to my parents' house," I inform him.

"You've left New York? Why would you do that? Your whole life is here!"

I explain it to him the best I can. "When Nan got sick, I started to realize her time is winding down. She could have died. That hit me really hard."

"Then visit her more often. But to leave the city you love and the business you've worked so hard to build? It seems extreme."

It does seem extreme, and when he says it, the gravity of what I've done really hits home. My stomach rolls over like I'm on

Space Mountain at Disneyland. So, I change the subject. "I wanted you to love my family as much as I do, Ethan. At the very least, I wanted you to like them."

"You wanted me to like them? How was I to know that? You never talked about them like *you* liked them. You always spoke of them as though they were an annoyance and an embarrassment. You were always so relieved to come home after visiting them." He seems genuinely confused.

Wow. I'm stunned silent, which is a rare event. What he says makes a lot of sense. How could I expect him to try to win my parents over when I was sending signals that indicated I didn't want that. I reply, "I don't know, Ethan. I really don't. But my leaving was only partially because of them. There were other reasons."

"Like what?" he wants to know.

"Like your hiding all my things when I was gone. How about that?"

He starts to talk three times before he gains traction. "Catriona, I have some problems of my own. Things I struggle with."

This is the first time I've ever heard him talk so openly. "What things?" I want to hear him say them out loud.

"I battle with my need for order. I have an intolerance for bright colors, and I fight to keep the noise of the world from overtaking my head. All of these things are physically painful for me. I'm at war with them on a daily basis."

His self-awareness is startling. When we were together, I was never consciously aware of those things, so I never actually put them into words, but what he says explains a lot. I thought those

226

were all just quirks of his, that he was completely fine with who he was. I didn't realize they were things he battled within himself. "Why didn't you ever talk to me about it?"

"I was always such an outsider as a kid. No one ever understood me. I figured if I was able to keep these things hidden, I could pass for normal. If I could do that, then it wouldn't hurt so much knowing I wasn't like everyone else."

My heart breaks for him. "I'm so sorry. That's awful to have to hide who you really are to protect yourself. Is there anything that can be done to help you? To help you tolerate the things that bother you?"

"I don't know. I'm going to see a psychiatrist tomorrow to find out." He confesses, "I also struggle with touch sometimes. It's why I don't like to hold hands and sometimes making love is difficult because of this, as well."

My world crashes in on me. "Ethan, I can't believe you never told me this."

"How could I tell you, when I couldn't even accept it myself?"

"But why now? You're almost thirty-five years old. Why are you finally addressing these things now?"

He exhales dejectedly, "Because the woman I love left me, and I'm miserable without her. I'm ready to do whatever it takes to win you back. I don't want to live my life without you."

Holy hell. I don't know what to say. I'm silent for a full two minutes after his confession before managing, "So much of this is water under the bridge. I'm not sure I can see us as a couple again."

"You can't see it now, but what if I fix myself? What if I get help and someone out there can make me better?" His voice shakes with so much emotion, I know he's crying.

"Oh, Ethan. I don't know. But whatever happens with us, you owe it to yourself to get help for you. You need to be in a world that isn't painful for you."

He won't hang up until I promise to talk to him again. And the truth is, I want to. I still love Ethan, although I'm still uncertain in what way. Even if I don't go back to him, I truly am invested in what happens to him.

My happy holiday spirit is taking a temporary hiatus. I don't currently feel like planning a party with my mom. I don't feel like running off to visit Nan. I feel like crawling back into bed and going to sleep for a week.

Life. What a journey.

Mad Money

I spend the majority of the day in my pajamas. Even after getting out of the shower, I opt for a fresh pair instead of clothes. Pajamas are comforting, like a big hug. They're underrated, and I think, as a society, we would be better off if we wore them more often. Maybe "Casual Friday" could be turned into "Pajama Friday."

I finally put on real clothes at five o'clock, but only because Sam is picking me up in twenty minutes to go Christmas shopping. We're driving to Champaign to the Market Place Shopping Center. If we're there by six, we'll have a full four hours to hit the mall before the stores close.

I keep thinking about Ethan and our conversation. To me, it sounds like he's suffering from some kind of autism, and while it's not Rain Man serious—and boy do I feel sorry for calling him that now—it's still a real problem in his life. I fell for him because he's sweet and kind and always made me feel safe. I'm very much second-guessing leaving him. Not that I can really see myself going back, it's just … heck, I don't know. It's just all so confusing.

When Sam picks me up, he can tell I'm out of it and asks,

"You doing okay, Cat? Something on your mind?"

Something is definitely on my mind, but Sam is not the right person to share it with. We agreed not to discuss the past and to take things from today onward. It's a good pact. My history with Ethan is mine. Sam has no ownership of it. Plus, he could never give me unbiased advice. So, I answer, "I'm good. Just planning my parents' Christmas party in my head."

He smiles like he accepts my answer but isn't buying it. "So, where do you want to go first?"

"Let's park in the Bergners parking lot and go in that way." This mall was considered big-city shopping when I was a kid growing up in Gelson. I laugh at the thought now, as I've grown accustomed to real big-city shopping. But there's a comfort coming back here. The little kid inside me is jumping for joy that the grown up me has come back with real money to spend. Note, the definition of real money for high-school Cat was anything over thirty dollars.

We decide to shop for Nan together before splitting up to take care of our families. I pick up beautiful silk pajamas and a robe. "I bet she'd love lounging in something so decadent while she recovers."

Sam agrees. He says, "I already know what I'm getting her. She's been complaining about cold feet, so I'm going to buy her some warm socks. Oh, and a bottle of perfume I read about. Its primary fragrance is heather, to remind her of the Highlands."

"That's really thoughtful of you. I'm sure she'll love them both."

Once we've finished with Nan, we go our separate ways, promising to meet at the Red Robin at seven for sustenance to fuel our spree. In the housewares section, I buy my mom a shortbread pan in the shape of bunches of wheat. It's a pretty standard one, but when I checked her collection earlier today, I didn't see one like it. I also buy her a citrus zester, a cherry pitter, and meat-shredding claws. God knows if she'll ever use them, but she'll love owning them.

I buy my dad club head covers for his golf clubs that say, "Kiss My Putt" and shot glasses that say "Sláinte," which is Gaelic for health. I have no idea what to get for my brother because I don't where he is or if we're even going to see him at Christmas. Also, because I don't know who he is any more, if he's not still a stoner. Once upon a time a bag of Doritos would have been a perfectly acceptable gift for him.

I head off to the restaurant, pleased by how much shopping I've done so far. I still need to get something for Jazz and Dylan. I'm thinking a gift card and a little something indulgent for the mother-to-be. I also want to get something for Sarah, and maybe even Sam. Nothing too big for him, just something that says I'm glad we've called a truce and are back in each other's lives.

Then I wonder if I should get something for Ethan. My gut says no, but my heart says, *why not get him something generic that won't get his hopes up*? I ask myself, like what, a blender? A toaster? What says, *I'm glad we're talking*, without saying, *let's get back together?*

The Gift

Once we're seated, Sam asks, "Remember when we used to come to this mall and our first stop always had to be Fannie May, so you could buy peppermint bark to eat while we walked around?"

I reflect in genuine delight as I begin to salivate. "And you used to get a soft pretzel and root beer?"

I think fondly of young Cat and Sam, so crazy in love with each other and full of dreams for their futures. "Did your life turn out the way you expected it to?"

Sam looks reflective. "Yes and no. I guess there's no way it could have turned out like I thought it would and still have included all the surprises along the way."

He doesn't need to explain what he means. I totally get it. I take a sip of water to push down the lump forming in my throat. I finally manage, "Life *would* be boring without the surprises." And I mean it. Even if we'd gone off to college together, and gotten married and had kids in our twenties, we still might not have stayed together. Maybe we needed to have our own adventures and then find our way back to each other if we were meant to be.

Then there's Ethan. He's a good man, even though he's dull.

His need for order is probably the only way for him to control his life and consequently his ability to live like a semi-normal human being. The question is, now that I know about his problems, does it alter my feelings for him. I love Ethan, but am in love with him?

I realize I'm totally lost in my thoughts and not a very good dinner companion, when Sam gets out of his side of the booth and scooches in next to me. He takes my hand under the table and whispers in my ear, "Stop thinking."

I look up surprised. "Easier said than done."

"I know. But sometimes you have to take a breath and live in the moment. The past is gone, the future is a question mark, all we can ever have possession of is what's right here in front of us."

I release a half-laugh. "The present really is a gift, huh?"

That's when he turns to face me. He looks lovingly and longingly into my eyes before ever-so-slowly bringing his lips to mine. He gives me plenty of notice to realize what his intentions are, so I can stop him. But what's about to happen is as inevitable as drawing breath.

Sam's kiss is achingly tender and familiar. It's home to me. It's where I am right now at this very moment. It's my gift in the present. After it ends, he pulls his food over to my side of the table. We sit next to each other in companionable silence and eat. Neither of us talks or even feels the need to. It's enough that we're together in this moment.

When the waitress comes to ask if we want anything else, we pass. We need to get back out into the mall if we're going to finish our shopping tonight. I tell Sam, "I want to get you something, but I don't want you to think it's a declaration of any sort."

"I guess you're not buying me a diamond ring then," he teases. "Darn it!"

I laugh, "Nope, not this year. How about a nice stethoscope or a pair of socks?"

He scrunches his face up. "Geez, granny, how about some underwear?"

"Too personal," I retort.

He raises his eyebrows suggestively, "How about no underwear?"

I smack his arm to let him know not to go there. "How about a new toothbrush?"

He shakes his head. "With all these rules and regulations, what in the heck am I going to get for you?"

"As you know, I love peppermint bark."

"But Fannie May isn't in the mall anymore."

"You might have to resort to ordering it online, Sam."

"I could do that. Or, we could just stop and buy each other tattoos on the way home. I could get you Sylvester the Cat."

"And I could buy you a great big Yosemite Sam."

He playfully bumps into my shoulder. "It's definitely something to think about."

I'll just add that to my list. There's so much going on in my head right now, it feels like a war zone. I decide to put Sam's gift on the back burner and concentrate on Jazz. Who knows? Maybe if I'm lucky enough, I'll be in her shoes someday. I can't help but wonder whose eyes my baby will have. Ethan's cat green, or Sam's sky blue?

Dust Bunnies and Ointment

You'd think my mother was about to give birth. She's driving herself and everyone around her crazy getting the house prepared. Except she's not readying it for a new life, she's busy getting it sorted for her Christmas party. We've decided on December 14th for the date. The thought being, it's early enough not to interfere with office parties and other already established holiday traditions, like getting out of Dodge to warmer environs.

I wake up early when I hear an annoying sound pulsing in the distance. I look at the clock to see it's only five forty-five. It's still dark outside, so it's probably not a snowblower. What the heck is it? My bed is so snug and warm I don't want to get out of it, but the noise is relentless. Finally, I throw the covers off with one quick movement and sit up.

I slip on my fuzzy socks with the rubber grips on the bottom, grab my robe, and creep cautiously down stairs. I find the source of the disturbance in the kitchen. My mom is standing in the middle of the room, with every drawer and cabinet wide open, holding a small cordless vacuum like she's Wyatt Earp in the middle of a gun battle.

"What are you doing?" I demand.

"Cleaning."

"At five forty-five in the morning?"

"There's a lot to do to get ready for this party, Cat."

I point out, "But, Mom, the kitchen will get dirty loads of times before the party. Don't you think you should start somewhere else? You know, like the basement?"

"Oh, I'm not cleaning the kitchen-kitchen."

I briefly entertain the possibility that I'm still sleeping and that this is just some bizarre dream. "I see." Which I don't. "If you're not cleaning the kitchen-kitchen, what are you doing in here?" I'm almost positive we're standing in the kitchen. I'm not quite sure where the kitchen-kitchen is, though.

She illustrates by going to the silverware drawer and revving her little machine before inserting in into the drawer. So, I guess, "You're vacuuming the silverware?"

She yells over the noise she's creating. "NO. I'M CLEANING OUT ALL THE CRUMBS FROM THE DRAWERS AND CABINETS."

I signal for her to turn the vacuum off. "Why are you doing that?

"So, if any party guests think to sneak off and peek in my drawers to see if I'm a bad housekeeper, they'll learn I'm not. I'll show them."

Wow, the insanity in this woman runs deep. "You're inviting friends to a Christmas party to celebrate and share in some holiday spirit. Am I correct?"

She nods her head. I continue, "Don't you think everyone will be too busy having fun and enjoying the celebration to care what your drawers look like?"

"No, I do not. Parties are the perfect opportunity to sneak around and get a true picture of who people really are."

"But you aren't really a person who keeps her drawers and cabinets crumb-free." In fact, I don't think I've ever seen this lunacy performed in our house before.

"I don't want them to know that. As far as everyone in town is concerned, I want them to think I'm a pristine housekeeper, a veritable Martha Stewart."

"You're not inviting everyone in town, and your friends already know who you are," I point out.

"Whose side are you on, anyway?" she demands.

"Mags, I didn't realize there were sides. I'm simply trying to point out that this might not be the most urgent item on our preparation list."

She points a finger at me. "You're wrong! Did you know that Stella James has a bag of mismatched socks in her laundry room cabinet so big she can barely shut the door?" She adds, "AND she has some ointment cream in her medicine cabinet to kill scabies? Scabies!" she spits out the last word like poor Stella has herpes or something.

I look side-to-side, searching for a hidden camera. This has got to be some kind of joke. "I did not know that," I finally manage.

She enumerates, "Debbie Swan keeps things in her night drawer that would make you blush, and Lisa Martin has a gun under her bed, out in the open, not even in a safe."

"Mom, how do *you* know these things?"

She looks at me like I've taken a nosedive off the clue bus. "Because I looked!"

"Ah, so what you're telling me is you're trying to protect your reputation from busybodies like yourself."

She doesn't even take offense, she merely exclaims, "Exactly!

So, while my mom is busy obliterating all traces of reality, by sucking out ten-year-old crumbs from the kitchen drawers, I'll be doing the real work like making sure we have something to eat and drink. Also, someone has to be in charge of finishing decorations. For all intents and purposes, I appear to be throwing this shindig on my own.

Strip Poker and Bingo

If there are no unforeseen setbacks, Nan should be home in three days. Over breakfast, Mom announces, "We should get the Christmas tree up and decorated before she gets sprung."

"Don't you think she'd like to be part of the process?" I inquire.

My mom puts her fork down in the middle of her scrambled eggs. "I don't care if she wants to be part of it. We've got too much going on this year, and Nan always micromanages everything I do to the tree. Not to be rude, but this is my party, and even though my mother could have died, it's still my house and I should be able to decorate my tree however I want." I'm starting to regret suggesting this gathering.

When I finally get out of the house, an event I've been anticipating since becoming aware of my mom's full crazy, I go straight to the nursing home. Sam is sitting with Nan, playing a card game in the recreation room. I wonder if he's moonlighting as her caregiver. He's always here.

I can't help but smile when I see them together. They're laughing about something, when I hear Nan yell out, "STRIP!"

I hurry over to find Sam sitting next to her without his socks, shoes, belt, and sweater on. "What's going on here?" I inquire.

Nan gives me a little wave. "Strip poker."

"I'm sorry, did you just say strip poker?"

My grandmother's face lightens up with an expression akin to lechery. "I did! Sam here told me if I got a good report from my physical therapist, he'd play any game with me that I wanted."

Sam looks up clearly uncomfortable and shrugs his shoulders. "How was I to know she'd want to play strip poker?"

"Nan," I suggest, "I don't think this is an appropriate environment for such a game, do you?"

A lady sitting at the next table shouts out, "Shut up, girl, she's winning! We're all waiting to see this stud muffin without his pants on."

That's all it takes for Sam to stand up and start looping his belt back into place. "Sorry to disappoint you, Mrs. Johnson, but the game's over."

Nan glares at me. "You see what you've done?"

"Nan, I don't think Sam was ever going to play long enough to take his pants off."

Mrs. Johnson yells out, "We'll never know now, will we? Party pooper!"

I offer to play Scrabble or good old-fashioned five card draw, but Nan exclaims, "Forget it. I'm tired, anyway. I guess I'll just go take a nap."

"Can I walk you to your room?" Sam offers.

"Don't bother. I'm supposed to do it myself. My therapist keeps telling me I need to walk more." She shuffles off, leaving a definite irritated vibe in her wake. I turn to Sam. "Nan seems a little bit grumpy today. What's up?"

"She's getting stir-crazy and wants to go home," he answers.

I can only imagine. Nan is not a person who identifies with other old people. She says they're boring, crotchety, and always complaining about their ailments. She claims to have better things to do than listen to that nonsense.

As soon as he's fully dressed, Sam and I walk out of the care facility together. I explain, "My mom's gone mental cleaning the house. What was I thinking suggesting a party right after Nan comes home?"

He smiles. "I think you were trying to do something nice but may have forgotten just how interesting your family really is."

"That's the truth. Mags is on a tear to get the tree decorated so Nan can't offer an opinion. I'm starting to feel stressed." Sam looks amused, so I add, "I've worked for a lot of high-maintenance hostesses, but my mom takes the cake."

"It's your lucky day," he declares. "I'm off today, so why don't we go get a tree and set it up? That'll give your mom a couple of days to finish it before Nan comes home."

"Do you ever work?" I demand. "How is it that you have all this free time to take me Christmas shopping and now tree shopping?"

He looks moderately offended. "I worked all day yesterday before we went to the mall and today truly is one of my days off." He adds, "Plus, I only work four days a week. Our little town didn't have need for another full-time doctor when I moved home. But once Doc Fischer retires, I'm next in line."

"So, what do you do when you're not working?" I inquire.

"I come over here to the nursing home and chat with people who don't have anyone. I somehow got coerced into being on the school board, and I call bingo at the Catholic church when I'm not scheduled at the hospital."

"You're a regular Boy Scout, aren't you?" I joke.

He shrugs. "I have a pretty charmed life. I just like giving back."

The more I learn about grown-up Sam, the more I like him. I might be starting to see the possibility of a future with him. It's still early days though, and I'm committed to taking things slowly, especially after talking to Ethan.

Worst Chaperone Ever

I call my mom to let her know Sam and I are on the hunt for the perfect Christmas tree and will bring it back later this afternoon. She's thrilled we're getting it because she's busy cleaning the grout in all the bathrooms.

"Why don't you drop your car at home, and I'll pick you up?" Sam suggests.

I thought he'd follow me, but it takes him twenty minutes longer than expected. When he pulls into my parents' driveway, I see why. He's not driving his SUV, he's driving Betty, his parents' old pick-up.

My heart rate increases to an alarming degree when I see it. Betty was with us through our entire high school courtship. Much to our delight, she was the worst chaperone in the history of the world. Things happened in, on, and against Betty that are better left to imagination. Nevertheless, images flash through my mind that leave me gasping for enough oxygen to keep from falling over.

Sam pulls up next to me and flings the door open from the inside. I step in like I'm entering a time machine. Everything looks the same as it did fifteen years ago. The red vinyl seats are slightly more faded, as is the dashboard, but the John Deere floor mats are still on the floor and the keychain is even the same as it once was.

My first boyfriend, stealer of my heart, and destroyer of my adolescent dreams, suggests, "I thought we'd drive to the Christmas tree farm in Decatur." Small towns usually set up Christmas trees in the parking lot of the local hardware store or have small pop-up stands in the country, without a large selection. Growing up, we always traveled at least a half hour to find a place with a bigger selection.

I merely nod in reply. Sam wonders, "Why so quiet? What's rattling around in that head of yours now?"

I answer in one word. "Betty."

His eyes sparkle. "Ah, yes. The old girl is still going strong." He glances at me out of the corner of his eye. "She sure saw us through a lot, didn't she?"

I try to swallow down the emotion forming in my throat but can't force out any sound. So, I simply nod in response. Sam instructs, "Open the glove compartment."

I don't follow his instruction immediately. Instead, I stare at the old key lock glove box like it's harboring poisonous snakes. Finally, I find my courage and flip it open. I reach in and pull out a stack of papers and assorted odds and ends.

It's full of Sam's and my history. He informs me, "There are stubs from concert tickets and notes we dropped into each other's lockers between classes. Be careful you don't crush my boutonniere from homecoming." I unearth a CD we burned together, a garter belt I wore to our senior prom, and a tassel from his high school graduation cap. It's like a time capsule of our best moments together.

I feel like I'm holding religious relics. Every single one is packed with its own special memory. Tears flood my eyes and I don't even bother trying to brush them away. "Why didn't your parents throw this stuff out?"

"They haven't used Betty as their everyday truck in years. Plus, I think they felt it wasn't their place to get rid of it."

"So, why didn't you?"

"I'm sure you know the answer to that question, Cat. These things, this truck, it's us. It's all I have left of our story. I kept it out of nostalgia."

I shake my head. "But you've been in other relationships. You were almost engaged to another woman."

"I suppose if one of those other women ever meant as much to me as you did, I might have seen my way clear to at least moving these things out into a storage box somewhere. But seeing as they never did, I didn't see the point. I like getting into Betty and remembering us. Sometimes I pretend I'm still sixteen, and I'm on my way to pick you up for something."

What a gut-wrenching thought. I can't believe Sam puts himself through that. God knows it would have been too much for me to bear. "Were you really going to interview at Lenox Hill, just so you could see me in New York?"

Sam hits a button on his phone in response. The air around us fills with an authoritative female voice, "Sam, this is Dr. Moskowitz, chief of staff at Lenox Hill. My assistant told me you were no longer planning to move to New York. I'm sorry to hear that and wanted to assure you that if you ever change your mind, we hope you'll consider us before looking elsewhere. Good luck to you and I hope to talk to you in the near future."

I have no words. Sam really was going to pursue me again, regardless of Ethan. He's not fooling around here. It's a thought that delights and terrifies me at the same time.

Douglas, Noble, and Fraser, Oh My!

At the Christmas tree farm, we buy hot chocolate garnished with whipped cream and chopped-up peppermint candy to fortify our search for the perfect tree. My parents' living room ceiling is ten feet high and Mom likes to use every inch of the space, so the tree-topper is brushing against it. This narrows our selection, but also increases the difficulty of finding a symmetrical tree.

We relay our specifications to the man working the area of the farm with the biggest trees. "Douglas or Noble?" he asks.

"Noble," we answer simultaneously. There was that one year when my dad brought home a beautiful ten-foot Douglas fir and you would have thought it was a *Charlie Brown Christmas*, the one where he brought home a pathetic stick to decorate. Mags moaned and groaned and sighed the entire month of December like she was carrying a cross around on her back.

We have a grand total of three trees to pick from, which is essentially three more than we would have had if we'd stayed in Gelson. We walk around them. We pinch the tips of the branches to make sure they bend but don't break—Freshness 101. We even smell them to see if one has a stronger fragrance than the others.

Once we narrow it down to two, Sam lays on the ground and looks up at them to check their symmetry from that angle. After several moments, he announces, "Ding, ding, ding, we have a winner!" He points to the tree that passes my mom's twelve-point inspection and while it's being wrapped it up, we look around some more.

"Let's get Nan her own tree," Sam suggests. "You know she's fond of Fraser firs. We can get a small one, a six-footer, maybe."

What a sweet thought. "Nan would love that, and so would Mom. That way Mags wouldn't have to argue over every ornament Nan wanted on the tree. Also, each one could use her own family plaid as their garland."

We pick out the perfect one and have it wrapped up, as well. I ask, "What about your parents? Do they need a tree?"

Sam shakes his head, "Mom's already got it covered. But I think I just might do a tree of my own this year. If Nan can have her own, why can't I?"

I laugh. "Do you even have enough decorations for your own tree?"

He looks at me like I've just asked if he has all of his toes. "Psh, I'm almost thirty-two years old. I've collected things."

I can only imagine. I'm looking forward to seeing what Sam's tree looks like when it's all done. I haven't even seen his house yet. He chooses a six-foot Douglas fir for himself. Once all three trees are secured in the flatbed, he asks, "Do we need to get a stand for Nan's tree or do you have a spare?"

I have no idea, so we swing by the store to get one just in case.

"If I remember correctly," Sam declares, "Nan prefers white lights, right?" He grabs several boxes as he asks.

"Yup, and my mom thinks anything but colored is an offense of apocalyptic proportion. Again, good thinking on getting Nan her own tree." I'm having such a good time with Sam. It feels like we've been doing this together for years.

Last year was the first time Ethan and I bought a Christmas tree together. I was shocked to learn he never put one up for his own enjoyment, instead he relied on his parents' tree to fill that need. When I suggested a live tree, he nearly flipped his lid. The thought of needles falling off that would need to be vacuumed was more than he could tolerate. In light of new information, I realize that was probably true.

We wound up with a very narrow four-and-a-half-foot tree that looked more like an accessory than the real deal. Ethan was so proud of it though, I didn't have the heart to show any disappointment.

When Sam and I get home, we discover my mom painting the spindles on the railing of the staircase. I ignore her as we carry the tree into the living room and begin to set it up. I know one thing for sure: I will never get married or even have so much as have an engagement party at my parents' farmhouse. It would be more pressure than old Mags could handle. She'd probably hire bulldozers to raze the place and rebuild it from scratch.

Diagnosing Ducks

Ethan calls at nine o'clock pm his time, eight o'clock mine, to tell me about his doctor's appointment. After talking to him for an hour, the psychiatrist was astonished he'd never been diagnosed as a child. Upon learning of his parents' unique traits, it became clear the entire household was a little off, and they just increased their limitations to include their son's peculiarities.

"I have ASD," Ethan announces. "That stands for autism spectrum disorder." This both relieves him (that there's a name for what he has) and disappoints him (that the diagnosis is autism.)

"I feel like a freak," he says. "I've always known I was different, but now there's no hiding it. I really am different."

"Is there some treatment?" I ask.

"Not as such. The doctor said there would have been things they could have done to help if I were a child, but as an adult functioning at a high level in the real world, there are no behavioral treatments other than simply pushing myself to increase my boundaries. He did say they could give me pharmaceuticals to decrease my anxiety, if I wanted."

"Are you going to try that?"

"If it will help me feel more comfortable in difficult

situations." He adds, "I bought a red blanket on my way home, and I put it on the back of the couch."

I'm touched that he's trying so hard to change, but I'm concerned I'm his sole motivation. "Ethan, you have to do this for you. Please don't do it for me because I can't give you any promises. A lot has happened between us that I'm just not sure is fixable."

"I know. But I might as well go for the ultimate win here. That would be getting back together and making you happy."

Ethan and I were mostly content as a couple. Yes, I was disappointed at times, but sharing your life with someone always involves compromise. I liked Ethan's controlled and regimented life because it fed something in me that yearned for structure.

I hadn't realized it was too much until I brought him home for Thanksgiving. Seeing my parents through his eyes made me realize my New York life had reached the opposite extreme of what I was running from when I met him. The question is, if he can really change, do I owe it to us to give him the opportunity to prove it?

Ethan tells me about the rest of his day, which encompassed ordering his Thursday lunch instead of his Tuesday lunch, to start pushing open his comfort zone.

"How did that work?" I ask.

"I couldn't eat it. I kept it on my desk for a full hour and couldn't bring myself to touch it." Then he quickly adds, "I shouldn't be telling you that though, because I want you to believe in me. I want you to believe I can do this."

"Why did you tell me, then?"

"Catriona, when you left, not only did I lose the woman I

love, I lost my best friend. Around you, I never felt like damaged goods." He confesses, "Sometimes I felt like I was letting you down, but you never made me feel like an oddity."

I'm glad I didn't. My heart constricts painfully, as I truly do love Ethan and I'm grateful for our time together. I realize how horrible it must have been for him to grow up never feeling like he fit in anywhere, always aware of his strangeness.

It makes me think of that childhood story, *The Ugly Duckling*. The poor little duck was always taunted for being different and not like all the other ducklings. He suffered from classic poor self-esteem and worked so hard to fit in. All he wanted was to be like everyone else. Yet, he was bigger, more awkward, and so obviously not the same.

Then came the day when he waddled off to the pond and caught sight of his reflection. He realized he was no longer a duckling. In fact, he'd never been one because his image told a different story. A beautiful, graceful swan stared back at him.

I want that outcome for Ethan so much I can taste it. I want this diagnosis and subsequent therapy to prove to him he isn't like everyone else, because he's not a duck. He's something unique and special in his own right. He deserves a happy ending. I just have to figure out if I'm going to be part of it in the way he wants.

Complementing Crazy

As soon as I wake up, I run downstairs to see how far my mom got on the tree. Before I left her last night, she declared, "I don't want any help. I want to decorate it myself, like I've always dreamed of."

What I see when in I walk into the living room is a horror beyond words. There are piles of tangled Christmas lights everywhere, ornaments strewn on top of every surface, and my mom passed out on the couch buried under a pile of three-inch wide Masterton plaid ribbon.

I'm not sure whether to wake her or just let her be. I opt for the latter and go straight to the kitchen to make an extra strong pot of coffee. I fear I'll need it. Over my first cup, I realize I haven't been part of my family's tree-trimming operation since I graduated from college.

I don't remember it being a traumatizing experience, but then again, we all had a part in it. My dad set the tree up and strung the lights. I wrapped the plaid garland around it in a whimsical, yet symmetrical, fashion. Travis set out all the ornaments, so Mom could see what she had to work with. Then it was all up to Mags to figure out which ones she was going to use that year and what their optimal placement was.

After two cups of coffee, I feel fortified enough to walk back into the scene of the disaster. My mom hasn't moved an inch, so I start with the lights. Before even trying to untangle them, I plug them in to see if they're still working. They aren't and there are no replacement bulbs.

So, I run upstairs, throw on a pair of yoga pants and tiptoe out the front door. I hit the Home Depot on Highway 47 because they open two hours earlier than anywhere else and grab fourteen boxes of colored lights in the same size as the piles all over our rug.

When I get home, I pick up all the defunct lights and put them in the trunk of my rental car. I'll throw them out in a city dumpster somewhere. Then I take all the new ones out of their packaging and put them in the same place the others had been. I hide the boxes in my trunk, as well. All the spare bulbs are thrown into the freshly vacuumed junk drawer in the kitchen.

When my mom finally gets up, I ask her how she's doing. She looks defeated and ready to cry. "I never realized what a big job decorating the tree was."

"Do you want some help?" I ask.

Her eyes brighten in excitement like I've just offered her the winning lottery ticket. "Yes, please! Your father put the lights away in such a tangle last year I could just hit him over the head with one of his spittoons."

I pull out the step-stool and carry it into the living room with Mags at my heels. When I unwind the first strand, she exclaims, "How did you do that so easily?"

I smile. "You just have to know where to start." She looks

confused but doesn't ask any further questions. I have all the lights on the tree inside of an hour. Then I do my job and wrap the ribbon around it. Mom excuses herself to get dressed.

While she's gone I put half of the ornaments back into their boxes and put them into the garage where they're stored. Mags has a habit of keeping every ornament she's ever received as a gift, purchased, or found discarded at a white elephant sale. She only likes half of them but is emotionally incapable of getting rid of the others. She doesn't want to hurt their feelings.

When she comes back down, we get to work. I share that I've been talking to Ethan on the phone.

She's surprised. "Why?"

I explain how he's just been diagnosed with ASD and that he's started to work with a psychiatrist to broaden his coping skills.

She doesn't say anything for several moments. Finally, she says, "Everyone's crazy in their own way. What makes two people compatible is finding someone whose crazy complements yours and vice versa."

"Are you saying that if Ethan's compliments mine, you wouldn't mind us being together?"

She fingers the lights on the tree absently. "The thing with you, honey, is you're so busy trying to compensate for everyone else's crazy, you haven't even bothered to discover what yours is." She adds, "I only want what makes you happy, Cat, and at the end of the day if you decide that's Ethan, then of course I'll support you."

It takes another hour with the two of us working together to finish the tree. It's our most beautiful one yet.

It All Comes Back to the Shuck and Chuck

I come downstairs after showering to find my dad hanging his own decorative touches from the chandelier—his mice. He's not done this before, so I question him, "Whatcha doing, big guy?" Even though it's clear what the answer is— hanging dead rodents from the light fixture.

He turns around with delight written all over his face. "Can you believe I've never thought to put them here?"

I smile like you would to a mentally disturbed person threatening to jump off a roof. "While it does seem like the ideal location in many ways, might I point out a small potential problem?"

My dad looks like he can't for the life of him figure out what that could be. "Shoot."

"Our guests probably aren't used to fully clothed mice dangling above their heads. I think you might scare the life out of some of them." Then stating the obvious, I add, "A good Christmas party doesn't usually end with people running from the house in terror."

My dad really thinks about what I just said before answering, "I'd agree if they were dressed up in something scary. I'm glad you mentioned it though, I can't wait until Halloween next year. I'm going to make them some monster costumes, Frankenstein, Dracula, The Mummy!"

I see we've gotten sidetracked and there's nothing I can do to change his mind. If my parents' friends ever experimented with drugs in the seventies, maybe they'll just chalk it up to an acid flashback. So, I smile in return. "I've always loved your Valentine's display, when you dress them up as Cupid and the great lovers of history." There's nothing quite like Romeo mouse and Juliet mouse in the throes of the famous balcony scene. It transcends belief.

While my dad is hard at work and mildly distracted, I ask, "What do you think of Ethan, Dad?"

"Ah, your mom told me about what's going on with him. Are you considering getting back together?"

I shrug my shoulders. "I don't know. We were happy for a long time. Part of me feels like I owe it to him to give him another chance, especially now that he really needs me."

"I can see where you might feel that way. But let me point out that you were part of what enabled Ethan to continue living his life *without* getting help. And you know how much I dislike those psycho-babble words like enable."

"Yes, but I'm also the reason he's getting it. He claims winning me back is giving him the strength he needs to change."

"Cat, you were the catalyst, but only once you left. It would be very easy for you to fall back into old patterns that won't help Ethan get better. I think he needs to do this on his own and then if you're meant to be with him, you can start fresh."

I consider what he's saying, but ask, "You're not just saying that because you don't like him, are you?"

My dad looks startled. "I don't dislike him. Of course, that doesn't mean I like him for you."

"Because of Sam?" I ask.

"I'd like nothing more than to see you and Sam together, but that's not my decision to make. Sam broke your heart. That's a hard thing to forget, even if you are capable of forgiving it."

My dad gets down off his ladder, takes my hand and leads me to the staircase. We sit on the third step. "What you have to remember is that you aren't seventeen anymore and neither is he. You've both grown up and have learned from your mistakes and experiences. Don't you think you owe it to yourself to find out who the grown-up Sam is?"

I nod. "I do, and we've been spending time together. I just don't want to jump into anything because of our past. I have to keep reminding myself we aren't those kids and that we don't really know each other."

"Not true. If you hadn't seen me for fourteen years, and I just showed up one day, would I be a stranger? It's the same with Sam. You grew up together, you experienced life together. While the relationship stuff is water under the bridge, the rest is still alive and well. Don't forget that."

"And if I wind up with Ethan?"

"Then you'd better teach that boy the shuck and chuck or we're going to have problems."

I love that my parents are both being so supportive. I know they want me to be with Sam, but I really do believe they'd both have my back if I decided Ethan was my future.

The Family Web

My days have been full since I've come home. If I'm not at the nursing home with Nan, I'm working on the party at home or spending time with Sam. I haven't had any time for myself, so I set aside the rest of the day to think about my life.

My first stop is the barn. I bundle up, grab a blanket and tiptoe out the back door. I sneak so my mom doesn't know where I'm going. If her focus increases enough to include the barn, she might decide it needs painting, too. If that happens, we're sunk. Better she concentrates on the minutiae in the house.

I have a thing for barns and always have. They're as much a part of the landscape of my childhood as the cornfields. In the midst of all the sameness are barns. They're all different to suit the individual farm's needs. There are new barns and old. Some for animals only and others to house tractors and farm equipment. I don't care what kind they are, they speak to me.

Our barn dates back to the forties when our farmhouse was built. It's a huge white structure that could hold a couple hundred animals, if necessary. Now, it only houses six chickens, a donkey, whatever farm cats have moved in, and my dad's taxidermied friends.

It's sad to see it so empty and my brain starts to ponder the possible uses for such a structure. It's in great shape considering its age. It just needs some basic TLC.

I climb the stairs to the loft, which is about half the size of the ground floor. When I was a little girl, this space was everything from my princess castle to the tallest peak of Mt. Everest. My imagination took flight up here. It's where I dreamed my best dreams.

Luckily all the hay has been swept out, so it isn't one great big rodent's nest. Although that would be a great source of material if my dad ever decides to expand his collection. The space is only used for storage now. There's an old spinning wheel from the time my mom was convinced she was going to add homespun wool to our farm's résumé. That pipe dream lasted approximately one summer. The magnitude of the job proved too much for us.

Not only did we shear the sheep and skirt the fleece, we sorted the finer bits from the courser ones and discarded the belly fibers that were too full of manure to use. Then we washed the wool in a detergent strong enough to dissolve any vegetable matter left. Finally came the picking, carding and roving—which readied piles of random fiber for the spinning process. It turns out we were all crap at spinning, and now all we have left of that venture is the wooden wheel.

Nan's old sewing machine is up here, as well, along with other random bits of furniture like a stream trunk, an oak vanity, and kitchen table and chairs. Over in the corner is the piece of furniture I'm looking for, an old army cot. I open it up, bang some dust out of it and then lie down.

Staring up into the rafters of this barn is where I've done my best thinking over the years and it's why I'm here now. I read the beams like a fortune teller reads tea leaves. Once I'm wrapped up in my blanket I begin the process of divining my future.

I ask, *why am I here?* My eyes are drawn to a huge cobweb in the corner of the ceiling. There are no spiders in it as I'm sure they're probably hibernating in one of the boxes. The web is starting to lose its grip on the top beam and is hanging by a thread in a couple of other places. Suddenly, the answer pops into my head.

My family is like that web. It was once strong and secure, able to capture and hold much in its solidity. But now it's getting older and starting to loosen. I'm home to help rebuild its infrastructure by spinning new connections to the support beam, to ready it for another generation.

It fits when you think of how close we came to losing Nan. Both of my parents are starting to unwind, too. They rent out most of their land and don't have many animals anymore. They live frugally off the rent they get while they either decide what to do next or until Social Security kicks in. Their connections to this world are definitely gaining slack.

I know this may sound fanciful to some, but I firmly believe God speaks to us in mysterious ways, and if he or she wants to speak to me through the beams in my family barn, who am I to question it?

Now I just need to lie here long enough to figure out if I belong with either Ethan or Sam. Unfortunately, this space is so full of memories of my childhood, which is full of Sam, that I can't get a clear answer.

Sam and I used to come up here and play house when we

were little kids. I was the bossy mom and he pretended to be the dad who sat in a chair and called for a beer. Neither of our parents modeled that behavior, so I can only assume we picked up on those dynamics from television.

When we were in junior high, we came up here to talk things out. We'd chat for hours about kids from school and how we fit into the mix. Sam was a geek during those years and often lamented he didn't feel like he belonged in any particular group. I was a cheerleader and confessed I felt the same way.

By the time high school rolled around, we came up here and played a different kind of house. We snuggled, kissed, and explored each other for hours. We fantasized about growing up and being together forever. I promised to learn how to cook and Sam declared he'd do all the yard work.

They were such innocent times, unbearably sweet and heartbreakingly naive. When you're a kid, you know with every fiber of your being that all you have to do is dream something for it to be yours. It isn't until you grow up and get hit in the face with reality that you begin to question your ability to have a happy ending.

I'm glad I came up here today. Not only did I gain some perspective about my family, I gained some insight about how I need to reprogram my thinking. I'm ready to believe in dreams again. It's time.

Running Out of Rope

Sam's mom, Liza, calls me on the phone. "I want to sign up to bring my yule log to the party. I'll make enough for sixty people."

I jump at the offer. "That would be perfect!" I explain, "Mom seems to have divorced herself from the idea of food preparation. She's busy with those all-important tasks like painting the mailbox and cleaning behind the washing machine."

"Can I help with anything else?" she asks.

"No. I've made several hors d'oeuvres and have gotten them into the freezer. I think everything else is under control." I say this as I pack up piles of my mom's discarded recipes to return to the attic.

Before I sign off with Liza, I declare I'm off to town to buy wreaths and garlands. I add, "I'm also getting outdoor lights. Sam is coming over after work to help Dad decorate the outside." My parents stopped doing as much exterior decorating once Travis and I weren't kids anymore, but Dad's excited to get back to it.

Before I can walk out the front door, my dad stops me. "What do you think about my moving Nan's stuff into the basement, so she can have her own little apartment? Now that Travis is gone, I think she might enjoy that."

"What a great idea! I'm sure she'd love it. We could put her Christmas tree down there, too, so she can enjoy it while she's lying in bed or watching TV on the couch." I advise, "I'm picking her up at two, so hurry."

When I was a kid, the basement wasn't finished, and it was spooky. We had a root cellar down there, otherwise it was used for storage and possibly as a ghost hangout. When I was in junior high, my parents decided to finish it off, so Travis and I had a place to spend time with our friends.

We used to have a ping pong table down there as well as a game table, and a television to play video games on. The ping pong table is gone, the game table has been replaced by a small dining table, and the television is now bigger and flat-screened, but other than that, things remain pretty much the same. Natural light pours through the rectangular windows near the ceiling, so after dad packs up Travis's stuff it's no longer a skeezy man-cave, I'm sure it'll look fabulous.

I run my errands on the way to the nursing home. The blinding white snow-covered fields hypnotize me and my mind drifts to books that I love. I always seem to be drawn to the common theme of coming home. I love to read about characters who venture into the world and ultimately find their way back to their roots. It doesn't matter if they do it figuratively or literally. I had a college professor who had us read *Gilead, The Song of Solomon*, and *The Mambo Kings Play Songs of Love*. I adored them all.

Then I recall favorite movies with similar themes: *Sweet Home Alabama, It's a Wonderful Life*, and *Hope Floats*. It seems a common thing for people to leave their place of origin in order to find themselves. For me, there's nothing sweeter than when they realize home is the best place to do that.

I've come to that realization with incredible clarity in the last few weeks. I thought my life was going in a completely different direction when it quite simply hit a wall. It's like I was on a lead tethered to my roots and suddenly ran out of rope. I couldn't go any farther, so I turned around and came home. Gelson, Illinois is where my story started, and while it might not be where it ends, it's once again an important stop on my journey.

I imagine what it would have been like had I never left here. I try to pick out the house Sam and I would have bought to raise our family in. I imagine what our children would have looked like and how old they'd be. And you know what? I can't. Because I suddenly know with complete certainty that I was one of those people who wouldn't have been able to fully appreciate home until I'd left it. I had to break away and try to find my own way before I could comprehend that everything I ever needed was right here in front of me the whole time.

I still don't know what man I'm meant to spend the rest of my life with. I just know that I'm meant to spend my life closer to my family. I forgive Sam, I really do. Without him breaking his ties, I never would have broken mine. And I realize to my very core, I needed to do that to get to where I am right now.

If You Can't Say Anything Nice

"Damn, girl, it took you long enough! I've been sitting here for three hours." Nan is in rare form.

I smile at the image of the shrunken matriarch of my family, stewing in the waiting room of the nursing home, with her suitcase case next to her and her winter coat on her lap. She's wearing a hat to cover her bandaged head that was probably at the peak of fashion in the nineteen sixties.

"Nan, you look wonderful. Just let me talk to the nurse and sign you out." She grumbles as I turn my back on her to secure her release.

"The doctor wants to see your grandmother in a week," the nurse informs me. "Make sure she gets plenty of fluids." She gives me a prescription for pain meds and cautions, "Don't let her use any recreational drugs."

I assure her my grandmother's pot-smoking days are over. Now that I know she's been fully in control of her foul-mouthed outbursts all these years, there's no need for her to be getting high all the time.

She also hands over an order for steroids—to keep the inflammation down, blood pressure meds—to keep any blood vessels from rupturing, and an anti-seizure medication. I'm starting to get a little nervous about taking Nan out of here.

I pull the car up front, and an attendant pushes my grandmother out in a wheelchair, so she doesn't slip and fall on the new snow. When she's secured in the front seat next to me, she demands, "I want pie."

"What kind of pie?" I inquire.

"Pecan and cherry. You'd better just take me over to the Snack Shack. That way you won't have to make it for me." This is my first glimmer into the high-maintenance patient Nan must have been at the nursing home.

"Let's drop your prescriptions at the pharmacy first, so they can get them ready while we eat."

"Fine," she grumbles. "I'll wait in the car. Don't forget to get my tissues with the lotion in them and a Mr. Goodbar for later. Oh, and I need a new romance novel. Men in kilts only, and make sure the boy on the cover has good calves. I loathe men with skinny calves."

I assure Nan I'll get everything on her list. Once we travel the two blocks down Main Street, I pull into a spot right in front of the pharmacy. I leave the car running to keep her warm. Then drop off her prescriptions and grab the items on her list— including a book with a long-haired man in a kilt standing in a field of heather with a red-headed woman lying at his feet. I can only imagine the plot of *My Bonnie Courtesan*, and smile at the thought of Nan reading such racy goings on.

When I turn around to leave, I run smack into the aforementioned grandmother. "What are you doing in here? I thought you were going to wait in the car."

"I would have, but it was taking you forever. I wanted to make sure you didn't forget me."

Ooooookay, so I've been in the pharmacy all of four and a half minutes. I have no idea how she translated that into forever. I take Nan's arm and loop it through mine, resting her frail hand on mine. "I'm sorry it took me so long. What do you say we go get that pie?"

We walk back out onto the frigid Main Street and cross the street to the diner. Once we're situated in a booth at the Snack Shack, Nan commands, "Come over here and sit by me like you did when you were a little girl."

I obey her immediately. "How's this?"

She leans her narrow shoulder into mine, and confesses, "I'm scared."

I put my arm around her. "I bet you are. That was quite an ordeal you went through."

I feel her head bob up and down. "I don't want to die yet, Cat. The worst part of this aging crap is that I still feel like I'm thirty-five in my head. Even though I can't remember diddly squat anymore. Then I look in the mirror and think, *who the hell is that old hag?*"

I smile. Nan has always seemed old to me. I used to look at pictures of her in her younger years and marvel that the gorgeous red-headed girl with sparkling blue eyes could have ever been the gray-haired grandmother ever present in my life.

"One day, you're vibrant and full of energy and sass and the next ..."—she sticks her tongue out and blows raspberries—"you're nothing. Just a shell of your former self. Then your husband dies, and you completely lose your identity. You haven't been just *you* in so long, you can't even remember who that is."

"Oh, I don't know, Nan. You seem to have plenty of sass to me. I bet if you asked any person in this town, they'd say the same thing."

She shakes her head. "They only know who I am because I decided to say my peace out loud and they're all afraid of me."

There's probably a lot of truth to that. "Do you really think the only way for people to notice you is to be outrageous?"

She gives me the side-eye. "Why else would they bother?"

"Why don't you try saying nice things to them and see what happens?" I suggest.

She considers my idea as the middle-aged server, with a tattoo of a grenade on her hand, comes over and asks what we're having. Once my grandmother orders her pie, she announces, "Nadine, that is one interesting picture on your hand." While not quite a compliment, it could have been an outright insult, and it wasn't. What we have here is progress.

The waitress looks a little bit afraid of Nan (as I'm sure the Snack Shack has been the location of dozens of her outbursts). She smiles shyly and responds, "Thank you, Mrs. McTavish, and might I say I'm right happy to see you feeling better after your troubles."

Nan acknowledges her sentiment with a sharp nod of her head. When the waitress leaves, I ask, "That wasn't too difficult, was it?"

Nan thinks a moment before answering, "I guess not. I suppose you've given me something to think about, young lady." Then she changes the subject. "Enough about me. What have you decided to do with your little ménage à trois?"

I'm about to point out that a ménage à trois is three people in bed together, not a love triangle, but that can only lead to uncomfortable conversation. So, I answer, "I don't know. I'm trying not to think about it."

She clucks her tongue in sympathy. "Don't worry, honey. I'm cooking up something I think might help."

I shake my head vigorously. "Oh, Nan, please don't. Let me handle it, okay?"

"Sure, honey. I'll do that." She smiles unconvincingly.

When the Cactus Goes Home

Nan hates that her things have been moved to the basement. She declares, "I feel like I'm being pushed out of the family and hidden away like some out-of-season decoration."

My mom counters, "We thought you'd like to have some extra space of your own."

"Why? So, you can forget I'm even here?" Nan fumes.

"Not at all, Nan!" Dad interjects. "You know how much we love you. I'll start moving your things back up to your room right away." He doesn't waste any time, either.

"Why doesn't Cat move down there?" Nan suggests. "After all, she's a grown woman and would probably enjoy having some privacy away from us old folks."

It's a brilliant idea. I find I'm not fitting into my old room like I once did. Sleeping on a twin bed again after all these years makes me feel like I'm camping, and the bedroom in the basement has a queen-sized bed I can stretch out on. I offer, "Nan, why don't we turn my room into a private sitting room for you?"

She shakes her head. "I don't want that, thank you very much. I want the time I have left spent with my family and not locked away like I'm a felon."

Nan has come home with a little bit of an attitude. Mags asks, "Mom, would you like to help us get ready for our Christmas party on Saturday night?"

"I would not. I'd be happy to come to your party, but I don't want to be your workhorse."

Oh boy, no one quite knows how to get on Nan's good side. So far everything we've done or said is ticking her right off. I suggest, "Why don't you go upstairs and rest for a while."

She snaps, "Why don't you get busy moving your things into the basement?" I'm happy to oblige.

When I take my worldly possessions downstairs, I unpack my boxes from New York. I put my red afghan on the couch, which looks perfect against the brown corduroy of the sofa. I put my blue vase out on the bookshelves, along with my matryoshka dolls. I even unpack my books. Then I place the basket of green and gold ornaments on the coffee table. By the time I'm done, I realize I've got the perfect little bachelorette pad for however much longer I'm home.

I go upstairs and find Nan sitting in the living room. "Would you like to come downstairs and help me decorate the tree we bought for you?"

She seems to have unwound a little bit and replies, "No, honey, you go ahead. I'd like to come down and sit with you from time to time, though."

"That sounds nice, Nan. You want to come down now?"

She doesn't quite seem to know how to answer. Just when I think she might, she says, "No, I think I'll stay right here. You go on. Let me know when you're done. I'll come take a peek."

I agree, but the first thing I do when I get back downstairs is to pick up the phone and call Sam. "I bet Nan's thrilled to be home," he declares.

I reply truthfully, "I'm not sure. She's prickly as a cactus and nothing anyone says seems to be the right thing. Do you think she's having some kind of side effects from her ordeal?"

"Irritability is very common after a brain injury. It also sounds like she's having some emotional adjustments. I should be over in about an hour to help your dad decorate the front of the house. I'll make sure to spend some time with Nan while I'm there."

I thank him before hanging up. It's nice to have someone outside our four walls to turn to in a situation like this. Sam loves Nan like she's his own grandmother, so I know he'll help us figure out the best way to get her settled back in.

The Boy Who Owns My Heart

I take a hot shower to help slough off the day. Opening the boxes from New York has brought back so many memories, like how much I had loved unpacking those same treasures at Ethan's apartment to help make it mine. We all know how well that worked out. Consequently, the need to wash away the past is intense.

I don't expect to walk out of the bathroom and find Sam sitting on my couch. I'm wearing a towel and he's wearing a smile. "Nan told me you were down here waiting for me. When I heard the shower running I didn't dare hope you were expecting me to join you."

"Good thinking," I reply. Even though the thought of Sam joining me in the shower is a delicious one. Goosebumps form all over my body and not in reaction to the cool air, either. "I'll be right out, just let me get dressed."

"Let me know if you need any help," he calls after me.

Nan appears to have herself a little plan. *Give the basement to Cat. She's a grown woman who needs her privacy.* My foot! That old lady probably couldn't wait to send Sam down here. I better keep a close eye on her.

When I come out of my new room dressed in my favorite yoga pants and fisherman's sweater, Sam pats the couch seat next to him for me to join him. I don't hesitate. He says, "I talked to Nan and I don't think her grumpiness has anything to do with the surgery. I think she's just a little bit frightened. What she went through was a real wake-up call. She's feeling her mortality."

"She told me how scared she was when I picked her up," I confirm. "What can we do to help her?"

He puts his arm around me. "Just talk to her and spend time with her." He cryptically adds, "And forgive her when she does things you might not approve of. She told me there are a few things she wants to see settled before she leaves this world and she's afraid they'll upset the people she loves."

"Dear God, did she say what those things were?" The possibilities are positively mind numbing.

"No, but I have to confess to being a little nervous, myself. That woman was a force of nature before the aneurysm. I can't imagine her upping her game."

I shudder at the thought. Then I smile up at Sam. "I spent some time in the loft today."

"Without me?" he pouts.

We truly did have some amazing times up there.

"I have some things to work through."

He starts to rub his hand up and down my arm. "What things?"

"We promised not to talk about the past, but there's something I want to tell you."

He arches his eyebrow in a question. "Lay it on me."

So, I do. I tell Sam all about Ethan's diagnosis and how he's getting help in hopes of winning me back. He doesn't say anything for a long time. He finally replies, "ASD isn't thought to be something that can be fixed. It's one of those things people are taught to live with. Ethan has already developed all kinds of behaviors and tricks to cope in the world. Some might think he's already gone as far as he can."

"Are you saying that from a medical standpoint or because you don't want me to go back to him?"

He shrugs. "I guess both, but the prognosis is real. It's not something I'm making up to win a game. Ethan is obviously highly functioning to be successful in the workplace. I'm not sure how much more his brain is going to be willing to change."

"And what do you think about him wanting to win me back?"

Sam looks deeply into my eyes. "I think he'd be stupid not to. Do you want to tell me what made you move out and come back to Gelson?"

I nod my head. "I really do, but I'm afraid I'm being disloyal by sharing that with you."

He smiles understandingly. "You're a faithful person, Miss Kitty, and I respect you for it. But know this, I'm not going to quit trying to win you for myself, just because Ethan is facing an uncomfortable reality about himself. I had nothing to do with him being born different, and I'm not handing over the woman I love without a fight."

My mouth goes dry. "The woman you love? How can you say that so soon? You don't even know me anymore."

"So soon?" he demands. "We've been in each other's lives since we were little kids. I loved you as a friend before I ever loved you as a woman. I've loved you forever, Cat, and I'm not going to stop." He takes a deep breath. "Are you thinking about going back to Ethan?"

"I don't know. I was content with him. It seems pretty low of me not to even consider it, especially now that he's going through so much. I was planning on marrying him less than a month ago. What does it say about my commitment to him for me to just drop him?"

"It doesn't say anything about your commitment, Cat. All it says is that you knew it was better to get out before it was too late. Couples break up all the time before they get married, and quite honestly that's the time to do it if you aren't right for each other. You don't want to wait until after you have children."

I retaliate, "Like how you broke up with me, when we didn't have anything to lose?"

He sighs deeply. "I don't think our situation was anything like yours and Ethan's. We were kids. We didn't even know what we wanted out of life, yet. You and Ethan are adults and you went into your relationship knowing things about yourselves that we never did at seventeen."

He gently lifts me up and slides me onto his lap. "Cat, I'm more serious about you right now than I've ever been about anything else in my life. My feelings for you aren't insta-love or love at first sight. What I feel has grown and developed over my lifetime." He adds, "Even though we didn't see each other for years, you've always been with me."

Then he puts his arms around me and draws me toward him. I'm on top, so I can pull away if I want to, but I don't want to. I feel the gentle caress of Sam's breath before his lips even touch mine. The first contact is so sweet and tender I want it to last forever. Then suddenly, it's not. It turns hot and wild and totally out of control and I realize my attraction for him is just as strong as it's ever been, quite possibly stronger.

If I had to choose who I wanted to be with right now, at this moment, there would be no contest. The boy who stole my heart before breaking my heart, is coming very close to owning it.

When Decisions are Made

After Sam and Dad put up the lights, we all go outside to praise their hard work. They've hung a giant wreath above the barn doors and another over the garage. They framed the second story in dangling white icicle lights, which I'm not sure how they managed in the dark. The large maple tree in front of the house is wrapped in red and white lights like a candy cane, and the bushes are twinkling with colored lights. Magical doesn't quite cover it.

Nan claps her hands together and squeals, "It's fecking awesome!"

I give her a look that suggests she watch her potty mouth. She just sticks her tongue out at me and grumbles, "I'm old enough to curse if I want."

My mom is in near raptures, as well. "It's just like it used to be when the kids were little!"

When Travis and I were young, we used to come out front at night when the Christmas lights were lit and run around in circles. We'd make snow angels and pretend the snowman was going to come alive and lead us in a parade. The memory is a wonderful one. It makes me hope that whatever my brother is doing, he's doing well. He was always full of such unrealized potential. I'm glad he's making an attempt to take charge of his life.

Mom makes us a little drink called Highlander Cocoa when we go in, which is just hot chocolate with a shot of scotch. Dad builds a fire and we all sit around the Christmas tree in harmony. When the fire is burning brightly, he picks up his mug and lifts it in a toast. "We're happy to have you home, Nan. It's going to be a very merry Christmas, indeed."

Nan smiles in return and mumbles something under her breath that sounds like, "Let's hope you still think so in a few days."

No one breaks the magical moment by asking any questions. Historically, when Nan thinks she's going to upset someone, she usually does. If there's any subtlety in that woman, it's yet to be discovered.

Sam and I sit on either side of my grandmother. He drapes his arm around her and runs his fingers lightly up my neck. His touch is electric and it's all I can do to keep from melting. I miss being touched. I know Ethan has real issues about physical contact, but I don't. I'm like a kitten. I'd be happy to always be curled up on someone's lap getting petted.

Mags toasts, "Thank you all for everything you've done to make this Christmas season the best ever." She turns to Nan. "We all love you, Mom. We're so happy you're home."

An hour later, it's nearly eleven and Sam announces, "I have to be at the hospital early tomorrow. I better get going."

"Why don't you spend the night?" Nan invites. "I'm sure the couch in the basement is comfortable." She does this with an eyebrow shrug and a huge wink for emphasis.

"Thanks, Nan, but I think I'm destined for my own bed tonight. It's been a long day."

He stands up and reaches for my hand to walk him out. Once we're on the porch, he nearly shouts, "Thanks for the great day, Cat. I'll see you soon!" Then he tilts his head to indicate the side of the house.

I step back before bending forward to see what he's pointing at. There, at the living room window, are three faces pressed to the glass trying to see what's going on.

I yell back, "I'll just walk you to your car to make sure you get there safely!" Inside we hear three sets of footsteps scurry through the entry hall toward the staircase. Those Nosey Nellies are running upstairs to get a better view of the driveway.

"They've been doing that since high school," Sam laughs under his breath. "You'd think they'd have caught on by now."

Without further ado he pins me to the side of the house and takes ownership of my mouth in a way that leaves me panting for more. The fire starts burning at my toes and quickly makes its way to more private places. When he finally steps back, the cold air rushes between us like an assault. Sam warns, "When I stay the night, Miss Kitty, I won't be sleeping on the couch." Then he turns and saunters to his car like the last man standing in a gun battle.

Between you, me, and the fencepost, my dreams are filled with what Sam will be doing when he's not sleeping on the couch, and for the first time in a long time, my body and mind start to hum with possibility. I'm full of anticipation for the future.

Dead Mice and Other Surprises

Waking up in bed after another night dreaming of Sam, I realize I've made my decision. I don't want my life to be full of lukewarm embraces and anxiety over whether my red afghan is going to set Ethan off. I wish him the best and truly want him to find happiness, but that's not going to be with me.

I don't know what the future holds for me and Sam, but I want to explore all the possibilities with him, every single spine-tingling one of them. I decide to get through the party Saturday night before calling Ethan and telling him.

I've hired a couple of high school girls, on Sarah's recommendation, to help serve hors d' oeuvres and keep things picked up. My friend knows these kids through a class she teaches at the community center on organics and is hiring them to work in her café when it opens in the summer.

When the night of the party finally arrives, we're all in fine form. The stockings are hung by the chimney with care, the pantry has been alphabetized in case some busybody bothers to notice, and dead mice are hanging from the chandelier in the entry hall. Check, check, check, we're ready to party!

Nan takes one look at me and whistles under her breath.

"Somebody's ready to have a good time!" I have on a black cocktail dress that hits right above the knee. It's elegant and understated, except for the fact the entire back drapes down below my waist. It's all business from the front and party from the back.

My dad is in his traditional Scottish dress; Nan wears her plaid, as well; but Mom has gone off script and is adorned in a long, red, Hawaiian Christmas dress that's decorated with palm trees covered in Christmas lights, hula dancers, and hibiscus flowers with tiny Santa Clauses in the center. It makes a statement, that's for sure.

I'm on door duty and Sarah is our first guest to arrive. She's wearing an elf hat, but she doesn't look happy to be here. I greet her with, "Merry Christmas, Sar!"

She grabs my hand, leans in, and rapid-fire whispers in my ear, "I'm so sorry, Cat. I didn't realize who she was when she made the reservation and I invited her to your party. When she checked in, I realized my mistake, but it was too late to disinvite her."

I have no idea what my friend is talking about until she steps aside, and I see the woman standing behind her. It's Ethan's mother, Natalie.

I'm speechless. What in the heck is Ethan's mom doing staying at Sarah's B&B over Christmas? I know she claimed to be leaving Jason, but I never expected her to really do it. Finally, I manage to ask, "Natalie, what are you doing here?"

She hugs me. "I hope you don't mind. I don't want to spend Christmas with my family this year. I needed to get away and when I started thinking about where to go, I remembered Sarah's darling B&B and it just felt right."

"I don't have to stay if it's too uncomfortable for you," she offers before I have a chance to reply.

It's plenty weird, that's for sure, but I think I can manage seeing her for one night. I welcome her in and send her off with Sarah to say hello to my parents. I'm too much of a chicken to take her myself.

The next guests arrive in a steady stream after that. Mrs. Bernhardt, the town librarian, is the only one who screams when she sees the mice hanging above her head. Everyone else seems to take it as par for the course with my parents.

When Sam arrives, he pulls me off into a quiet corner to greet me properly. He's particularly delighted by my backless dress and finds every opportunity he can to touch my bare skin. It's a delicious torture. While I'm still locked in his embrace, he croons, "I'm taking your choice of dress as an invitation to caress you."

I don't disabuse him of that notion. I just smile coyly, "Merry Christmas, Sam." Then I add, "Ethan's mom came with Sarah."

He jumps back. "What?! Why? How?"

I give him the elevator version of the story. He doesn't quite know how to respond. "She warned you not to marry Ethan, so she obviously knows we still have feelings for each other."

I nod. "That would be a good guess. Be sensitive, okay?"

"Of course. I mean, sure. I mean, God, I don't know what I mean, but I promise to be nice."

I know he will be, but it's still good to hear. I'm hoping there are no more big surprises tonight, but with the way things have started out, I'm not holding my breath.

Mystery Guests

At eight o'clock, the party is in full swing. Spirits are flowing like water and food is consumed as if it's being devoured by a pack of starving wolves. All signs point to it being a very successful gathering.

At eight twenty—I know this because the grandfather clock chimes ten minutes before the hour and half hour, a tribute to my father's ability to fix things— a rather striking woman walks in. She's got gorgeous red hair all done up in a french twist and is wearing a green cocktail dress, showcasing alarmingly muscular calves. Her fingernails look like red daggers. I have no idea who she is, but she's so dazzling it's hard to look away.

Nan greets her warmly with a hug and kiss, so I assume she's someone my grandmother has picked up in her travels. God knows where, though, because Nan doesn't travel. I temporarily forget the mystery guest while I chat with people I've known my whole life.

Jessica Handler is here with her parents. She and I were in the same class at school. I offer her a drink and say, "It's nice to see you, Jess. What have you been up to these days?"

She smiles shyly. "Just working at the flower shop on Main

Street." She adds, "I was in Waterloo until my dad had a heart attack a few years ago. I decided to move

home and help my folks. I never left."

I nod my head knowingly. "I've been in New York City for the last decade, but I'm in the same boat. Nan just got out of the hospital and I suddenly feel like it's time for me to come home for a while."

Sam joins us and wraps his arm around me. "Jess, it's nice to see you!"

"You too, Doc." Then she looks between us, "It looks like you two have found each other again."

I glance up at Sam. "You could say that." Before the conversation can progress, I spy the redheaded woman in different clothes. This time, she's wearing a gold sequin dress and her hair is down. I briefly wonder if it's the same person, but those calves are a giveaway, unless she's a twin—which is an alarming thought. One of those creatures is an anomaly, two would be downright miraculous.

Nan is still at her side, introducing her to different people. I announce to Sam and Jessica, "I need to go check something in the kitchen, if you'll excuse me."

I walk straight toward my grandmother, but by the time I get to her, the strange woman is nowhere to be seen. "Nan, who were just talking to?"

She looks confused. "Mrs. Gilford?"

"No, not her. Who's the tall, red-haired woman?"

Nan looks uncomfortable. "Oh, her? She's no one, just a friend from bingo."

That woman at bingo would cause a stir I'd like to see. I don't believe Nan for a minute, but I don't pursue it. Instead, I ask, "Are you having fun?"

"I sure am, honey. How about you?"

I confirm I'm having a good time, as well. "I was just on my way into the kitchen. Can I get you anything before I go?"

My grandmother shakes her head. "Nope. I'm good." I give her a little squeeze before heading to check on the food situation.

When I get to the kitchen, the hired help seem to have everything in order. I'm about to walk back to the living room when I catch a glimpse of gold swishing through the door to the basement. We've opened the downstairs to the party. With over sixty people in the house, we needed more room to keep the flow.

I decide to follow the unidentified woman downstairs to introduce myself to her. But Martha Simms, an old friend of Nan's, corners me to tell me about her rheumatism and asks if I have the name of Travis's pot dealer. She's heard the MaryJane is good for pain.

"Sorry, Mrs. Simms, I don't know who my brother's supplier was." Then I offer, "Maybe I can get you an ibuprofen?"

"No, dear, thank you, though. I need something that'll pack more of a wallop."

As soon as I disengage from the drug-seeking octogenarian, I look for the redhead again, but can't find her anywhere.

Just When You Think It Can't Get Any Weirder

At ten pm, my dad brings out his bagpipes. I cringe knowing what comes next. I wish my brother were here to protect us all from the forthcoming assault to our eardrums. Dad stands by the Christmas tree and announces it's time for the entertainment. The people who haven't heard him play yet look on with anticipation. Those of us who know better refill our glasses.

As soon as he begins "Greensleeves," the doorbell rings.

I make my way across the room and Sam wraps an arm around my waist to join me. When we get to the entryway, he maneuvers me under the mistletoe and dead mice for a quick kiss. Then he grabs the doorknob and opens it. While one might guess it's Jolly Old St. Nick on the other side, it's not. It's none other than Ethan.

My mouth hangs open like I'm seeing a ghost. The first words to fall out of it aren't a welcome. "What are you doing here?"

The smile on his face disappears when he sees Sam's arm around me. "I thought I'd surprise you. I thought I'd show you I was learning to be spontaneous."

Sam, who you'd think would remove his hold on me out of deference to Ethan's feelings, does no such thing. Instead he pulls me closer and welcomes, "Come on in, Ethan. The drinks are in the dining room."

I push Sam away and suggest, "Why don't you go fetch us all a great big one?"

I don't take Ethan's coat. Instead, I grab my own out of the closet and drag him outside. A party is no place for what's coming. He looks so sad when he asks, "So, you've replaced me already?"

"Ethan," I begin, but I don't really know how to continue. I finally settle on, "Sam and I were together throughout high school. We have a history."

"So, do we," he responds.

"Yes, we do," I agree. "But our history needs to remain such. Ethan, I love you. I really do, but I'm not in love with you."

"We were engaged."

"True, but I think I agreed to marry you in order to live a drama-free life. When I got home from Thanksgiving, I realized I needed more. I was giving up a lot of myself to accommodate you and what you wanted. I can't live like that anymore."

"But I'm getting help," he pleads. "I came all the way here without even planning it first. I only had ninety-eight minutes from the time I booked my ticket to catch my flight. Surely, that shows I'm making headway."

My heart hurts so badly for him. "Ethan, I'm thrilled you're trying to help yourself. I really am, but it's too late for us. I don't want to live in New York anymore. I want to be here with my family. I don't want to worry whether something I'm doing is making you uncomfortable. I can't go back to that." I ask, "Were you planning on staying here?"

He nods his head in affirmation. So, I add, "I don't think that's going to work. But why don't you come in? There's someone here you need to see and I'm pretty sure you can stay with her."

I lead Ethan back inside and take his coat. Then I take his hand and lead him into the other room to find his mother.

The Unwelcome Guest

Natalie is not happy to see her son. "What are you doing here, Ethan?" she demands.

"What am *I* doing here?" His arms start to twitch. "What are *you* doing here?"

"I've checked myself into Sarah's bed and breakfast through the New Year."

He seems stunned. "You're going to stay in a yurt in the middle of a corn field, in the middle of winter for two weeks, leaving your husband alone for the holidays?"

"I thought the two of you would be together," she replies.

"I had, as well, but things aren't going very well in my own life right now. I need to focus on those."

"Ethan, I don't want to live like I was living anymore. There's got to be more to life than what your father and I have, and I want to discover it before it's too late."

"Why don't you try to discover it with Dad?" His feet shift from side-to-side like the floor keeps moving beneath him. This is obviously a very uncomfortable conversation for him and it's manifesting in physical behaviors.

Natalie's face is so flushed she looks almost magenta.

"Because he's not interested! I've pleaded with him for years to try new things and go to new places, but he never wants to. I've decided if I'm ever going to have the experiences I desire, I'm going to have go after them on my own."

I slip away when Ethan begins to tell his mother about his diagnosis. I don't think I should be around for that conversation. It's no longer my place. I decide to go downstairs and try to collect my thoughts. I feel horrible for Ethan, but I'm also relieved to have told him how I feel. At some point I'll offer him my friendship, even though I'm not sure he'll accept it.

Sarah is fast on my heels as I descend the stairs. "Holy hell! What's *he* doing here?"

I exhale loudly, "He's here to prove to me how much he's changing. He wanted to surprise me."

"Well, damn, he succeeded there. Where's he staying?"

I clear my throat. "As to that …" I pause out of trepidation. "He thought he would stay here, but clearly that won't work. I was hoping he could stay with his mom at your place."

She shakes her head. "The yurt she booked only has one bed and all the other ones are taken through Christmas Eve."

Trying to gather my courage, I finally ask, "Are your parents still in Florida?"

"Yup. They'll be there until March."

I boldly forge ahead, "Any chance he can stay in the house with you?"

My friend's mouth hangs open, then closes, and finally opens again. "You have got to be kidding me. You want your rude ex-boyfriend to stay with me, in my house, after the way he treated me?"

"I know it's a lot to ask, Sar, but I'm sure he'll only stay for a day or two. Now that he knows I'm not going to get back together with him, there's nothing keeping him here."

She rolls her eyes. "If I agree to this—and it's a big if—you're going to owe me."

"I'd agree to just about anything right now. There's no way he can stay here. Talk about awkward."

"Fine," she concedes. "Let's go tell him before I change my mind." She none-too-gently grabs my arm and drags me in her wake.

When we reach Ethan, he looks pretty strung out. I smile tentatively. "Sarah says you can stay in her house with her while you're visiting your mom. She doesn't have any other yurts available right now."

He looks at me hopefully, but when I shake my head to indicate he will not be staying here, and I meant what I said about not taking him back, he turns to my friend and graciously accepts, "Thank you, Sarah. I'm very appreciative of your hospitality. Of course, I'll pay the going rate."

"You got that right," she replies. Then she walks away so as not to have to endure another moment of awkwardness.

Ethan turns to me. "Catriona, Cat, if you change your mind, I will always welcome you back."

"Oh, Ethan, don't say that. I'm not going to change my mind. Our ship has sailed. I want you to find someone else to share your life with. I don't want you holding on to false hope as far as I'm concerned." I want to reach out and comfort him, but I don't dare as he might see it as a sign that I'm wavering. Which I'm absolutely not doing.

"I don't want to live without you," he says pleadingly.

"You don't have to. I'd like for us to stay friends, but only friends."

"I'll take it," he agrees. "That doesn't mean I won't still be hopeful. You're the only person who's ever made me feel somewhat normal."

I take his hands in mine. "Merry Christmas, Ethan. I hope the New Year is full of wonderful new things for you."

He tries to smile, but he looks so lost. Life gives, it takes away, it breaks hearts, and brings new loves. One thing is for sure, these past few weeks have been packed with more surprises than I ever expected. I hope they're finished because I'm not sure I can handle any more.

Bleeding Ears and Bagpipes

When my dad starts to play "Highland Laddie," Nan makes her way across the living room to stop him. "For the love of God, Dougal, my ears are going to start bleeding any minute now! I think you'd best take a break."

My dad appears to be slightly offended, but he tries to shrug it off by announcing to his guests, "I'm just going to go get a wee glass of water."

The crowd applauds politely. I'm guessing more out of relief than in appreciation of his talents. The redheaded stranger walks into the room and approaches Nan. She's changed dresses, again. This time she's in a red number with a Masterton plaid silk scarf around her neck. The slit on her skirt is high enough to indicate her thighs are just as impressive as her calves.

Nan embraces her and says something that clearly upsets her. The stranger shakes her head and Nan stomps her foot in response. Before I can guess what's next, my grandmother moves to the front of the fireplace and whistles like she's trying to hail a taxi cab in Times Square during rush hour.

Everyone stops talking immediately. "I have a dear friend and relative I'd like to introduce you all to," she announces. Then she throws her arm out toward the lady in red. "I'd like you all to meet Rhona." She doesn't offer any more information than that.

Rhona hesitantly joins Nan amid the approval of our guests. "Rhona plays the bagpipes like a dream, and she'd like to regale you with a couple of numbers."

While I have no idea how we're related to Rhona, I'm delighted for her to take over for my dad. If he'd kept playing much longer, people were going to start leaving in droves.

The mysterious Rhona picks up the pipes to prepare herself. The crowd is quiet in anticipation of hearing the instrument played well. They don't have long to wait. The mystery woman begins the haunting strains of "Amazing Grace." The hair on my arms immediately stands on end. This chick knows what she's doing.

People from all over the house make their way into the living room and foyer for the concert. The tune is as beautiful as I've ever heard. It's played with a depth of feeling that is nothing short of profound.

When she's done, Rhona moves into "Eibli Geal Ciuin Ni Cearhaill," which is a Gaelic number that translates to "Bright Quiet Eileen O'Carroll." Then she plays" "Auld Lang Syne."

Everyone is positively enthralled by her performance. When people start to sing along, my parents walk into the room together. Their eyes are transfixed on their guest. My poor dad, he'll never be able to play for this crowd again, now that they've heard how it's supposed to be done.

They continue toward the woman who's performing one of their favorite songs, like she's an angel fallen from heaven. When the last note is played, Rhona puts the pipes down and looks at my parents before she hangs her head. They obviously know each other.

I feel like the whole room is a bunch of voyeurs, myself included, like we're witnessing a very private scene not meant for our eyes. My dad sniffs, and pulls out a hanky to wipe his face, before he holds out his arms. "Son, we're so happy to have you home."

Holy crap. I look closely and wonder how I didn't see it before. Beyond her magnificent calves, it's plain as day. Rhona isn't some long lost relative. She's a very recently lost relative. She's Travis. My brother has come home for my parents' Christmas party dressed as a woman. Nothing about my history with him has prepared me for this moment. My mom throws herself at her child with happy tears coursing down her cheeks.

Both of my parents seem as surprised as I am by this new development, but there's no judgment in them for their child. They're simply delighted to have their son home. I look over at Nan, who appears darn proud of herself. She's smiling from ear to ear like her face is about to split in two.

I'm frozen in place until my dad announces, "Everyone, I'd like you to welcome our son, Travis ... err, Rhona ... home for Christmas. Isn't he, or she, a wonder on the pipes?"

Our little town is not known for their ability to incorporate change of any great magnitude. Hilda Ransom once wore a sequined tube top to a holiday party hosted by the president of the bank and it was the talk of the town for a full year after. Hilda is a woman. The tube top, while not in the height of fashion, was not particularly offensive. Hilda is an A-cup at best. In retrospect there was nothing overtly shocking about her outfit choice.

Travis, a.k.a, Rhona, is sporting a chest so large I'm guessing she's got a couple of grapefruit stuck down her dress. How did she get the better rack between the two of us?

Images click rapid-fire in my brain—Travis dropping out of college doing every drug he could get his hands on, his hiding out in the basement for the last several years. My poor brother. Nan's aneurysm seems to have sparked a courageous change in him, as well.

I push people out of the way to get to him or her, and when I do, I throw my arms around her and declare, "I'm going to need to borrow that dress."

Travis, now Rhona, picks me up as tears are unleashed for both of us. "Anytime, Cat, anytime."

While I'm sure we've just given our little town enough to gossip about for the next ten years, I think this is the best Christmas party I've ever been to. I can't wait to talk to my sibling and discover what's been going on in that head of his. Or hers.

The first thing we need to finalize is what I should call her. I would say it's confusing, but for once, things are starting to make sense. And in the meantime, it seems like we should enjoy the rest of this party before the night ends.

When the Bird Leaves the Cage

The last guest doesn't leave until one o'clock. We all turn in without having the big family discussion I assume we'll now be having over breakfast. After all, it's not every day your brother comes home as the sister you've never had.

I offer Travis the use of his old bedroom in the basement, but he says he's just as happy to sleep upstairs in my room. I don't fall asleep right away. Instead, I lie awake reliving different scenes from the night. My ex-fiancé and his mom showing up unexpectedly; my brother and his ever-changing, eye-catching new wardrobe; the mice dangling from the chandelier ... One oddity after another fills my head.

I finally close my eyes somewhere around two and sleep like the dead. The good news about sleeping in the basement is there isn't a window in the downstairs bedroom, so no light comes pouring in at the crack of dawn—or eight, being that it's winter. I sleep until one p.m. and when my eyes finally pop open, it takes more than a few minutes to gather my bearings.

Questions like *Where am I? What day is it?* and *What in the hell happened last night?* pop into my head.

When I finally haul my butt out of bed and up the stairs, the kitchen is empty. Even the coffee in the coffee pot has been cooked down to dregs. I start a new one, pour myself a bowl of cold cereal, and sit down to take stock of everything.

I've successfully broken all romantic ties with Ethan, which is a load off my back. I'll make a point to talk to him before he goes back to New York. It's the least I can do. I feel like I was treading water the two years we were together, slowly and steadily using all my energy to just keep myself from drowning. Then fatigue set in and I couldn't keep my head above water any longer.

I didn't even know I felt that way until I stepped onto shore. Shore being Gelson, of course.

Travis walks in as I pour my first cup of caffeinated wonder. He's wearing a pink silky robe but doesn't have his wig or makeup on. His nails are still red and claw-like. The whole picture is a bit jarring. I ask, "Can I pour you a cup?"

"Yes, please." Then he sits down to join me.

I put a mug in front of him before plopping in the chair across from him. "Want to fill me in on what's happening?"

"Yeah, I do." After a few moments of silence, he asks, "Remember when we watched *The Birdcage* when we were little?"

I do remember. I was eleven and Travis was eight. Nathan Lane positively took our breath away. "Best movie, ever."

"It is," he agrees. "Do you remember what I did after we watched it?"

I smile as the image pops into my head. My brother ran upstairs and found Mom's highest heels, then he strapped them on and proceeded to effortlessly prance around the house. "I sure do. You were a natural in those shoes! I used to be so jealous because I couldn't even shuffle two steps in them without falling over."

"That movie changed my life. I watched those men transform themselves into women and I wanted to do the same thing with everything in me. I used to lock myself in the bathroom for hours and practice putting on makeup."

"Is that what you were doing in there? We used to worry you were going to hurt yourself," I tease, implying there was something a bit more sordid going on than that.

He laughs. "Well, yeah, that too, but I was mostly learning how to put on false eyelashes and contour my face, so it was more feminine."

"Why didn't you ever tell us?"

"I didn't know how," he answers. "I've lived in this little town my whole life and the only time I ever saw a man in drag was at Halloween and then it was always a big joke. I didn't know how to express that I wanted to dress like that in everyday life. I couldn't imagine anyone taking me seriously."

I ask the obvious question. "Are you gay?"

He shakes his head. "Not even a little bit. Not that I think people can be a little bit gay. I'm pretty sure you either are or you're not."

"You just want to dress like a woman." When he nods in confirmation, I ask, "All the time or just some of the time?"

"I'm not sure yet. Up until a few weeks ago, I never dressed like one in public. I'm just now experiencing the freedom of expressing myself the way I've always wanted to."

"You should have told us. We're the weirdest family in town. Dad has worn a kilt since we were kids."

"Oh, believe me, I know. I used to take a lot of ribbing at school from the guys about that." He adds, "And wearing a kilt is a manly thing. Imagine how they would have reacted if I'd upped the game by dressing in sequins."

"Who cares about them? Did you really think *we'd* judge you?"

He shrugs his shoulders. "I guess I was just hoping it was a phase and one day I'd wake up and be normal."

"A phase that's lasted the majority of your life?" Then I ask, "How did Nan find out?"

He explains, "She came downstairs one day while I was posting on my YouTube channel. She watched me without letting on she was in the room."

"You have a YouTube channel? What do you do on it?"

"I teach men how to dress in drag." Then he says, "I know you think I've just been living off Mom and Dad all these years. But truly, I've mostly been paying my own way."

"How do they think you've been making money?" Because I know for sure, my parents have been concerned over my brother's apparent lack of focus.

"I'm pretty sure they think I'm a drug dealer. They've never come right out and asked me, but really, what else could they think?"

I have about a thousand more questions, but my most immediate one is, "What's your new job?"

"Most of the money I make on my channel comes from cosmetic companies for mentioning their products. One of those companies is starting a line of theatrical makeup. They've brought me on board to teach them what kind of cosmetics would be needed. Basically, I just go to work every day as a man and let them watch me transform myself into a woman. Then I help them transform other men. The thinking being if the makeup is strong enough to work on a man, it'll work on anyone."

"Where is this? Where are you living?"

"Chicago. I was considering their offer when Nan got sick. The day that happened, I called the CEO and accepted the job."

I'm kind of speechless. Here I thought my brother was a deadbeat loser for the last decade and it turns out he's been doing okay for himself in a field he's never felt he could tell anyone about. It's an odd twist for sure, but not a bad one.

"What do I call you? Travis or Rhona?"

"When I'm in drag," he answers, "call me Rhona. When I'm not, call me Travis. Does that work?"

"What about when you're half and half like now?" I indicate his female dressing gown and make-up free face.

"Call me anything you want. I'm just glad that you all finally know my secret."

I get up and give my brother a giant hug. "I'm so proud of you, Travis. And I'm glad you're finally letting us share your life with you."

He hugs me back. "Thanks, Cat. I'm grateful to be a part of the weirdest family in town." In that moment I feel real pride that my family marches to their own tune, regardless of societal norms. How boring to be like everyone else when that isn't what your heart wants.

We all sit down to a family dinner with Rhona later that afternoon, and my parents beam with joy and relief that their son isn't a drug dealer.

"Rhona," my mom announces, "you have to promise to be home for Christmas."

She agrees and declares, "Wait until you see what I bought to wear!" We're all abuzz at the possibilities.

My family is a marvel. They had the hardest time accepting Ethan, who in their eyes, was stuffy, boring, and entirely too buttoned-up. But my brother comes home in a dress and they don't even blink an eye.

Hocus-Pocus and Other Woo-Woo Rubbish

Now that the big Christmas party is over, I'm not quite sure what to do with myself. There's nothing looming over me. Yes, I eventually have to figure out what to do for employment, but I'm trying to make it through the new year without feeling the need to make plans.

A new way of life in my post-Ethan existence.

I resolve to drive out to Sarah's to see how she's doing with the Crenshaws. I feel bad about forcing her to shelter my ex. I know he's not her cup of tea, and I'm sure she can't wait to get rid of him. The least I can do is check on her and see if she needs anything.

I'm not sure what to expect when I knock on her front door, but I don't expect to open it and find Ethan and his mother sitting on the floor under an open-sided copper pyramid with Sarah burning a wand of dried sage around them.

When my friend spots me, she puts her fingers to her lips to indicate I shouldn't make any noise and interrupt whatever's going on. She's speaking in soothing tones to them, "All of the bad energy surrounding you is being cleansed away. The negative thoughts, fear of change, inability to be flexible, all the things that are imprisoning your chi. Release that which is weighing you and your spirit down. Let go of the obstacles keeping you from experiencing the life you were meant to live."

I expect Ethan to open his eyes at any moment and demand Sarah quit talking nonsense. But he doesn't. Instead, he seems rather content and peaceful. He's not even complaining about all the smoke. Sarah continues, "I want you to continue to sit in the pyramid of enlightenment and visualize the toxic energy leaving your body. I'll be back in a few minutes." Then she signals for me to follow her.

Back on her front porch I start to laugh. "What are you doing to them?"

She shoots me a dirty look. "I'm opening their minds to the possibilities of life. They're both so locked up by anxiety and fear, they've completely closed themselves down. Their chakras are so dark, neither of them has an obvious third eye anymore."

It's no wonder Sarah and I became friends. There isn't a normal bone in her body, which is apparently something I attract. "Yes, well, how in the world did you get them to go along with your little exorcism?"

"Natalie is actively looking to enact change in her life. She's open to almost anything I suggest. Maybe not the naked snow roll, but almost everything else."

I want to ask what the naked snow roll is, but honestly, I'm kind of afraid of the answer. So, I say, "I can see where it might be too soon for that. But what about Ethan? This is so not his thing. He thinks this kind of stuff is just a bunch of hocus-pocus and woo-woo rubbish—his words, not mine."

My friend shrugs her shoulders. "He was really shaken up last night when he got to your house to find you and Sam were together. He's pretty raw and he's really questioning a lot right now. I assured him this was the perfect time to really capitalize on change, if he's serious about doing it. I offered my services while he's here."

"Your services?" I ask. "I thought you just gave people a place to stay and fed them breakfast. What else do you do?"

"SO much more!" she exclaims. "I read their auras and help pinpoint problem areas, then I recommend dietary changes and do guided meditations. I'm pretty good at reading their tarot cards, as well."

"Sar, Ethan isn't just buttoned up and rigid. He's not that way out of spite. He was just diagnosed with autism spectrum disorder. It makes a lot of sense when you think about it. Did he tell you that?"

She tips her head back and forth. "I don't really put too much stock in those medical diagnoses. Western medicine is famous for coming up with umbrella mumbo jumbo to cover a bunch of things they don't understand."

"Ooookay. What do you suggest Ethan does to help himself?"

She smiles excitedly. "First of all, he needs to purify his body from all animal products. He needs to go vegan for a full two weeks before he can do that. It will bring his vibration back into alignment, which will blow open his mind to change."

"Sarah, I don't want to rain on your parade, but there is no way Ethan is going to become a vegan for two weeks. He might last the rest of the day, or however much longer he's staying here, but as soon as he gets home, he's going to go right back to his own routine." I share, "He can barely eat if the food varies too much from his set menu."

"That's what he said. So, I convinced him to stay through the New Year with his mom. I'm working out separate therapies for them, as well as joint ones like the pyramid meditation."

"What? Why? You don't even like Ethan. He barely tolerates you. Why would you want to help him?"

"Cat, the people who need the most help are often the most obnoxious. It's my duty as an enlightened soul to help shed light for the troubled. How is this world ever going to evolve into something beautiful if we don't reach out our hands to those in need?"

"But you can't stand him," I accuse. "You were mad that I even asked you to let him stay here."

"I can see where you might have gotten that impression. But just because I'm enlightened doesn't mean I'm perfect. My spirit guide came to me last night in my sleep and set me straight. She told me if I don't share my talents for the good, my light will start to dim, and my vibration will decrease. I don't want that to happen."

If I didn't look like a Masterton so darn much, I might start to wonder if my parents and Sarah's had mixed us up as infants. Like they went to the same party and let people hold their babies and then never noticed when the wrong one was handed back to them.

All I can do is shake my head and say, "Good luck to you. Let me know if you need any help finding either one of them when they run off screaming." Hopefully not when they're stark naked after a snow roll.

Vegan Vacation

After leaving Sarah's, I drive to the hospital to see Sam. The nurse at the front desk pages him while I wait in the lounge. When he shows up, he has a huge smile on his face. "You came to see me at work!"

I laugh. "Is it that shocking?"

"Kind of. It just seems like a giant step for you to make considering you keep telling me how slowly we have to take things."

"I do want to take things slowly, but now that I've told Ethan it's over once and for all, well, I guess maybe we can speed up a tiny bit."

"You ready to set the date, then?" he jokes.

Pretending ignorance, I ask, "For what?"

Sam pulls me to my feet and wraps me in a bear hug. I feel right at home in his arms like they were designed just for me. "Miss Kitty, we belong together and we're eventually going to make things official. I know it's too soon right now, but one day it won't be and we're going to run off together and live happily ever after."

"That sounds like a dream come true. But for the moment, do you have time for a cup of coffee?"

He looks at his watch and replies, "I do. Just let me alert the nurses' station where I'm going."

When we get settled in the hospital cafeteria, I tell Sam that Ethan's staying in town through the New Year. I expect him to be irritated, but he surprises me. "If he's staying with Sarah, that's probably not a bad idea."

"What? Really? Why?"

"I went through Sarah's boot camp after I moved back to Gelson. I even lived out there in one of her yurts while I was doing it. I did the whole clean living, meditation, vegan diet thing. I never felt better."

"Really?" I just can't see it. "But you're a doctor. She was just telling me she doesn't buy a lot of Western medicine mumbo jumbo. I thought you guys might not see eye-to-eye on a lot of stuff."

He shakes his head. "Just because I practice Western medicine doesn't mean I buy all the mumbo jumbo, either. For instance, I'm not a fan of prescribing drugs for things that should be handled on a more holistic level. When a patient comes to me with high cholesterol, I tell them how to modify their diet and order them to start exercising. Some doctors just give people drugs right away and don't address the effects the patient's lifestyle has on their health."

"Where do you stand on meditation?"

"I'm all for it," he answers. "Calming the mind is extremely healing when you consider what a killer stress is. It wouldn't surprise me if anxiety is a big issue for Ethan. Meditation, mindfulness, and even aromatherapy are all effective ways to deal with it. I think it could be very good for him." His eyes widen like he's just had an idea. "I'll tell you what, as soon as Ethan and his mom go home, I'll take some time off work and we can do a retreat out there ourselves. It'll be fun."

"Is this your way of getting me to go away with you?"

He winks. "Maybe." But then adds, "In all seriousness, Sarah's really good at this stuff. She didn't even tell me about what she does; I read about it in *Chicago* magazine and thought, why not?"

"I had no idea. I thought she just had a B&B and sold organic produce. She never mentioned anything else."

"Nope, there's a lot more to her than that. In some circles she's considered a miracle worker. I've even sent patients to her boot camp who I think could benefit from a lifestyle makeover."

I'm shocked. "You prescribe it?"

"No, but I recommend it. Change is hard for people who are set in their ways. Having someone prepare healthy meals and show you how to do it for yourself, having someone talk to you about the benefits involved in calming your mind and caring for all aspects of your life—it's pretty incredible."

I'm going to have to think more about this. My friend has a lot more going on than I ever gave her credit for. I'm kind of excited to see what she does firsthand. Not until Ethan and his mother leave though, which I kind of hope is sooner rather than later.

Destination Barn Dance

When I get back to my parents' farm, I don't go inside. Instead, I sit out on the front porch and try to still my mind. If I stay in Gelson, I need to figure out what I'm going to do here. I know I said I'd wait until after the New Year to even think about it, but I'm just not a person who can sit still without knowing what direction I'm headed.

No grand ideas are coming to me, so I decide to take my question to the barn rafters. They haven't failed me yet. I grab a blanket out of the old tack room before climbing up to the loft. I set up the army cot, lie down, and bundle myself up. Then I ask, "Okay, God, rafters, whoever's listening—what the heck am I going to do with myself in this little town in the middle of nowhere?"

I stare at the ceiling for so long, I fall asleep. It feels like I drop into some kind of alternate universe. I see the barn completely transformed. It's clean and free of clutter. On the main floor there are three chandeliers hanging from the center beam. Round tables, set with linen and fine china occupy half the space, while the other half has a stage for a band and a dance floor. There are people everywhere dressed elegantly in gowns and suits. I'd call the overall look rustic chic. It's positively gorgeous!

Then the scene shifts to show the main area sporting bales of hay surrounding picnic tables. Saddles are used for seating along with wooden benches and stools. Fiddlers play country music and people square dance in merry circles. This would fall under the category of a good, old-fashioned barn dance.

Different images keep popping into my mind and I realize this barn, while no longer housing the trappings of a working farm, still has a lot of life left in it. I could take a page out of Sarah's book and advertise country-themed weddings to people in Chicago. Maybe she and I could team up and I could send revelers to her farm to rent yurts to make this destination idea more marketable to the city crowd. Our closest hotel is about twenty-five minutes away, and that's probably too far for most people. Sarah's farm is seven minutes away, which seems perfect.

When my eyes pop open, I can't wait to run my idea by my parents. I know the farm has been getting to be more work than they want. Maybe turning a profit on it again will be enticing enough for them to jump on board.

As soon as I get into the house, I call for my mom and dad to meet me in the kitchen. Then I go there myself only to find them already sitting at the table. They're drinking tea and my dad announces, "Beat you!"

I chuckle. "Smarty pants. Listen, I want to talk to you guys about something." The look on my mom's face is as serious as a heart attack, so I add, "But, only if it's a good time."

"It's as good a time as any," Mags answers. "We wanted to talk to you about something, too."

I nod. "You go first."

My dad starts, "Your mom and I have been talking for a couple of years about moving into a smaller house in town. This place is a lot of work and we're getting tired of maintaining it."

"I have the perfect solution!" I interrupt. Then I rush in and explain, "I think we should rehab the barn and turn it into a party rental venue. We'd primarily advertise it for weddings, but we can do family reunions, office parties, all kinds of things."

My parents share a look that indicates they aren't too excited about my proposal. My mom finally says, "That sounds great, honey, but it also sounds like a lot of work. We're hoping to simplify our lives and free up some of our responsibilities."

"That's why we were going to tell Travis he had to leave after the New Year," my dad adds. "We want to list the house and property. There's a cute little place in town your mom has fallen in love with. If we can get our asking price here, then we can buy that place and still have a good chunk left in the bank."

"What about Nan?" I ask.

"It's a two-bedroom, two-bath house," Mags answers. "We'd take her with us."

"Does she know what you're planning?" I can't imagine my grandmother living any other place than right here.

Dad nods his head. "She does. She's not as excited about it as we are, but she's happy at the thought of not having to climb stairs anymore."

I feel totally and completely deflated. I was so sure my parents were going to love my idea and we were all going to go into business together. I have to do some quick thinking. I tell them, "I totally get it, and I'm behind you all the way. Just don't list the house until we talk about this again, okay?"

When they agree, I run up the stairs to get my laptop. I have a couple things I need to look into.

Finalizing the Future

I call Jazz before I do anything else. There's so much to catch up on, what with Sam and Ethan and all the personal life drama. Once we cover that, I find out her pregnancy is going great and that they're having a boy. I tease, "People will look at him funny with the name Catriona, but sometimes in life sacrifices have to be made."

She giggles. "I think I just peed a little."

"Way to make pregnancy look glamorous, my friend." Then I segue into my plan for my parents' barn.

Jazz screams in my ear, "Oh, my God, I LOVE that barn! What a fabulous idea!" She's quiet for a minute before adding, "Of course that means you won't be coming back to New York. Dammit."

"Jazz, I don't want to wait to have you buy me out. I want to offer to buy my parents' house, and then I can live here and rent out the barn. I should be able to swing the price because real-estate is just a fraction of the cost of what it is closer to the city. Apparently, no one wants to move here and that has a way of keeping the prices down."

"Remember when we promoted Jen to vice-president?" my friend asks.

"Yeah, what about it?"

"Well, I've recently found out that she isn't the struggling young woman we always pegged her for. It turns out she's something of an heiress. She approached me last week to ask if you were coming back. I told her I didn't know. She said if you weren't, she wants to buy your half of the business and become a full partner."

I'm so excited I can hardly stand it. "You're kidding! How do you feel about that? I mean, I know we both like her, but is she someone you can see yourself working with as a partner?"

"That's essentially how we've been working since you left for Thanksgiving," my friend answers. "While that hasn't even been a full month, it's our busiest time of year and we're getting on great. Based on our revenue, and her ability to pay cash, you should easily be able to afford your parents' place."

Sometimes life rewards you for all the crazy it puts you through. Nan's illness and breaking up with Ethan have been unexpected. Yet they've brought so much good into my life. I appreciate my family more than I ever have before, Sam is back in my world after way too many years apart, and now I'm going to start my own business in the house I grew up in. It's staggering to think about so much change in such a short period of time.

"Go ahead and offer Jen the deal," I tell Jazz. "You have all the paperwork on our value. Tell her I'll call her tomorrow to hammer out the details. And Jazz, I love you. I wish we could still see each other every day, but I've truly landed where I'm meant to be."

"Oh, Cat, I love you too. Just because our lives have separated us by a couple of states doesn't change the fact that you're my sister. You're my family and I'd do anything for you."

We talk for a few more minutes before hanging up. I promise to throw Jazz the best baby shower in the world and she threatens that I'd better. I send love to Dylan, she sends it to my family, and then we say goodbye.

Nothing has ever transpired this easily in my life. I can only hope it's because it's meant to be and not some awful cosmic setup. But even I can't imagine the universe being that cruel.

I go downstairs and get some steaks marinating for dinner. Then I throw some baked potatoes in the oven and get to work on a tossed salad. When my parents, Nan, and I sit down to eat, I announce, "I'm going to buy the farmhouse from you myself. I hereby offer you your asking price."

My mom drops her fork. "How can you afford that?"

In that moment I'm nervous I underestimated their price, so I ask, "How much are you asking?"

She gives me the number. It turns out the opposite is true. They're asking a significant amount less than I thought they would. I assure them, "I should be able to pay cash after the first of the year as long as everything moves smoothly with transferring my shares of Cat Jazz Productions to Jennifer."

"This calls for a wee dram of the Glenfiddich in celebration." my dad announces.

After we move the party to the living room, Nan sidles up next to me on the couch and asks, "Would you mind if I stayed on with you for a while?"

My mom swivels her head quickly. "Mom, we want you to come with us!"

"I thought you were tired of climbing the stairs," my dad adds.

She shakes her head. "I didn't want you to feel bad about leaving so I said that to ease your minds. I don't want to leave here, especially now that there's going to be some excitement going on."

Three sets of eyes turn expectantly in my direction. I smile bigger than I've ever smiled before. "I would love nothing more, Nan. I can't think of a better roommate than you!"

While most people might not want to room with their eighty-year-old grandmother, mine is one of the biggest reasons I came home. I'm finally going to get a chance to make up for some lost time with her and I'm going to take that time anyway I can get it.

The Next Chapter

I call Sam and tell him. "Get your butt over to my parents' house. I have some news for you."

He doesn't ask any questions, he just says, "I'll be over in ten minutes." Eight minutes later, he pulls into the driveway.

When he arrives at the front door, he looks nervous and a tad bit apprehensive. "Is everything okay?"

I grab his hand and pull him in the direction of the barn. "I want to tell you in here."

We trudge across the snow and climb up to the loft the same way we used to all those years ago. We sit facing each other like we're twelve, about to share a great secret. I announce, "Sam, I've thought long and hard about where I want to live."

He looks worried again. "Am I calling Lenox Hill back looking for a job again?"

I shake my head. "Not on my account, you aren't. I've decided I want to stay right here in Gelson. I want to be near my family as long as I have them. So, I'm going to buy my parents' house and use the barn for destination events. I'm going to stay in the party planning business. I'm just going to bring the parties to me."

He looks as happy as I feel. "Cat, that's the best news ever! Are your parents staying on with you?"

I shake my head. "No, they have their eye on a little place in town, but Nan wants to live here."

"She should. I couldn't imagine this house without her." Then he leans in until our noses are almost touching. "But let's see if we can't entice her to move to the basement apartment for privacy's sake." Then his lips are on mine claiming ownership and I hand myself over with no reservations.

Ethan is no longer part of my journey and neither is New York. My life has come full circle since I left here fourteen years ago. In that time, I grew up and faced challenges that only made me stronger. I fell in love and out of love. I made a name for myself and in the process made enough money to afford a bit of stability.

Yes, I'm trading in the excitement of big-city living for life in a small town, but I'm more than ready to make that change. The next part of my life is about family. It's about renewed love and starting over. It's all about me and what makes me happy.

Sam pulls away and says, "Welcome home, Cat."

And just like that it feels like I never left. I'm exactly where I belong.

The End

I would be SO grateful for review on Amazon! You can also leave one on Goodreads. If you want to learn about the next book in the series, please sign up for my newsletter at https://whitneydineen.com/newsletter/.

Thank you, lovely reader. I appreciate you!!

Keep reading for an excerpt from Cat and Sam's next adventure in **Relatively Sane.**

Prologue

As a kid, I had an ongoing fantasy. I'm waiting for the school bus to pick me up in front of my family farm, when a shiny black Lincoln Town Car pulls up next to me. A very attractive woman in the back seat rolls down her window and bursts into tears. She gasps, "Buffy, is that you?" (Note: I might have been enthralled with the television show, *Buffy the Vampire Slayer* at the time. I was definitely a fan of the name.) The woman and her equally handsome husband leap out of the car and throw their arms around me, engulfing me in a cloud of Chanel Number 5 and Versace Man.

Between sobs of joy, she calls to her husband, "Charles, it's our baby. It's really her!"

They tighten their embrace and I become the filling in a Pendleton wool sandwich. This wonderful, loving, perfectly ordinary couple, decked out in city clothes, explains how there was a mix-up at the hospital where I was born. Their baby and another were returned to the wrong bassinets after feeding time. They only discovered the truth when the person they thought was their daughter ran off and joined the circus as it passed through their town.

The woman says, "We knew then and there a mistake had been made. A child of ours would never dream of such nonsense."

In retrospect, I realize I hadn't thought this through very well. I should have wondered what kind of parents wouldn't go after the child they'd raised and save her from a life of carnie living. At the time, I was too involved in my fantasy and the comforting explanation of why I was growing up in a near-insane asylum—a.k.a. Masterton Hall, a.k.a. an old farm house in Central Illinois. It was much easier to convince myself that I didn't belong to the people who laid claim to me. I was Buffy Summers and my real family wasn't embarrassing in the least.

This fantasy got me through some tough times. Like when my grandmother Nan called my little league coach a fukakta screwball who needed his eyes examined, I consoled myself that we didn't share the same blood. As such, the shame I was feeling wasn't really my own.

When my dad showed up to all my school functions wearing a kilt and boasting about the joys of being Scottish, I was comforted that the wrong girl was being called Catriona Masterton. When my mother bought six sauerkraut crocks because they were on sale, even though she hated sauerkraut, I said to myself, "Cat, these aren't your people. Don't lose hope. Your real parents will find you and take you away from all this." When my brother Travis started to walk around the house in my mom's high heels, I reminded myself that Buffy was an only child.

It wasn't until high school that I finally accepted that the Summers were no more than wishful thinking on my part, and that I belonged to the Masterton clan, hook, line, and sinker. Part of my acceptance was because I'd fallen head over heels in love with my childhood playmate, Sam Hawking.

Sam and I frolicked in the mud, learned to play cards, and studied for science tests together before discovering more adult games in the hayloft of my family barn. He gave my life meaning. He was enough reason to give up my dream of belonging to a normal family. If I wanted a life with him, I needed to stay right where I was. Goodbye, Summers Family! Hello, kooky Mastertons.

Sam made me feel things I'd never felt before. My body blossomed under his touch, my heart filled to the point of bursting, and my dreams shot out of the stratosphere. There was nothing he and I couldn't do, be, or achieve as long as we were together. While my family was as odd as they came, around Sam I felt relatively sane. I'd even given us a celebrity couple name, SamCat.

Tragically, as often happens with first loves, we ultimately went our separate ways. The end of high school was the end of us. I was crushed, as it wasn't my idea to break up, but college eventually softened the pain and my life moved on. My subsequent move to New York City propelled me into adulthood, which is where I met Ethan.

For two years, Ethan and I were a good couple. We were grown-ups together. We paid a mortgage, put money away for retirement, and we planned a wedding. Ethan was as different from Sam as I could find in a man. He's what I thought I wanted, what I thought I needed. I was wrong.

I brought Ethan home to meet my family over Thanksgiving,

and it didn't quite go according to plan. My parents surprised me by inviting Sam to join us. It had been fourteen years since I'd laid eyes on my first boyfriend. The feelings I thought were long dead, began to revive. The life I had mapped out for myself was sucked into a blackhole, never to be seen again. My past and future collided in such a way a whole new universe was born.

Pet Cemetery

"Cat!" my mom screams from the rafters, "come up here!"

"Where are you?" I holler back.

"In the attic."

The entrance to the attic is in the upstairs hallway, via a skinny staircase that drops down from the ceiling right next to the bathroom. I want to go up there about as much as I wanted to go into strangers' basements as a child—or now for that matter. In general, I'm not a fan of the creepy nether regions of old houses. Upstairs, I see my mom Maggie, or Mags as her friends call her, has started to clear out the garret for the move to town. My parents have finally decided to downsize to a more manageable house. This one is too big for their needs.

Mom's been dropping stuff willy-nilly from the opening in the ceiling and as a result the hallway is full of an array of treasures. I jump aside to avoid being hit by an ancient dressmaker form from the seventies that's still wearing a half-made patchwork skirt. I step around a pile of old Halloween costumes from Travis's and my childhood, and trip over a brown corduroy beanbag chair I don't think I've ever seen before.

I have to shove stuff out of my way to make contact with the floor. I had no idea my parents had such a collection up there. Having said that, my mom recently told me she's storing fifteen banker boxes full of recipes she's clipped from newspapers and magazines, mostly stolen from the library and various waiting rooms around town. The woman is like an onion. You pull back one layer and there's a whole new layer of crazy just waiting to make you cry.

When I finally ascend the rickety stairs to the attic, I'm greeted by a sight so startling, it renders me speechless. Mags is standing next to the oval ox-eye window with light streaming in on her, showcasing a moose head she's wearing. Big, black, shiny marble eyeballs stare back at me. I eventually tear my gaze away from her to look around. The whole space could double for an animal sacrifice scene straight out of a horror flick.

There are squirrels, deer, and even a buffalo head. A beaver with little buck teeth and a demented smile leers at me. "Wow, who knew you guys were this kind of nuts? This is beyond the bounds of even my imagination, and I grew up with you."

My mom pulls off the moose head. "Oh please, this is nothing. Your dad has gotten rid of most of the good stuff over the years. He sold the French mountain sheep when we needed money to repair the tractor and the Indian leopard so we could take that trip to Alaska." She takes a breath and appears to be preparing herself for something. Finally she spits it out, "I thought you might be able to use some of this in the barn when you fix it up for your parties."

Now might be the time to mention I'm the one purchasing my parents' farm. I'm a party planner by trade. Despite having a successful business in NYC, I've realized it's time to build my nest closer to home. A lot closer to home, if you consider that I'll be hanging my shingle on the barn in the field out back. Timing was on my side, as one of my employees was in a position to buy me out, which is funding this adventure of catering to the cool millennial Chicago scene. Barns are the new "it" thing. As long as they don't have dead animals in them.

"How do you envision me doing that? Maybe by prying open the beaver's mouth and stuffing an apple into it before using it as a centerpiece on the buffet table?"

"Don't be ridiculous," my mom sputters. "I was thinking you could hang the heads on the walls and strategically place the squirrels and smaller animals so they're peeking around corners. It would be totally authentic, don't you think?"

"Manure piles and livestock would be authentic as well, but I don't see that working. Thanks for thinking of me though."

"If you won't take them, what am I supposed to do with them?" my mom demands.

"Put them on Craigslist."

"You mean, sell them?" she gasps.

"Actually, I meant you should give them to anyone insane enough to haul them away."

She visibly jolts as if this is the most absurd idea she's ever heard. "Give them away? We have thousands of dollars of preserved wildlife up here. You don't just give that away."

"So, take it with you," I suggest.

"And put it where?"

"Hey, lady, you're the one who wanted to scale down and move to a smaller place."

She smiles at me sweetly. "Do you think we can leave them

up here while we re-home them?"

"Nope." I shake my head. "Because I know re-homing isn't your goal. You're hoping you can leave them here and I'll forget them, but that's not going to happen. Now that I know *Pet Sematary* is right above me, I'm going to have nightmares until it's gone. I may even have to have Reverend Abernathy perform an exorcism."

"Don't be ridiculous." She smiles, trying to charm me. "Can you help me move them downstairs?"

"No can do, Mom. I'll go get Dad for you, though." I have an aversion to touching taxidermied creatures which, I assure you, made my upbringing quite a challenge.

"Don't bother," she snaps. "I'll take care of it myself."

Her ploy is to leave everything up here in hopes I'll forget. She couldn't be more off base. There's a lot to do to get this house into good enough shape for my new venture. Extermination of critters, both dead and alive, has just been bumped up to the top of the list.

The Naked Snow Roll

After graduating college, my childhood friend Sarah, began cultivating her organic farming empire. She now supplies some of Chicago's swankiest dining establishments. Demand for her organic farm-to-table fare has taken off, propelling interest in her farm stand and yurt-style B&B. Her next venture, the vegan café, opens this summer. Her farm has become the mothership for the nutty-crunchy crowd in our neck of the woods.

Sarah calls and asks, "Want to come over and try some of the new recipes I've been working on?"

"I'd love to," I declare. "You would not believe what's going on here today." I tell her about my parents' collection in the attic.

Sarah, a lover of all creatures great and small, says, "Your parents aren't normal. I've accepted your dad's many taxidermied rodent decorations over the years, but really, where does it end? Are they going to stuff Nan when she dies and keep her around for company?"

Just thinking about what my parents will do with my grandmother when she sheds her mortal coil sends a shiver through me. "I know you're kidding, but promise you'll never bring the idea up to them, just in case they glom onto it."

It's a distinct possibility that they would.

"No worries. I was only half-joking. I wouldn't put it past them." She continues, "Come by at noon and I'll have food ready for you to try."

In addition to having an established sustainable organic empire, Sarah also helps people with their health issues by running an alternative, all-natural boot camp. She detoxifies their systems with a two-week diet of pure vegan living. She isn't always vegan herself, just vegetarian, but she claims complete abstinence of animal products is necessary to cleanse impurities from the body and align the spirit. While that's occurring, she walks her guests through guided meditations, aura cleanses, and God knows what else.

"Ethan and his mom have gone back to New York, right?" *Please God, let them be back in New York!* Nerves ping pong across my stomach as I wait for my friend's reply.

Available now!

About the Author

Whitney Dineen is an award-winning author of romantic comedies, non-fiction humor, and middle reader fiction. She lives in the beautiful Pacific Northwest with her husband and two daughters. When not weaving stories, Whitney can be found gardening, wrangling free-range chickens, or eating french fries. Not always in that order. She loves to hear from her fans and can be reached through her website at https://whitneydineen.com/.

Join me!

Mailing List Sign Up
whitneydineen.com/newsletter/

BookBub
www.bookbub.com/authors/whitney-dineen

Facebook
www.facebook.com/Whitney-Dineen-11687019412/

Twitter
twitter.com/WhitneyDineen

Email
WhitneyDineenAuthor@gmail.com

Goodreads

www.goodreads.com/author/show/8145525.Whitney_Dineen

Blog

whitneydineen.com/blog/

Please write a review on Amazon, Goodreads, or BookBub. Reviews are the best way you can support a story you love!

Other books by Whitney Dineen:

Romantic Comedies
Relatively Normal
Relatively Sane
She Sins at Midnight
The Reinvention of Mimi Finnegan
Mimi Plus Two
Kindred Spirits
Going Up?

Non-Fiction Humor
Motherhood, Martyrdom & Costco Runs

Middle Reader
Wilhelmina and the Willamette Wig Factory
Who the Heck is Harvey Stingle?

Children's Books
The Friendship Bench

41000503R00192

Made in the USA
Middletown, DE
02 April 2019